Advance praise for Joanne Skerrett and *Sugar vs. Spice*

"*Sugar vs Spice* is a powerful story with a strong and timely storyline. The author does an impressive job of keeping the focus on the sensitive plot as well as the main character's relationships with co-workers, family members, and peers. I was captivated from the first page. Joanne Skerrett offers a fresh new voice in fiction that will be around for a long time to come. I highly recommend this one!

—Mary Monroe, author *God Don't Like Ugly* and *God Don't Play*

"A powerful story of change and courage in the face of adversity. Told with class, skill and grace. The mark of a gifted writer. Skerrett's characters bloom with life and complexities. Their struggles and their evolution forces you to look at your own life and pray that if ever faced with the trials of her heroine Tari Shields you, too, will discover the strength you never knew existed within."

—Donna Hill, author of *Getting Hers* and *In My Bedroom*

"A witty story full of laughs and moving dialogue that will have you wondering what's next!"

—Maryann Reid, author of *Marry Your Baby Daddy*

"A poignant look at relationships between women, the loves of their lives, and the many priorities that compete for their focus. Brilliantly executed."

—Leslie Esdaile Banks, author of *Betrayal of the Trust*

And outstanding praise for Joanne Skerrett and her debut novel *She Who Shops*

"A classic underdog story that will leave you rooting for Weslee as she struggles to keep her head above water in African-American society."

—Patrick Sanchez, author of *Girlfriends* and *Tight*

"*She Who Shops* is a charming novel—I laughed, I cried, I had an overwhelming urge to shop!"

—Kalyn Johnson, coauthor of *The BAP Handbook: The Official Guide to the Black American Princess*

"Joanne Skerrett has written an engaging novel about New England's black upper-middle class and what happens to one young woman after she's drawn into their world. Her story will inspire readers to follow their dreams, as well as their hearts."

—Karen V. Siplin, author of *Such A Girl*

"*She Who Shops* is an entertaining story of friendship, love and romance. The characters are introspective and well drawn and it is an interesting examining of the new race relations and social class within the Black Community."

—Nina Foxx, author of *Going Buck Wild*

"A charming debut."

—Kayla Perrin, author of *Gimme An O*

Books by Joanne Skerrett

SHE WHO SHOPS

SUGAR VS. SPICE

Published by Kensington Publishing Corporation

Sugar vs. Spice

Joanne Skerrett

Strapless

KENSINGTON BOOKS
www.kensingtonbooks.com

KENSINGTON BOOKS are published by

Kensington Publishing Corp.
850 Third Avenue
New York, NY 10022

ISBN 0-7582-1153-8

First Kensington Trade Paperback Printing: June 2006
10   9   8   7   6   5   4   3   2   1

Printed in the United States of America

In Memory of Holly Berinbaum-Silva

and Hewins Street neighbors, a Nubian Notion, the Knights at Uphams Corner and Codman Square libraries, Reggie Cummings of the Inner Circle, the folks in the MEEI O.R. who keep asking my Dad for more books. My editor John Scognamiglio and agent Frank Weimann. My old friends from the Dominica Grammar School who haven't forgotten me. And Jason.

Last but not least I'd like to thank the extraordinary team of women who took care of me when I was sick: Dr. Bita Tabesh, the baddest (in a good way) oncologist in the whole world; my surgeon Dr. Diane Lockhart (what scar?), N.P. Joan Sully (I only threw up a couple of times and I didn't always take the pills) and the nurses and staff at Harvard Vanguard in Kenmore Square and West Roxbury. Also, thanks to Sue at the radiation center in Quincy (those creams really did work wonders). I salute all my sisters who are living with breast cancer; we are strong, phenomenal women. And a question for my readers, when was the last time you gave yourself a breast exam?

Joanne Skerrett, September 2005

ACKNOWLEDGMENTS

I'll start by thanking God because He's the reason I'm here today. Then there's my family: From Citronier to Bath Estate, the chemo room to Kimball's, and all points in between we've always hung tight; let's keep it that way. Thanks to everyone who bought and read *She Who Shops*, especially those who wrote those nice e-mails!

Thanks to my wonderful, supportive friends and colleagues at the *Boston Globe:* Dave Beard, my unofficial publicist for *She Who Shops* (you really should start your own company). Jim Concannon and Debbie Jacobs in Books. The night and financial desk folks: Christine Murphy (I miss dinnertime at Café Globe), Paul Makishima, Jesse Harris, Matt Bernstein, Dave Gillis, Al Rudnic, Meghan Irons, Eileen Woods, Jill Marquard, Dorothy Clark, Rose Foley, Charlie Mansbach, Beverly Cronin, David Jrolf, Dave Yee and everyone else I'm forgetting. The CCI team: Those long months (or was it years?) in the (most likely toxic) basement were, um, fun: Paul McGeary, John Vitti, Greg Lang, Bob Scherer-Hoock, George Patisteas, and Lylah Alphonse. Phyllis and Cynthia Winfield (thanks for the bike!), Shirley Jobe, Diane Lewis, and Glenda Buell (for all your support at my tedious events).

Huge thanks to my Chicago girls Rebecca Little and Diane Hawkins; Dr. Lisa McCoy (for the stack of books and pamphlets and your kindness). Can't forget Cameron Prior, Simeon Olowere, Marylene Boucher, Arthi Subramaniam, Pam Sansbury, Donna Bains, Nancy Sullivan, Paula Bouknight, Johnny Diaz, Janine Rodenhiser, James Bailey, Peter Loblack, Ms. Marjorie Hicks, Ms. Sarah-Ann Shaw, Mrs. Best

CHAPTER

1

She was one of those girls—the tiny ones whom the cute boys called *midget* back in high school, and who never quite got over it. Maybe that was why she drove that monstrous SUV; it probably made her feel less insignificant.

Tari was careening from lane to lane in city traffic, talking into the headset, oblivious to fulminating drivers swearing at her imposing truck that interrupted their line of vision and stole their lane. She was in a rush, with one hand on the steering wheel and the other on a Starbucks cup—black with a Sweet'N Low. And she wasn't too shy about leaning on the horn if the guy in front lingered on the green.

Everything a person could suspect about Tari Shields was probably true. She was a cute, short, tightly wound girl-woman. One of those in that extended, self-indulgent adolescence that they thought was not really of their own choosing: thirty years old and up, quite single, with a good, well-coiffed head on her shoulders and a sweet career that might as well be called husband. You could say that Tari was all of the above. But what you saw was what you didn't quite get.

What you did see was a brown girl, with big, lively eyes over a wide nose and a bow-shaped mouth. Pretty, in a girl-next-door sort of way. She would catch your eye with that tight body and those obsessively whitened teeth whenever it occurred to her to flash them. But she wasn't smiling as her Toyota 4Runner sprinted toward the expressway that Saturday morning.

If she was only a few minutes late for kickboxing, she'd lose her spot in the front of the class. If that happened— well, she'd never let it happen. To her, the back of the class was for gadabouts and slackers, those chatty Cathys or panting, baggy-sweatpants-wearing girls who were always self-consciously struggling to keep up with the front of the pack.

She didn't have time for the back row. She was too serious, too driven. Nothing she hated more than disappearing into the furniture of any room, and at 5'2", shorter than her thirteen-year-old nephew, she had her work cut out for her when it came to standing out.

"Denise, have you heard anything about MetroBank filing Chapter 11?" Tari sipped her coffee with one hand and steered the truck off the I-93 exit with the other. No, her contact at the rival bank answered, not a thing. "Call me if you hear anything this weekend. Okay? Please, D. My editor's breathing down my neck."

Honk, honk! She resisted the urge to give the driver behind her the one-finger salute.

When Tari took her place in the brightly lit aerobics studio at World Gym, she surveyed the room through the mirrors looking for the regulars. She only nodded at the other women with whom she sweated three times a week for ninety excruciating minutes of side kicks, squats, jabs, and uppercuts. A cluster of them chatted while they stretched, and Tari allowed herself into their inane conversation. They never talked about anything she ever wanted to listen to, but she played along, feigning interest. Most of them were Lean Cuisine moms desperately trying to hold on to their figures so they would not fit the old-wife stereotype. The others were flashy, clubby, designer-clothes-wearing chicks and plain-vanilla singletons like her in compulsive pursuit and maintenance of the hottie body.

It was always the same with the mothers: how Junior was dealing with his cold or teething or taking his first few steps. And with the singletons: that guy never called again or he turned out to be married or where did you get those cute earrings. Most times she had to physically restrain herself from rolling her eyes. She couldn't imagine having a serious conversation with any of these girls, as much as she loved sweating with them. She pulled her shoulder-length hair into a ponytail high on her head, hoping that the sweat would not frizz her hair into cotton candy.

When Donna, the instructor, entered the room, the jockeying began as everyone took their usual spots. Dagger looks flew as the newcomers broke protocol and had to be sarcastically told that they were standing on ground that had already been claimed. The new girls were always so clueless. Tari shook her head.

The music, 178 beats per minute of remixed R&B and trance, was ear-splitting, but it sent Tari's adrenaline spiraling. Donna, a more muscular version of Gabrielle Union, was already in the zone, screaming cues at the class of fifty or so women. Donna hardly ever counted down or made cute jokes to force her students' minds off the intensity of the workout. Instead she yelled war chants and had the women repeat after her as legs and arms, glistening with sweat, assaulted the air. "Kick it. Kill 'em. Kill 'em."

When the class began to wilt she became a drill sergeant, berating them: "Come on, what's going on here, you guys? What is this? High tea at the Ritz? Y'all better pick it up before I make you do one hundred more!"

The room began to heat up after just a few minutes, and some of the women in the back row began to eye their water bottles, looking for some reassurance that relief was still in sight. Fifteen minutes into the class, many had stopped to just catch their breath and grab a drink of water; a couple of them had walked out in defeat.

Tari hadn't even warmed up yet. She moved in Donna's orbit, muscles tensed, going kick for kick and jab for jab. She never let up, never stopped to drink. Sweat poured from her skin, ran down the sides of her face, and left dark spots on the red Nike tank top and sports bra.

By the time she began to feel winded, the hard part was over. The ninety minutes had flown by, and her entire body was soaked but cleansed of a week's worth of stress. Donna high-fived her and the other gym bunnies in the front row.

Minutes later, she lay on the floor for the fifteen-minute stretch, the real payoff for all of this loud music, high kicks, and Donna's lighthearted verbal abuse.

She only allowed herself to think positively during the stretch. And her thoughts fast-forwarded to the evening ahead. She imagined herself having a good performance that night. A representative from a small but respectable jazz label would be coming to hear her sing, thanks to a good word the jazz critic at work had put in for her. Maybe she would try to squeeze in a massage before rehearsal with the quartet this afternoon. And no, she wouldn't make any more useless calls, tracking down that MetroBank story. Obviously, there was nothing there.

She reached her left arm all the way across her body and took in a long breath. The stretch soothed her aching triceps, and she let her arm relax on her chest for just a few seconds. She felt something. It was a hard spot that contradicted the smooth softness of her right breast. She looked around at the women on the floor in similar poses. This was not the time to feel her breast. *It's probably nothing,* she mused. Stupid cysts! She hadn't had one in years, and now was not a good time to get herself or her doctor all excited over nothing. It would go away once this horrible fat week, or PMS, was over with. *Pain in the butt, or boobies,* she sighed as she moved her spent body into the next stretch sequence, thinking only good thoughts.

At the showers, she stripped without an ounce of self-consciousness. In fact, she liked the fact that she could walk around the locker room completely naked and not worry about the bumps and bulges that terrified some of the other girls into hiding behind their towels. She noticed the surreptitious stares. *Yeah,* she thought. *I worked hard for this body; go ahead and stare all you want.*

"You look so great," said one tall and sinewy girl, who also looked as if working out were her other full-time job.

"Thanks, babe." Tari smiled. "So do you."

She raced toward the showers, edging out another girl who was ambling toward the stalls and clutching her towel to her soft body for dear life. *You snooze you lose,* Tari thought as she claimed her favorite stall and undressed quickly. She ran her hand over her breast again as the water poured over her, and it was still there. *Dammit! This thing had better go away by next week!* Ten years ago she'd had one, and that had been scary enough. She couldn't bear the thought of going through another painful biopsy. "Some women just have lumpy breasts," the doctor had shrugged after the ordeal was over. But she hadn't shrugged. It had been scary.

At least she'd been down that road before, she thought as she pulled on a pair of low Chip & Pepper jeans, tank top, and some flip-flops. Her I'm-real-cute-without-even-trying look. She sighed. Just another annoying cyst that would probably require another annoying, time-consuming visit to the doctor. She looked in the mirror and frowned. *You look like a twelve-year-old,* she thought. Oh, to be taller; she glanced at the tall girl who had complimented her earlier. Oh, well.

She looked herself over again. She preferred to be all dressed up, but it was Saturday and she had a lot of errands to run. She applied some lip gloss. *You can't always look like a diva, hon,* she told herself. *Gotta get going.* She almost bumped into Donna on her way out of the gym.

"Slow your roll, girl," Donna said. "You kicked butt today."

Tari smiled as she headed for the exit and toward the parking lot. Phase one of the day was over. Now she had things to do. Tonight would be a big night. She couldn't wait.

CHAPTER
2

Self-doubt seldom found a comfortable place in Tari's mind. But tonight she would be under professional scrutiny from that Mars Recording rep, and that warranted an extra effort. She took an extra-long bubble bath, ginger and citrus bath oil, complete with aromatherapy candles, to relax her. She had dabbed on a new eye shadow, caramel ice, though not without some trepidation, and drank more lemon juice than usual. She was not nervous, she told herself, just being extra cautious. *This could be the break. Gotta look good; gotta sound even better.*

She made one last phone call to Manny. The gruffness in her piano player's voice told her that he was not in the mood for a lecture.

"Tari, how long we been doing this, huh? Gimme a break. We'll do what we've been doing the last four years, and we'll sound as good as we always sound."

Manny, forty-two years old and a part-time professor at the New England Conservatory, was the backbone of the quartet. He played every instrument there was, wrote most of the music, made all of the arrangements. She had approached him at the conservatory one evening, years before, after his lecture on early Coltrane. She'd told him how impressed she was with his knowledge and his talent. It could have been the compliment or maybe it was the way she had smiled, but he gamely agreed to hear her sing. Months later she was the voice of his band, Loose Change.

"I'm just saying, Manny, that tonight just feels different to me. You know?"

"Uh-huh." He didn't sound too convinced. "Relax, okay? My wife's on my behind about something. I gotta go. I'll see you in a few."

Tari sighed. Why did he never listen to her? One last appraisal in the full-length mirror in the foyer rated a satisfactory nod. And a final tug at her bra straps to make sure her girls were standing at attention, then she was on her way.

Manny's ambivalence about the future of Loose Change was a sore point between them. From where Tari could see, the man obviously had no ambitions beyond teaching jazz at the conservatory and being a good family man. *That's all well and good*, she thought, *but what about me?* It wasn't as if she herself were searching for major stardom, trying to be a Diana Krall or a Cassandra Wilson. He knew that. It was just such a waste to not take advantage of an opportunity when it presented itself. For goodness' sake, how many local bands got Mars Recording reps to come to their gigs? All she asked was that he tell the other guys in the band, especially the drummer, to not drink so much tonight and to try a little harder.

She allowed herself to daydream as she drove through the congested streets of Roxbury. It was Saturday night and everyone was going somewhere. Boys driving loud, low-riding cars punctuated the streets along with crowded, brightly lit MBTA buses and pedestrians putting their lives on the line to cross to the other side. Blight was in the immediate picture on Warren Street, but the city skyline appeared almost within grabbing distance, the lights of the Pru tower twinkling like diamonds. What if? Tonight could be the night that she got an offer—one she could dangle in front of all of those doubts that told her she couldn't.

The traffic thickened at Huntington and Mass. Ave. as a crowd of mostly white-haired, sports-jacketed folks lined up outside the symphony to see Keith Lockhart work his magic wand.

But it could turn out to be just another tiresome event. She hated being background music for the crowd. What she would be up against tonight would be inane conversations: "What I'd really like to do is join the peasant farmers trying to reclaim their land in Bolivia before I start law school." She would read her audience's lips sometimes as her voice competed with and lost to the attentions of the shiny, smiling date across the table or the woman in the low-cut top and tight jeans leaning over, dangerously, at the bar. They, her audience, never *listened* the way she wanted them to.

She parked her 4Runner in the back lot of Rico's off Inman Square. The familiar crowd, out for a Saturday night of meeting, eating, drinking, and wishing, was walking into the building, which really was an old Victorian gutted and rehabbed into a restaurant with average food and a decent-size stage and tiny dance floor. But she couldn't complain too much; Rico's was one of the few places she could get gigs these days. There was always "real talent" in Boston, and no one had room in their establishment for a virtual unknown like Tari Shields. Yes, she could sing, really sing. But she was still a nobody, according to them, anyway.

But back when she'd started singing as a four-year-old in church, she'd been a star. Her mother, Coletta, had decided that her daughter had talent, and Tari always found herself on display, whether it was in her parents' living room or in front of the church, singing gospel songs for old church ladies, who swayed and closed their eyes as she belted out those old hymns.

By the time she was in first grade, she'd already decided

that she wanted to become a famous singer, but not the kind that sang to churchified old ladies. She fantasized every Sunday in front of the small church that she was on a big stage and that those people in the pews were her fans. She could go from imagining herself Whitney Houston to Brenda K. Starr. In ninth grade, she started a group called Apex, a really bad rip-off of the girl group Klymaxx. But they broke up after about a month because none of the girls could get along with her. And only two of them could play an instrument. Tari saw this as confirmation that she was not meant to share the stage with anyone else.

In college, she gravitated toward the artsy types who spent little time in class and plenty of time writing songs, poems, short stories about the cruelty of love, life, and poverty. She found herself singing backup for a jazz funk band led by one of her classmates at NYU. They played little clubs in New York's outer boroughs and a few gigs in small Village bars. Her roommate, a Kansas native who wanted to be an actress, dragged her along to audition for small parts in off-Broadway plays. As humiliating as Tari found the audition process, she always went along. It was good practice, she told herself. Someday, someone would recognize her talent and give her the break she deserved. It hadn't happened yet, but she'd still kept on singing. As the years went on, she began to see the dream as something un-attainable and sometimes even silly. Like a thirty-year-old man still holding on to a nine-year-old's aspirations of mak-ing it to the major leagues.

I may have sold out, but at least I never gave up, Tari always told herself each time she wondered what would have hap-pened had she really worked hard enough or fought hard enough or stayed in New York or kept on going to auditions. *I am still singing,* she thought. *It could be worse; I could be doing nothing at all.* Small stage or stadium, she suspected that it would be the same feeling: having all eyes on her, everyone listening to her, feeling what she was feeling. She was a small girl who always struggled to be seen and heard, and when she was onstage, even here at Rico's, her audience had no choice but to look and listen.

CHAPTER
3

The spotlight glinted off the highlights in Tari's bottle-chestnut hair. It was a carefully planned effect on her part, but it wasn't enough to win the full attention of the audience. They rebuffed her advances as she flirted with the microphone and moved her hips to the midtempo jazz beat, a classic that Manny had improvised with his crazy, genius fingers. She was exasperated, though you could not tell from her face. Her big brown eyes were smiling as her voice rang out over the smoky bar.

". . . No, I never heard them singing / till there was you."

The way Manny had reworked the song, it sounded more like something you would hear from Jill Scott than Sarah Vaughn, and Tari loved it. They had practiced that song over and over, and she wondered if the audience even cared how long and hard they had worked to make the thing sound this good.

She surveyed the room. It was a full house of young, mostly single folks, many of them grad students out for a cheap night of entertainment. That she could discern from their abused Garment District garb. Sprinkled in were more polished professionals who had made the trip to Rico's to hear some real, live jazz, probably because someone else had told them Rico's only allowed the best local talent on his stage. None of them seemed to be true jazz fans, Tari thought, because if they were, they would have been captivated by her voice.

She wanted to throw the mike at them. *Hey, look at me!* If it were up to her, she'd be at Scullers or the Regatta bar tonight. Sure, the crowd would be older, but that was where the true jazz aficionados, the connoisseurs, went. At least *they* would recognize and appreciate her talent.

It was just like Rico's to attract such pretentious, citified, up-and-coming phonies, Tari thought as her efforts to captivate her oblivious audience subconsciously grew less and less fervent.

A rowdy table, probably celebrating a birthday, loudly made toasts. The entire room looked their way as the laughter rang up to the mural-painted ceiling. Tari's hand tightened around the microphone stand as the distraction stung, but she sang with half her heart. So rude.

After the weak applause ended and she'd taken her bows, she realized that the Mars Recording rep had left halfway through the first set and had not returned, though a half-full glass of something brown and alcoholic still sat on his empty table. She had sung *to* the man, a short, jumpy-looking type with thick black hair and Coke bottle glasses. But he had only stayed through the fourth number, "My Funny Valentine." Maybe she shouldn't have sung standards. Maybe she should have tried one of her own songs. This was where she and Manny had disagreed. But she had decided not to get into it with him again. And she didn't meet his eyes as the set ended.

She kicked off her shoes in the tiny dressing room backstage. She was so tired of these gigs at hole-in-the-wall places, where people really didn't come to see her. They wanted to drink, hook up, see and be seen by others. She felt about as significant as the peeling paint on the wall. It was enough to make her want to give up. But the thought of having only journalism to look forward to for the rest of her life was like dying itself.

It was supposed to be a temporary thing. She'd started writing for the paper at NYU by mistake. They were looking for a nightlife columnist, and since she felt she knew New York nightlife like she had invented it, she took the job. She didn't expect to like it or even be good at it. But within six months she'd already scored an internship at the *Daily News*, and the following summer at the *New York Times*. By graduation, top newspapers were fighting over her, and she'd chosen to return home, a decision she sometimes still questioned. Yes, it was nice to be in a smaller, more manageable city, closer to family. But New York had been fun. Crazy. But fun.

The tiny dressing room smelled musty, of wet laundry and stale cigarettes, and the lone lightbulb above the mirror flickered as she changed quickly from black cocktail dress, her stage dress, to yoga pants and an NYU sweatshirt. She looked almost as tired as she felt, and that nagging pain on the right side of her chest forced her to take deep breaths every few minutes. She paused; what was that, anyway? Was that related to the cyst, or had she been hitting the cardio too hard again? *I really need a break*, she thought. *From everything!*

Away from the spotlight, her big brown eyes dulled and her tweezed eyebrows lost their symmetry after she pulled the sweatshirt down over her head. She noticed that there was the beginning of a crack at the left top corner of the mirror. That hadn't been there the week before. Hmmm. Rico was now letting these young college rock bands play on weeknights. *He must be really desperate*, she thought, as she wiped off the shiny lipstick and applied Sephora lip balm with her fingers.

Stupid man, she thought, as her mind wandered back to

that Mars Jazz rep. There had been times when she had brought the house down with "My Funny Valentine," when people turned away from their beers to find out where that voice was coming from. Then they couldn't take their eyes off her because that big, powerful, yet smooth voice pouring from that petite, pretty black girl would just grab them by the throat and hold them there until the last note. Oh, well, she sighed, tonight hadn't been one of those nights.

There was a knock on her door as she put on her sneakers.

Her bass player, Marvin, poked his head in.

"Can I come in?" Marvin was the father of four sons and worked as a mailman, doing the Financial District route during the day. Manny said he'd found him playing on a sidewalk four years ago, hawking his homemade CDs, all bass solos.

"What's up, Marvin?" Tari asked wearily, tying the laces of her Sauconys. "Did you see that guy walk out in the middle of my set?"

Marvin nodded sympathetically. Something was on his mind. He stuttered uncomfortably as he complimented her performance and the dress she had worn, one he had seen several times before.

He cleared his throat. "Well, Tari, I've been wanting to tell you this for a couple of weeks, but I've been putting it off."

He paused, and Tari's heart sank.

"I got a regular gig on Saturday nights with the house band down at Harper's in Allston. Uh . . . So I won't be able to, uh . . ."

"You're quitting?" Tari asked incredulously.

"Well, not really. I mean, if you have gigs on Fridays or Sundays I could probably . . ." Marvin's voice trailed off.

Tari held up her hand. "It's okay, Marvin. Thanks for letting me know."

When Marvin left the room, Tari closed her eyes and sat still. She wanted to scream. Where would she find another bass player, a good one that she could afford? Manny certainly wouldn't take the task on himself, nonchalant as he'd been lately. She said a silent prayer, asking God to give her control over the anger that was rising inside of her. She did not want to make a total wreck out of an already ruined night.

She took stock. Breathed. It had been a long, trying week. And with this bomb from Marvin, the next week suddenly did not look any better. All she could see in addition to more fruitless phone calls about a rumored bankruptcy filing by the city's biggest bank was a long, tiring search for a bass player. She could feel another overwhelming wave of fatigue coming over her, and she leaned back heavily in the creaky chair. Where could she find herself another bass player in two weeks? She had another gig in two Saturdays.

As she tried to make her way out the back of the club, she noticed her drummer, Albert, feeling up one of the waitresses. She detested the man, and the sight of him with the young woman who was not his wife disgusted her. She averted her eyes and walked past the couple groping each other.

She reluctantly chatted with Rico, just wanting him to give her her money quickly so she could go home to bed.

"You sounded really good out there tonight," Rico said in his gregarious yet fatherly manner.

She decided not to tell him just yet that she was losing Marvin. She didn't see Manny and assumed that he already knew and was avoiding her; he was much closer to the guys than she was. Rico chatted on about his new chef and other topics Tari did not care about. It was another ten minutes before he finally gave her an opening in the conversation to make her exit. *Free at last*, she thought as she made her way to her truck.

The pillowlike breeze coming into the open windows of her truck did not sting as it had just weeks ago. It had been a long, brutal winter, and the city was finally shedding its layers of packed ice and snow in preparation to bloom.

The winters. That was the reason she gave people who asked her why she needed the truck. One kid, obviously fresh from a freshman environmental science class, even tried to give her a lecture once on her inefficient gas mileage as she was leaving the Body Shop in Harvard Square.

"You'd better get out of my way," she had snapped at the dreadlocked idealist and snatched the parking ticket off her windshield, making sure to slam the door hard to show him how little she cared about the Green Party gaseous emissions spewing out of his mouth.

Tari loved her truck, though it seemed to swallow her up. But this was what she had always wanted, a big, bad car that made her feel on top of the world. They called it command seating, and that was how she felt behind the wheel of the truck.

She drove quickly down Massachusetts Avenue, which at three A.M. on a Sunday was nearly clear all the way to Commonwealth. There the traffic would pick up because the college kids were still getting out of the bars and clubs, and the taxis would be lining up to take them back to their dorms. Other partiers would be staggering off the sidewalks and stumbling into the streets. Oh, to be in college again. Well, maybe not, she thought as she saw a group of young girls screaming and carrying on in an obvious attempt to get the attention of a group of boys nearby.

When the light turned red at Boylston, she looked up at the Virgin Megastore and pressed play on one of her fantasies, the one where she could just walk in off the street and find her own CD in the jazz section under the Ss. Or the other one where fans would be lined up at midnight, spilling onto Mass. Ave., the day before her new CD hit the shelves. *So stupid,* she thought, *especially after tonight's let-down. But it would be nice. . . . .*

She sped up as the streets cleared on lower Mass. Ave. She quickly glanced at the crowd that was still hanging outside the legendary Wally's, a more downscale, grittier version of Rico's that had seen its share of jazz greats grace its cramped, formerly smoky, yet renowned stage. It always took a while for that group to break up, and she looked at the place longingly. The demographics were a bit different from Rico's crowd: browner, edgier, less likely to have delusions about saving the Third World. Her kind of people. But she knew that she would get only respect and street cred from singing there, little else. She wanted more.

She hummed to Nina Simone's "Fodder on My Wings" as the streets grew darker and more deserted. Skyscraper lights grew fainter in the rearview mirror as she headed into the neighborhood, swallowing up another night of high hopes.

Minutes later she turned the key in the door of her house. Even though she had been in it for over a year, she still loved the feeling she got when she set her own burglar alarm and surveyed her living room and her big staircase. She would never regret ignoring those who told her to wait until she found a husband before she bought it, that it was too big for her and her alone. She loved the nearly eighty-year-old three-bedroom Colonial that had cost her $300,000, a veritable bargain in Boston.

The blinking light on her Caller ID turned out to be yet another frantic call from work. She quickly dialed into her voice mail. Joe Martone's raspy voice came over the line: "Listen, Tari. I heard MetroBank is about to make a big announcement on Monday morning. I need this on page one in Monday's paper. So do what you need to do and give me something. I need something by Sunday night, before first

edition. Okay? Don't call me back until you have something for me."

Tari slammed the phone down. She felt the urge to do
more damage, break something, but she checked herself.
How many times and how many ways could she tell this
man that this rumor was going absolutely nowhere? She
walked up her staircase, fuming.

She would take a quick shower and let the spray soothe
her tired chest muscles, say her prayers, and then wrap herself in the covers. Sunday would take care of itself. She was
too tired to drive herself crazy over a story.

CHAPTER
4

"Is that cigarette smoke I smell in your hair?" Melinda eyed Tari, nose wrinkled, her large eyes questioning.

Tari scanned the crowded church parking lot to see if anyone else had heard her sister. The ten A.M. service at the New Covenant Church had just ended and the entire neighborhood came alive. With five thousand members, it was as close to a megachurch as Massachusetts would ever see. But the fact that it was smack in the middle of one of the hottest spots in Mattapan made it special. Crime and miracles on the same block. Good and evil, sharing turf peacefully. The congregation comprised everyone from former crack addicts to MIT professors.

"I had a gig last night, and I just didn't have the energy to do a wash and blow this morning," Tari said, her hand smoothing the hair that Melinda wrinkled her nose at. It was so like Melinda to always find something amiss with her, and Tari eyed her sister, hoping to point out something lacking, but not a hair was out of place even in the stiff March wind. Melinda's gray cashmere coat complemented her crisp gray skirt suit; a severe string of pearls around her neck with matching earrings and sensible suede pumps completed the look. Melinda wasn't just well put together, she was armored for success. Every day. Tari, on the other hand, was always throwing something on at the last minute, zipping up in the car, putting on earrings as she walked into the office.

But that had always been the case: Melinda, prim and perfect, always admonishing and wagging her finger at the less orderly and more scatterbrained Tari. They were only five years apart, but Melinda had always made it seem like an entire generation. "Because I'm older, that's why!" was the stock answer she gave Tari when she'd gotten—in Tari's opinion—the prettier doll, the nicer dress, the bigger dessert, the new bed. . . .

Now, after a lifetime of living in Melinda's shadow, Tari had begun to grudgingly accept her place in the family. Little pain-in-the-butt sister. She bristled when Melinda lectured her about her dating habits, her spending, her tight sweaters, her high heels, and the fact that her spiritual life left a lot to be desired. Every now and then there would be a blowup and someone's feelings would get hurt. Usually Melinda's. But that was nothing compared to the hair pulling, scratching, and screaming that went on in the Shields household when the two of them grew up together in the same room. Age and maturity shaved a tiny bit off the friction that still chafed below the surface of their now-calm relationship.

"Tari, do you really think that it's right for you to be singing in those places?" It was one of Melinda's favorite questions and one of the reasons Tari tried to avoid her sister as much as possible.

Tari rolled her eyes. "Melinda, I told you, it's only until I get a recording deal. I don't want to be in those places any more than you want me to be, but that's how the business works. I'm not going to get discovered in a church, am I?" She looked at her watch. *Can I go now?*

Her sister just shook her head and sighed.

Melinda Shields-Jones was a tall, Swiss Miss cocoa–

skinned woman whose presence commanded all to see and hear her. She was the supersista, born to be a wife, mother, big sister, and best friend who baked perfect pecan pies, kept detailed scrapbooks on herself and her children, could converse about the political problems in Kyrgyzstan and the sorry state of the consumer class. She would not hesitate to tell you to dump that no-good boyfriend of yours because you deserved so much better. And you believed her and did it! As a child, she took on many of the responsibilities in the home, edging her mother out of the way sometimes, as if rehearsing for her role later on in life.

She dressed well, cooked and cleaned elegantly, smiled at all the right moments, and made all her friends feel that if she could do it, they could do it too. It was her goal in life— to be inspiring. Supersistahood was her calling in life. She never tired, at least not as far as anyone else could see. She had a full roster of patients as a couples psychotherapist, taught Sunday school, and led the church's toy drive every Christmas. Her husband, a perennial master's degree candidate, was a deacon. They were a formidable couple, towering over other people not just physically but spiritually. The pastor often held them up as examples of a good marriage, a good Christian family. They were widely admired, and envied.

Tari suspected that it was this flawless exterior of a life that made Melinda more than a little self-interested in seeing her little sister follow in her footsteps—and at least sing with the choir. It was as if Melinda wanted her to be an accessory, like that godawful old-lady gold jewelry Melinda wore, something that would make her look even better to her stupid, self-righteous friends. Tari was so tired of explaining herself to people like Melinda who failed to realize that she could have a close, personal relationship with God even though she sang in clubs where people smoked and drank—things her church frowned upon. Tari would tell them that the fact that she was living right was enough and that there was nothing wrong with her music itself. She would quote scriptures, telling them how Jesus consorted with criminals while he walked on this earth. In Tari's opinion, Melinda and others like her were just Pharisees—too righteous for their own good.

She was wearying of Melinda's critical eye and was about to say good-bye, when her brother-in-law approached with her niece and nephew, Taylor and Jared. Tari's exasperation melted as she scooped up Taylor in her arms. She temporarily lost her worries as her five-year-old niece chattered on about Sunday school, and her thirteen-year-old nephew showed her the newest gospel rap song he had written.

"Sister Tari," she heard a voice behind her say as she blew into Taylor's ear, making the five-year-old shriek. It was Violet Mathers, a sister who sang in the choir. Tari groaned inside. "Tari, we're still looking for another soprano, girl," Violet said after she'd greeted Melinda and Michael with the breathless reverence and unspoken but obvious admiration of a lonely single woman seeing her dream marriage materialize right before her eyes.

"I know, Violet," Tari said patiently. "But work is really crazy right now. I really don't have the time to commit to rehearsals and everything."

Violet nodded, but her expression screamed *liar.* "Okay. But we're here anytime you find the time."

Melinda looked at Tari disapprovingly as Violet waddled away in search of more prey to recruit for church work. "You don't have the time to go to choir rehearsal once a week?"

"Don't start with me, okay?" Tari said, beginning to feel closer to the edge. "I have a lot of stuff going on right now. My bass player quit last night."

"Hmmph," Melinda said. "Maybe that's God trying to tell you something."

Tari placed Taylor down. She had hit her tolerance limit.

"I'm gonna get going. I have to go home and make some calls. I'm chasing a story."

She walked away fuming. Melinda had always been judgmental, but it seemed that the older the woman got, the worse it became. *Who anointed her head of the family, anyway? Might as well have Mom here always giving me a hard time,* Tari grumbled. She laughed when her younger brother, Jeffrey, who was at divinity school in North Carolina, called himself Melinda's third child, but she could see where he was coming from. She'd been trying not to let Melinda's motherly behavior get under her skin, just to avoid the fights, but it was easier said than done.

Her heart flipped as she noticed who was standing next to her truck. They'd exchanged well-planned nonchalant glances and faked ignoring each other for months now. His car was parked right next to hers. She looked down and fumbled for her keys. *When are we going to stop playing this game?* she wondered.

"Hey, is that your car?" he asked.

He speaks? She held in her stomach. She looked up—nonchalantly, she hoped—and noticed that he had straight, evenly set white-white teeth. She wondered if he had laser treatments to get them that shade. Teeth were her obsession, and she could not just let those kinds of things pass by without giving it some deep thought.

"Um, yeah." Her heart skipped, but she willed herself to look calm and collected.

"You left your window open." His voice was deep and rich like chocolate mousse. She noticed that his eyes were brown enough to catch the sun and sprinkle amber rays everywhere he looked. *What did he just tell me?*

"Oh, did I?" She felt foolish for thinking that he was trying to strike up a conversation, make a move. "Yeah. . . . Thanks."

"You're welcome." That voice again. She reflexively

looked for a wedding ring as he fished for his keys and slid into his car. None, but she already knew that. He smiled as he backed out of the parking space. She half smiled back, standing there with her keys in her hand.

"Aaack!" she exclaimed as she got into her car. She just knew how stupid she must have looked, standing there gawking at him. He was fine, fine, fine, she thought. *Too self-assured for me. And he really isn't my type.* Too dark, for one thing. And she'd made up her mind after Roger that she would not date another tall man ever again. Tall women were always giving her dagger looks wherever she and Roger went, as if it were her fault that she was only 5'2". Who wouldn't want to be 5'8"'?

She shook her head and for a second smelled the smoke that Melinda had complained about. Yes, she did need to go home and wash her hair. But more importantly, she had to make those phone calls. She had to have a story for Joe before ten P.M.

CHAPTER

5

Radio noises and kid clatter crowded the space in Melinda's head, but she did not ask Michael to turn down the volume of the stereo. What was the use? It would only start another fight. The kids were causing havoc in the backseat of the Suburban, and she let them. She was in no mood to be the enforcer today.

All she could think of was her sister. That Tari was going from bad to worse, in Melinda's estimation. The girl had one foot in the world and one pinky toe in the church. Who did she think she was fooling with her churchgoing and her self-righteous attitude? Melinda sure wasn't taken in by that act. If Tari truly loved the Lord, she would not be singing in those bars. She certainly would not be single and going out with that worldly Indian girl she called a best friend and those other girls she hung out with. Melinda knew what her little sister's problem was. She was just too ambitious. The girl always wanted to have everything, and not just every old thing, the absolute best of everything. She wouldn't date Michael's friends because they didn't read the *New York Times* or they had never seen *Les Misérables*. And she wouldn't sing in the choir because the women in choir were just not the kind of people she hobnobbed with at her invitation-only restaurant openings, charity events, and such.

Melinda had given up trying to convince her younger sister that she had to be satisfied with what God provided. Even her mother, tenacious Coletta, had given up, it seemed. She and Melinda could agree on one thing: Tari needed to just settle down and stop pushing so hard for God only knew what. Many times Melinda suspected that Tari had not the slightest idea of what she was fighting for—all those aerobics classes, as skinny as she was; she never had enough brand-name clothes; and someone at her job was always trying to steal her story or whatever. The girl just needed to stop. Just stop. Find a man, get married, have some kids, and be happy.

She herself, Melinda, had stopped trying to make her own life perfect. She fully accepted now that Michael would always be lazy. That he might never finish that degree and start working again. That he would always forget to put the mortgage payment in the mail on time. That he would never fix that broken window in the basement. That was just how things were with him, with them.

She was not surprised when people told her how much they looked up to her and Michael and their successful marriage. It wasn't as though those people were wrong. They were not seeing an illusion when they looked at her and Michael Jones. Her marriage was working, and quite well at that. But Melinda believed that it was because of God and the clarity he had given her. She could see now, clear as a Steuben glass filled with Iceland clean spring water, that this was her destiny.

Sacrifice and self-denial were not new to her. She had worked and put herself through graduate school and then through her postdoctoral studies while Michael stayed home with the kids. That was when she began to describe him as a "stay-at-home dad."

Her hard work had gotten her a nice office downtown with Blue Cross. Her patients were mostly married couples seeking ways to delay the inevitable. Half the time she could extend the life of a bad marriage a few months, maybe a year, but that had been a record. But it gave her some satisfaction to see those couples trying. Helping people. It's all she ever wanted to do in life.

Sure, she got angry sometimes when Michael wouldn't pull his weight. When he spent all day Saturday playing golf when he should have been doing something with his son. Or when he would forget to pick up the kids from school, forcing her to bolt from the office early and rush through traffic. He had been laid off for five years, before the baby. Five years since that day IBM handed him that pink slip. All the plans about finishing his engineering degree and working again, maybe teaching, had gone out with yesterday's newspaper. A stay-at-home dad? Hardly. He only stayed home when the weather was not conducive to a day at the links or on the squash court. But Melinda hardly ever got upset over things like that anymore. She was patient.

She was no Tari, always flying off the handle, mad at everybody and not afraid to let them know it. Melinda kept things under control. She had become adept at rationalizing. The twenty pounds she could lose, well, she carried them well at five foot ten inches. The fact that she fantasized about leaving Michael and moving to France for a year or two, well, everybody had silly dreams. She was no impulsive, selfish woman out to satisfy just her own needs. Melinda put her family first because that's what God called her to do and it's what she was happiest doing.

Michael ran through a red light, causing their son to gasp from the backseat.

"Dad, the light was red!"

Michael laughed carelessly. "Relax," he drawled.

Melinda rubbed her right temple. *Patience develops experi-*

ence and experience, hope. That was fast becoming one of her favorite scriptures these days.

"What's the big rush, anyway?" she asked, trying to keep her voice level as Michael tore through another yellow light.

"The Knicks are playing the Spurs."

"And that's worth killing your family?"

He sighed and shook his head.

Yeah, I'm now the nagging wife, she thought resentfully.

Later that afternoon, she laid out the kids' uniforms for the next day, making sure that Jared was on top of his homework. Taylor was with her father, watching basketball. She contemplated dinner. It had been a long week, and she was exhausted. But she wanted her family to have home-cooked meals. Together. It was the way her mother had done it, and by God, that's the way she would do it. As a psychotherapist, she knew the value of spending quality family time together, so she had to do this no matter how tired she felt.

She placed a whole chicken in the oven and started peeling potatoes. She loved her kitchen. It was spacious and modern, everything she always wanted. She just wished that she could spend more time in it. She'd dreamed of having a kitchen like this when she was younger, and a husband who made enough so she could stay home and cook wonderful meals for him. Dreams always seemed to turn out that way, she mused. Halfway, half-right, and half-baked sometimes. She was so disappointed in Michael. All she ever saw in him was potential, still did, but he wasn't half the father or the husband she'd dreamed he could have been.

An hour later they sat down to dinner, and she tried to make conversation, but Michael seemed distracted.

"Who won the game?" she asked, not quite caring but trying to connect even on this most desperate level.

"Spurs."

"Oh." She wondered if she should ask what the score was, but who cared? She most certainly didn't.

"Taylor, don't do that!" She wiped her daughter's face, which was half covered with potatoes.

Jared laughed. "Taylor, you so nasty."

"Jared, don't tell her that! And it's not 'you so nasty.' How many times do I have to tell you not to talk like that?"

Jared looked down at his plate. She knew he was grumbling. He would only do that when she corrected him, not when his father did. Never mind that she was the one footing the bill for his private school and all his extracurricular activities. She felt guilty sometimes for the resentment she felt toward her own kids. It wasn't their fault that she was overworked and underloved, as that old R&B singer put it. God, they were her kids. She loved them with everything inside of her. That's why she did everything she did. So they would have a good life, a nice house, go to good schools, have great careers, and hopefully have better sense than their mother when it came time to pick a mate.

"There's another game starting in a couple of minutes," Michael said, looking up from his empty plate.

"Can I watch, too?" Jared asked.

"Did you finish your homework?" Melinda asked, noticing that Michael was about to nod his head. *Sheesh! Am I the only adult in this house?*

Jared didn't answer. "Go upstairs and finish your homework and you can watch after you're done," Melinda ordered.

Without missing a beat, Michael got up and loped off to the living room, where his beloved TV awaited. Jared ran upstairs to his room. Taylor sat in her high chair, playing with her food.

Melinda surveyed the messy table in front of her and the sink full of pots and pans. *Perfect*, she thought, *just perfect*.

CHAPTER

6

The Sunday-afternoon blahs were competing with Tari's work ethic. *Why am I here staring at this screen when I could be outside doing stuff? Having fun? A life, even?*

She closed the Word file and went to Bluefly.com, where a whore of a banner ad beckoned: Cashmere Sweater Sale. Up to 75 percent off! *Resist, resist.* Then, *forget it.* She had to change the scenery to something less distracting. This story was not going to write itself.

The office was quiet and deserted, except for a few copy editors whom she nodded at as she perched at her overly neat desk. Those people weirded her out sometimes, the way their eyes always seemed to accuse her of a dangling modifier or run-on sentence.

She immediately went to the list of contacts she had painstakingly compiled over the years. Not that she expected to get far on a sunny spring Sunday afternoon. Heck. This office was the last place she'd be if she'd had any real say in the matter. Surely the rest of the civilized world had to be out enjoying the sun after being cooped up inside all winter. She sighed. Unfortunately, it was her job to be here and to persevere.

After her fifth fruitless call, hope began to dim and flicker like an old lightbulb. She looked at the story on her screen. It was full of expectant gaps where she would put the quotes from pending sources. But after three hours, no one had called back, and all she had was the skeleton of a story with a lot of expectant gaps. She began to see the day slipping away. She put her head down on her desk in defeat.

She summarized what she had on MetroBank: It would restate profits for the last four years because of accounting errors that the bank's officials were failing to quantify or describe in any great detail. That was last week's news. It was a $4.5 billion hit for the bank, and bankruptcy seemed inevitable. But no one was confirming anything yet. Also, no one was saying much about how these errors had slipped by in a bank of this size. There were a lot of holes to fill, and she needed someone to call her back. Bad. Now.

In the meantime she poured on more foundation, layering her story with facts that would fill it out but not add anything of significant value: MetroBank was one of the oldest in the country, begun in the early 1800s by a WASPy New England family who wanted a financial institution that would cater to the needs of monied yet frugal Episcopalians like themselves. As the bank grew over the years, it changed hands many times, going public in 1975. But descendants of the original family still laid claim to its history, if not some of its scattered yet ample assets. It had long been a formidable institution in the city, one that donated millions of dollars to charitable causes, bailed businesses out of trouble, approved an entire generation for mortgages, and sponsored many a political career. But over the last two decades, as the banking climate changed, MetroBank began to lose much of its power. All of the majors were caught up in merger frenzy. Venerable institutions like Bay Bank, Shawmut, and Bank of New England had now been bought and sold so many times by giants like BankBoston and then the monster FleetBank that most customers had lost track of where they originally opened their checking accounts. MetroBank's refusal to join the merger party threatened to leave it standing alone and weak in an era of megabanks. It had already lost many of its customers to the gigantic Fleet, which was about to be swallowed up by Bank of America. And there was little chance of survival for the bank unless some wealthy suitor came along and snapped it up. But this potential financial scandal would certainly tarnish its allure. She saved the file. "God, make one of these people answer their cell phones!"

On a whim, she dialed for the third time the number of a vice president at MetroBank who had recently quit the company. The guy was notoriously brusque, and she hated to deal with him, but he was her only hope. He had quit the company with more than a little acrimony involved, so maybe he had an ax to grind. An ax she could wield to her advantage. She half hoped that he wouldn't answer, as he had a reputation for being a loose cannon. But he did.

"Bill Boggs," he said gruffly after only one ring.

Tari introduced herself, trying to sound upbeat and confident. "So, Mr. Boggs, I hear that MetroBank will announce its Chapter 11 filing tomorrow. Can I get a quote from you?" It was one of the oldest tricks in the book. Pretend that you already had the information so the source would give you the confirmation you needed.

"Where did you hear that?" Boggs's voice demonstrated his suspicion.

"Oh, I've heard it from a number of places," Tari bluffed.

"Those jerks," Boggs said, barely loud enough for Tari to hear. "Yeah, I have a quote for you, but you can't use my name," he said.

Tari sat upright in her chair. "Well, sure, but you're gonna have to tell me something really good for me to guarantee that, Mr. Boggs," she said, her heart beginning to race.

"Oh, this is good, all right," Boggs said.

Tari set her fingers on her keyboard, ready to type.

"Okay, here's your quote: MetroBank thinks that filing a Chapter 11 will solve its problems and cover up all of its lies, but it won't. The bank has been mismanaged by some very unscrupulous people for decades, and they won't be able to hide their crimes forever. When this is over, some very important people will be going away for a long time. This is going to be the Enron of Boston."

Tari typed carefully, not wanting to get a single word wrong. "Can you tell me more, Mr. Boggs?" she said almost breathlessly. Joe was right. If this guy was telling the truth, this could be a huge story.

"No, I can't tell you more right now. I'm about to get on my sailboat. But I'll talk to you after I see what you've written in the paper tomorrow."

He hung up. At first Tari didn't know what to do. She had gotten a scoop. This MetroBank thing could be way bigger than just a bank in financial trouble after some accounting mistakes. Boggs was alleging mismanagement and potential criminal behavior. The Enron of Boston! She picked up the phone with a new zeal. If only she could get just one more person to corroborate these allegations, she would have a story, a big story, and be the star of the newsroom on Monday.

Darkness had fallen outside, but her determined eyes failed to see beyond her mission. She dialed number after number, her fingers flying a mile a minute across the keypad. The few people who bothered to answer, angry over being interrupted at dinner, didn't want to talk with her, and to her this only confirmed Boggs's comment. Once she stated the allegations, they quickly made an excuse to get off the phone. Something was up at MetroBank. Could it be, she wondered, that this story that had served to be nothing but a thorn in her side over two weeks had suddenly be-

come something that could take her career to an entirely
new level?

She called Joe, who answered the phone with his mouth
full. "Are you serious?" he said. "Boggs said that? My God,
I'm coming in. I'll make some calls, too."

Tari held the edge of her desk and breathed out.

"Thank you, God," she whispered. "After last night, I
needed this."

She began to fill gaps with Boggs's words.

No one in the newsroom of the *Boston Statesman* would
ever describe Tari as nice, sweet, or great to work with. She
was known as pushy, a bit overbearing with her opinions,
and always quick to put her foot in her mouth. But that was
only among her peers. Her editors loved her dogged determination, her keen nose for getting a story, and her sharp
writing, plus her ability to almost always turn in a story on
time.

So she did not expect much patting on the back as she sat
at her desk that Monday with the day's paper on her desk,
her story in the lead position. She was still cautious. And
the message she deduced from her colleagues' icy green
stares was *don't get all bigheaded just yet*. All she really had was
an allegation from a really good source. But as the day went
on and the local TV stations picked up on the story, more
people were coming forward. Former employees of Metro-
Bank were alleging stealing by management and wrongful
firings of those who asked too many questions. Tari was
calm on the outside, but inside she was dancing a jig. This
was huge! She finally had herself a story that could keep her
name on the front page for weeks.

Mariska Lunes, who had sat next to her for four years but
who had never taken any kind of liking toward Tari, was
doing her best to ignore her even more than usual. Mariska,

who had recently married the man she had been not-so-secretly dating the last seven years, was still a blushing bride with an acute case of myhusbanditis. Tari suspected that Mariska had probably been waiting her entire thirty-four years on this planet to be able to begin every other sentence with, "My husband . . ."

Being a sometime pragmatist, Tari had asked herself why it was that this bothered her so much. She had even entertained the thought that she might have been jealous of Mariska's wedded state. But no. Mariska's marriage only came about after her husband's former wife finally, after three years of rancorous resistance, decided to grant him a divorce. As far as it was known, most of Mariska's husband's paycheck went toward supporting the four children that he had with that former wife. So what Mariska had for a husband was a dependent. And Tari couldn't help but admire the woman for being so in love with a man twenty years her senior.

Sadly, the import of Tari's story only served to flare up Mariska's myhusbanditis, and she spoke loudly into the phone, most likely to ensure that Tari heard her every word.

"My husband is taking me out to dinner tonight, so I won't be able to stay late. I've told my editor that my family comes before work. I'm not spending all my nights and weekends here for a story just to go home to an empty house."

Tari brushed off the obvious dig. If she had been the Tari of two years ago, she would have waited till Mariska got off the phone and then told her a thing or two about going home to an empty house. Instead she got up and walked away, heading to the cafeteria for more coffee.

She smiled as all six foot seven inches of Roger Levine, not including his hair, lumbered toward her.

"Hey, you kicked rawhide on that story."

Tari took the compliment gratefully. It was the first genuine one of the day.

During their best days together, Tari would have bet her beloved home that she would someday be Mrs. Roger Levine, with three or four little biracial children running around her suburban yard, attending temple and church on alternating weekends. But the relationship took several wrong turns, and then it finally crashed and burned.

It had been easy for Tari and Roger to ignore or forget about their status as an intercouple, interfaith and interracial. The stormy relationship was beset by so many other issues that were certainly more pressing. Her friends were used to her rainbow of boyfriends, from Tunisian to Guatemalan, so they did not blink when she introduced Roger to them. Her parents were more concerned that Roger was not Pentecostal.

But it was not as simple with Roger's family. Roger, an unabashed mama's boy, was the type to go home to Brooklyn at least twice a month. He spoke to his parents almost daily; most times they did not have to call him because he called them. His mother decorated his apartment, right down to placing her framed picture on his living-room wall. At first, Tari thought those were just cute little quirks that were holdovers from his being an only child. But she was wrong.

Roger's parents, once they realized things were quite serious between their son and Tari, began to wear him down. At first Roger confided in Tari, laughing at his parents' obvious attempts to derail their relationship. But as time passed and his parents' criticisms began to take root, he began to see faults looming in Tari that they pointed out: her short temper, her stubbornness, her tendency to overspend, her commitment to her career, her unrealistic dream of becoming a singer, and her competitiveness. Those were not the qualities of a good wife, Roger was warned. And the more he thought about it, the more right his parents sounded. It wasn't his fault. Roger wanted someone more like his mother, a selfless and patient martyr who wouldn't mind sacrificing her own dreams and desires for those of her husband and children. He didn't see Tari that way; she wouldn't even give up her kickboxing class so they could have breakfast together on Saturday mornings. So after Thanksgiving that year, when Tari was slipping him hints about her ring size, Roger broke things off.

Once she'd gotten over it, Tari began to call it the Roger fiasco, and sometimes the whole thing was so distant a memory it was almost as if it had happened to someone else. But every now and then she was reminded that he had been the last "boyfriend." There had been no one to speak of since. And it scared her that she was getting so used to being alone that the pangs of fear that had plagued her mid-twenties of never, ever wearing something white and beaded from Amsale and saying "I do" had ceased to exist. Yes, she had hit the big 3-0, but she was no serial-dating, party-hopping, Match.com–slumming, speed-dating singleton taxiing on the relationship runway, hoping to take off into wedded bliss. She suspected, hoped, that it would come eventually. Coletta and Melinda threatened her all the time that it would. So what was the hurry?

As she walked away from Roger she felt no stirrings, no desire, and that in itself was a major achievement, like finishing the Tufts 10K race last year. She had trained just as hard to get those thoughts out of her head, purge those needs from her body, force her eyes to see just plain old Roger and her brain not to wander off to all the wrong places.

Now they could work together, talk, joke, without the drama. And there was no there there. It was a good feeling.

Her cell phone rang as she climbed the stairs to the company cafeteria. The smell of the coffee made her quicken her steps. "We're still meeting up later, right?" Rebecca, her best friend, wanted to know.

"Yeah, but I'm running late. That story's gonna explode

girl." Tari lowered her voice as she walked into the crowded cafeteria.

"Talk to me about it at dinner, then," her best friend said. "I'm having a hell of a day over here, too."

Tari grabbed her coffee and dumped in skim milk and two packets of Sweet'N Low. She looked over at the rows of tables and noticed a group of her colleagues peering over the front page of the paper and talking animatedly. She strained her ears to listen. Then she walked over.

"I don't know why they're allowing her to use an un-named source in a big story like this. I wouldn't put that kind of trust in her. She just doesn't have what it takes—"

They must have felt her presence, because the table suddenly went silent.

"Hi, Dan." Tari summoned her perkiest voice and stood over the table as faces went red and throats were cleared.

"Hey, Tari. Great work there." Dan Silver gestured to the front page in front of him, a cubic zirconium smile on his face.

"Thanks, dude," she said, returning his fake smile.

"Jerks," she muttered as she walked away.

Like hell I don't have what it takes, she fumed. *If they're so much better than me, why didn't they break the story? Why aren't their names on page one?* Her heels clicked furiously against the hallway floors as she recalled years of sarcasm and condescension from the likes of Dan Silver. The man still thought he was some kind of golden boy, but everyone, including him, knew his time had long come and gone. Tari snorted as she remembered the look on his face as he looked at her story. Pure jealousy, she thought. Dan used to be a big-name reporter back in the day, but now he was just a bitter, balding, potbellied shadow of what he used to be. Now all he could do was pick on the younger reporters and editors to cushion his crash landing into a world of senior citizen discounts, pension payments, and idle irrelevance. *I don't want to be mean,* Tari thought as she walked back to her desk. *But these folks can get to a sister sometimes!* She took a deep breath as she approached her desk. *Doesn't matter,* she thought. *Criticism is good. It only makes me work harder. I'll show them who has what it takes!*

CHAPTER

7

The yoga studio was small, the mirrored walls steamy, and the twelve women who lay on purple plastic mats on the Pergo wood floors could have been dead, so quiet and motionless they appeared.

Tari could almost hear her mind straining to arrive at that place of serenity where she imagined everyone else had beat her to. But she couldn't free her mind of thought. The excitement of this week was not exactly something she wanted to just let go of that easily. Since Monday her office phone had been ringing off the hook and e-mails had been pouring in from all over. Even some of her more competitive colleagues were beginning to congratulate her on her big scoop. The MetroBank story was the talk of Boston. She mentally replayed the telephone call with the mayor. She hadn't talked to the man in years, since her early years on the crime beat, and back then she'd been a bumbling, stuttering rookie. Now the man was congratulating her for breaking a story! Ah, she would savor this week forever. It was even better than having the attorney general tell her, "Thanks for doing my job for me, kid."

The CEO of MetroBank was holding up under the pressure, refusing to apologize or resign. But Tari knew that his days were numbered. Bill Boggs was not the only one making allegations, and those were feeding more speculation that there was a pile of hidden misdeeds at the city's largest bank. The story had also brought about a total change in outlook for Tari. She looked forward to, even daydreamed about, work now, the same job that in the last few months had begun to feel as exciting as a midmorning shift at a Walgreens in Worcester.

This yoga class was part of the midweek routine, yoga and dinner with Rebecca. She'd wanted to put in another late night at the office, but Mariska's taunting forced her to get up and leave. The woman was a twit, but she was right; it was pathetic to spend all day and half the night in a musty newsroom. Besides, Tari couldn't very well forgo the weekly tradition since it was the only time she got to see Rebecca, and they had a lot to catch up on.

The instructor silently signaled that the quiet period was over, and the women, unprompted, went through a series of stretches. Dee, a limber, 5'11" biracial goddess hailing from Vermont and somewhere in Thailand, was ethereal and patient, a contrast to hard-driving Donna in kickboxing class and the perfect balance for Tari's exercise routine. She quickly glanced at Rebecca on the purple mat to her left. And her friend's eyes were still closed.

Tari's arms stretched way above her head, heels dug into her mat, breath swished in and then out. She released her arms and let them flow down to her sides. As she pressed her arm into her side, she felt the softness of her breast on the side of her right bicep. Then she felt an unfamiliar interruption. She pushed her bicep into her breast again, and again she felt it. It hadn't gone away. Was anyone looking? Her eyes scanned the room. She had to touch it this time. For certainty's sake. Rebecca, still holding the full body stretch, had her arms fully above her head and her eyes closed. No one was looking.

Tari reached her hand up to the side of her right breast and squeezed. It was a lump. Big. Bigger than a quarter. She sighed. What a nuisance.

Tari tried to visualize what was in her Palm III. She would have to schedule a doctor's appointment, probably a mammogram, and then an excision. It, the cyst, could be gone in two weeks. Then she could go back to the MetroBank story, finding a bass player, and her life. She sighed. Some things happened at the most inappropriate times.

Later, as the women changed in the tiny locker room, they chatted amiably, all the while surreptitiously taking inventory of one another's bodies. The really thin ones, who could never be thin enough, complained about those last five pounds they couldn't lose. Those who were merely thin heaped plaudits on the complainers for their stellar efforts to starve and exercise themselves into walking cornstalks. The ones who were just normal, or who in the thinner girls' opinions had "just given up," got dressed quickly, not wanting to dwell on where they obviously fell in this pecking order of thinness. They didn't even feel quite worthy enough to tell the very thin and the merely thin that "no, it's me who should lose ten pounds."

Tari and Rebecca were out of there in fifteen minutes, laughing at the other women's hypomaniacal narcissism as they walked into the clear evening. "Hey, I'm self-absorbed, too, but at least I'm self-aware enough to admit it," Tari said.

"That doesn't make you any better than them." Rebecca laughed.

Rebecca Ashad, of Port of Spain and New York City, loved to eat, and it showed nicely. Luckily, she wasn't the type of person who grew too dismayed over her five or ten pounds over the weight ideal set by the American Heart

Association or whoever it was these days who decided such things. Rebecca, who had managed to parlay a law degree from New York University into a job in fund-raising for Harvard Law School, was a food writer at heart. She had stuck to Tari like glue when they were introduced at a party in New York. They both had trouble now remembering the name of the mutual friend who had brought them together, though they did remember how bad that party had been.

At that point, Rebecca was following her parents' dream of seeing their eldest daughter join the legal profession. But she always knew that eventually she'd get around to her first love of writing about food for *Bon Appetit* or *Gourmet* or even the Dining Out section of the *New York Times*. But it hadn't happened. Not yet anyway. Having journalist friends had been part of her strategy to get her work into print. And the strategy had worked, to a certain extent. Tari did use her shaky contacts at work and in the Boston media to throw Rebecca the occasional restaurant review or a piece on Asian, Indian, or some other ethnic or exotic cuisine. They had both been mildly surprised that an alliance born obviously out of professional convenience had turned into a real friendship.

As usual, Rebecca was recommending a new restaurant. "Are you listening?" she asked as Tari idly turned her 4Runner onto Massachusetts Avenue heading up to Cambridge.

"Did you say Central or Harvard Square?"

"Harvard," Rebecca said, furrowing her thick but neatly shaped brows. "Are you okay?"

Tari sighed. "It's just this story. It's taking so much out of me. I haven't had a full night's sleep all week."

"Oh, you know you're enjoying this. Stop complaining." Rebecca always saw right through Tari.

She was right. But Tari couldn't help but feel that it was all too good to be true. And this lump in her breast was just so ill timed, so inconvenient. She didn't even want to bring it up with Rebecca. It would only ruin dinner and her semi-good mood.

The Thai restaurant that Rebecca had been raving about all week was in the basement of a building on JFK Street. Tari walked behind Rebecca, glancing in the window of the shoe store next to the restaurant.

"You're not buying anything," Rebecca warned.

Tari laughed, embarrassed and a little peeved at the motherly admonition. "I was just looking in the window, for chrissakes." It was Rebecca's calling in life, she had said many times, to save Tari from overspending herself into bankruptcy. She'd suggested that Tari sell all the clothes in her closet with tags still dangling from their sleeves on eBay. Tari had yet to do any such thing. As far as she was concerned, she could not pass up a sale because, well, you just never know when you might need a blue beaded tank top. Rebecca, on the other hand, saved every penny and had been wearing the same clothes since her freshman year in college. To her, a day spent shopping was a waste of time. Why shop when she could be haunting through Central Square for rare spices from India, the Caribbean, or China, or chatting with chefs at ethnic restaurants trying to glean recipes that she could try out on her fiancé, Ravi?

Tari felt a tiny pang of familiar envy as Rebecca bent so as to not bump her head as she descended the stairs leading into the basement restaurant. Oh, to be taller. Tari often felt that they made an odd pair, she petite, black, and so American, Rebecca, tall and unabashedly Hindu, sometimes wearing a sari when they went out. But the friendship worked because their personalities melded into equilibrium. Rebecca looked up to Tari because she always seemed so daring, so unafraid to do whatever it was that she wanted. Tari looked to Rebecca to rein in her impulsiveness and to remind her every now and then that the whole world was not waiting on the sidelines to cheer her inevitable downfall.

As they ate their salmon and vegetables sautéed with joom jeem sauce, Rebecca complained about her boring work at the university and Ravi, who had left his job on Wall Street to pursue an MBA. The hostess looked at them as she sipped tea out of a tiny yellow china cup with no handles. Tari was only half listening. She needed to find a bass player. She needed to start thinking about how she would find one. And she needed to call her doctor. Her mind couldn't focus on one thing. The hostess. What was she staring at? Legs of passersby hurried past the window on JFK Street above. It was peculiar, she thought, to look out a window and just see legs walking by, and Tari interrupted Rebecca's tirade about Ravi's latest transgression to tell her that. Rebecca looked at her as if she'd just landed from Mars.

"Tari, are you sure you're okay? You're so scatterbrained today. Maybe you need to take a day off from work."

Tari was taken aback. "I'm fine. I just have a lot on my mind."

"Why don't you place an ad on the Web for a bass player?"

Tari rolled her eyes. It wasn't that simple. She would rather have someone come to her through word of mouth.

Rebecca shrugged her athletic shoulders. "Just stop stressing out, okay? I'm stressed enough as it is. I need you to be calm for me right now. This wedding thing is going to drive me crazy."

Tari nodded absently. She had grown used to Rebecca's histrionics about her year-away wedding that her parents in Port of Spain, Trinidad, and Ravi's parents in Philadelphia were up in arms about. Rebecca's family wanted a full, traditional Hindu celebration on the island, and Ravi's parents, who had lived in the United States for over thirty years, wanted their son to marry in the Catholic Church where Ravi had been baptized. Ravi wanted to elope. Rebecca just wanted to be able to make a decision.

"Ooh, I have an idea!" Rebecca shot upright, fork pointing up in the air.

Tari tried to show some interest.

"Let's go to the Good Life."

Tari's face shifted into confusion. "Why? We just ate."

"They have live jazz tonight."

Tari hesitated. "I don't know if I'm in the mood. I should go home and get some sleep."

"No, Tari," Rebecca said, shaking her head, her massive curls lashing her cheeks. "They have these local guys playing on Wednesdays now. It's a new thing they're doing to fill up those tables on weeknights. You could probably find a bassist."

Tari was touched by her friend's attempt to help her. "But those guys are real amateurs," she said.

"No, I went last week with Ravi, and the band sounded really good—as good as the guys who play with you."

Tari reluctantly agreed to go, promising that she could only stay a few minutes, but only because the Good Life was only a few blocks away. When they entered the place, Rebecca took a seat at the bar and Tari followed reluctantly. She felt that familiar tug of guilt that arose every time she entered a bar or nightclub. She had to remind herself, *I'm not doing anything wrong.* Even during her college days when she was far away from home and the watchful, judgmental eye of her preacher father, she still felt fear before she took a sip of beer or let a man unhook her bra. To her, that fatal bolt of lightning was always just one sin away.

Rebecca was right, the band did sound good. Though it was still early in the evening, the room was semifull with an after-work crowd. She took in the stage—small. The band was made up of mostly old-timers, most likely retirees pursuing their hobby of playing drums, saxophone, and piano. And bass? He was no old-timer. And he looked familiar.

"Oh, my goodness!" Tari hit Rebecca on the arm. "It's

the guy from my church I was telling you about the other day!"

"Where?"

"Playing the bass, the stand-up bass!"

"Oh! Go talk to him after the set," Rebecca said. "It must be destiny. Besides, he's cute."

"Are you nuts? I can't let him see me in here. Let's go!"

Tari jumped off the bar stool and grabbed Rebecca's elbow. Rebecca followed her out the door. "What do you mean he can't see you in here?"

"It's a church thing," Tari said, hoping Rebecca would drop the matter.

"Oh, so I wouldn't understand?" her friend said sarcastically.

"I need to get home," Tari said, wanting to avoid an argument.

Rebecca held up her hand. "Fine. I'm walking. I'm in no hurry to get back." Rebecca's apartment was a ten-minute walk away, but Tari, guilty, still begged her to get in the car. Rebecca waved her hand dismissively and walked away.

Tari looked in her rearview mirror to see her friend, all nerdy-chic glasses, denim jacket, long, flowered skirt, and clogs. Rebecca's offbeat, untrendy style never ceased to amuse Tari. But today, it made her feel worse. Rebecca was her unpretentious rock of a friend; she hated it when they argued. But she couldn't let Rebecca into that part of her world—her church world that meant so much to her. That would mean philosophizing about religion with Rebecca. They had gone there a few times, and the result had not been pretty. It wasn't that Rebecca did not believe in God—or Jesus Christ, for that matter. It was just that she had questions. Lots of them. Some that Tari could not answer and would not even dare ask herself. "Let's just not talk about it anymore," was Tari's solution.

But Rebecca did not want to give up that easily. She just had to know. "Tari, you're so smart; why do you believe in all this evangelical stuff? It's so . . . not you," Rebecca had said many times.

Tari had tried to laugh it off. "And it's so not you to be so narrow-minded. You think all Evangelical Christians are illiterate rednecks or poor minorities. Look, there are a lot of intellectual reasons to believe in God. I just don't want to get into all of them with you."

"Whatever," Rebecca had said. "Why don't you just admit that your parents put the fear of hell in you since you were a kid, and at thirty years old you're still terrified that you'll die and end up in a pit of fire for all eternity?"

"Ha! Even if that were the case, at least I'm safe. And just for saying that, I won't put in a good word for you when I get to heaven."

Rebecca had sighed. "You're an idiot."

That's how those conversations always ended—with a joke or a wisecrack. It was a gulf between them that Tari didn't necessarily feel a need to mend. She couldn't explain the comfort she got from knowing that something greater than humanity was responsible for the sunshine, snow, babies being born, takeoffs, landings, colors, tastes, smells, and all the other miracles of life. Those things couldn't be all random, no matter what Darwin or any other science book said. Else what would be the point of even living?

Her faith was her anchor, and it didn't matter that none of her colleagues or friends understood. It was the first thing she'd known as a child, the foundation her family was built on. God was as much a part of her as her vital organs. She'd struggled with Him in high school while her friends went to beach parties and she was forced to go to vacation Bible school. She'd been laughed at when she'd told a college roommate that she thought premartial sex was wrong. She was ashamed, then she was defensive, then defiant. So she embraced it, and she decided she'd never let anyone make her feel ashamed of it anymore. So Rebecca didn't understand? Tough. *Who said we have to understand everything there is about life?*

CHAPTER

8

As Tari drove through the early-evening traffic, she pictured his face over and over again. No, he wasn't really her type. But he was fine. And he seemed to be working that cool, aloof thing really well. *Yeah, he'd make someone else a really good boyfriend or lover or hookup. Whatever. Not me, though.* Her cell phone rang. She rolled her eyes as she looked at the display; it was Melinda.

"I saw you on the front page today," Melinda said. *Wow, she's actually calling for a good reason,* Tari thought.

"Yeah, that's what I was working on all day yesterday."

"Congratulations," Melinda said in a clipped, tight voice.

"What's up?" Tari asked.

"Nothing. Just stressed out."

"You and Michael fighting again?"

Melinda laughed. "No. I just had a busy day at work. Where are you?"

"Coming back from yoga and dinner with Rebecca."

"Oh, you single girls have all the fun."

Tari rolled her eyes. "Nobody's stopping you from having dinner and doing yoga, Melinda."

"True. But where would I find the time?"

Oh, here we go, Tari thought. *She wants to bemoan the fact that she's so busy being superwoman, she doesn't have time for such frivolous pursuits as I do. Lay it on me, big sister.*

"I mean, it's not easy raising two kids, taking care of a household and working full-time. . . ."

Tari rolled her eyes again and silently mouthed the words along with Melinda. How many times did she have to hear this?

"So, Melinda," Tari said. At this point she'd have done anything to shift the conversation. "I found something in my right ta-ta."

"Huh?"

"Breast. Boob. Titty."

"I understood the first time, Tari. What do you mean you found something?"

"I think it's another one of those cysts."

"Really? Did you make an appointment?"

"Not yet."

"Not yet?" Melinda sounded surprised. "What are you waiting for?"

"I . . . This MetroBank thing. . . ."

"Is more important than your health?"

"It's just a cyst, girl. Chill out. That's why I didn't want to tell you."

"Well, if it's a cyst, go and have it taken care of, then. Why are you always playing around like that, Tari?"

"What do you mean playing around?"

"I mean taking things so lightly. You're just so blasé about everything."

How can she take one incident and generalize it into I'm blasé about everything in life? Tari sighed. "I'm working on a big story, Melinda."

"I know. I know. Just call the doctor and get that thing biopsied."

"Okay. Fine. I gotta go."

Tari hung up, shaking her head. *Why did I even tell her? This girl needs to stop acting like she's my mother!*

Melinda sat in her office waiting for her last couple to come in. They were late. She hated being the last one in the building to leave. And what was with Tari, anyway? Why would she be so unconcerned about something like that? Melinda's secretary had been diagnosed with breast cancer just two years ago, and she'd been only twenty-five when she'd gotten the diagnosis. Anything could happen. She checked herself. *What am I thinking?* This was Tari the workout freak. She was still too young, too healthy, and too mean for anything bad to happen to her. Yep, definitely too mean. Melinda laughed.

Her secretary, now in remission, told her that the Sellerses were ready for their session. Melinda opened their file and winced. This guy, Muhammad Sellers, had been cheating since day one of that marriage, and three years later his wife, Celia, was still holding it together. That woman was an idiot. But she'd never tell her to leave him. The patient had to make the decision on her own. They were her least favorite couple. She hoped she could make it through the session without throwing a lamp at Muhammad.

Rebecca walked away, angry. She could not understand why after all these years Tari would not let her into this one part of her life. She suspected that it might be some irrational shame, but she was never sure. Rebecca was eager, dying to know what had brought about this change in her high-strung friend. When she had first met Tari, she'd thought that this live wire was what she needed to fully assimilate. To leave her quiet, dowdy foreign-student-self behind and become a true sophisticate. Tari was like that then. Always wanting to party. Always dating someone interesting. Now her friend had changed, for the better in some ways, but Rebecca wanted to know how she really managed to do it. How she never talked about sex anymore, never drank, and hardly ever went out at night unless it was to one of her gigs. It couldn't be just the yoga classes. Rebecca took yoga, too, and most nights she couldn't wait to get home to jump Ravi's bones. So it had to be the religion.

Rebecca, who had been raised devoutly Hindu in Trinidad, had chosen the path of ambiguity over allegiance to any faith or deity when she moved to New York in 1994. She remembered being one of the *onlys* in her high school full of black and Indian children who were mostly Catholic and Protestant. The other Indians who practiced Hinduism stuck close together. But she was bookish and awkward and never stuck to anyone in particular. It had been an easy move to go to college abroad. There was no best friend in Port of Spain to weep for at the airport or to exchange letters with. Just her little brothers and sisters, who were patiently awaiting their turn to escape.

She'd never looked back, not even when her parents came to visit and criticized her Americanized lifestyle. It was only to appease them that she planned to have a wedding in full Hindu tradition. Because for her it was just that, tradition. She did not go to Mass with Ravi on the few Sundays out of the year that he went. For some reason, cathedrals terrified her. Something about the painted windows and incense seemed so gothic and old-worldly to her that she always felt she was in the scene of a horror movie where all hell was about to break loose. Of course, she never told Ravi those things.

He was waiting for her when she walked into the tiny apartment they shared. She grimaced at the McDonald's bag on the coffee table.

"Rav, you should have told me to pick you up something. You know how I wish you wouldn't eat that stuff."

He looked up from the thick investment management textbook, his dark hair falling all over his wire-rimmed glasses. "What took you so long?"

She told him about Tari's search for a bass player. He rolled his eyes and grabbed a few French fries. "Another day, another Tari crisis." Rebecca had laughed at Ravi years ago when he'd said that Tari terrified him. "She's just so sure of herself." Now he and Tari joked around like old friends, though he still thought her a bit of a drama queen.

Rebecca sat on the couch near his feet with their mismatched socks. "She makes me so mad with that shady religion thing of hers."

He shrugged. "Why don't you just leave her alone? Let her be a holy roller if she wants to be. Why do you have to *understand?*" His eyes said, *Why are we having this conversation that I really don't care for yet again?*

"It's not that. She gets all self-righteous . . ."

Ravi sighed. "Becks, I gotta finish reading this chapter."

"Fine, fine." She slapped his foot playfully and left him in the company of his textbook. He didn't have to tell her that he was tired of hearing about Tari's problems or metamorphoses.

"How would you feel if she kept getting on you for being Hindu?" Ravi said as she walked toward the bedroom.

"It's the not the same thing," she retorted.

Ravi elected to bury his head in his book instead of taking Rebecca up on this argument.

Whatever, she thought. She wasn't quite ready to buy Tari's argument that Christianity was so sacred, so holy, that it could only be talked about in reverential, hushed tones. She had begged Tari to take her along to church sometime. But Tari had refused. "This is not a science project," she had scolded. "It's sacred."

She only wanted to go to Tari's church, to know more about her and to find out whether it would change her, too.

She knew that Tari thought it was just her curiosity about experiencing "a black American church" but it was much more than that.

Rebecca was searching for truth, too. All her life she had done what her parents wanted, even coming to the States to study law when she had wanted to stay in Trinidad to teach English literature. But now that she was a free and independent woman in a country that she truly felt was her home, she wanted something deeper. What she wanted was to write about food. Every day, all the time.

She longed to be one of those people who loved everything about their lives; jobs, relationships, all of it. She had fallen into fund-raising because it was the best thing she could find when Ravi decided to move to Cambridge to get his MBA. The dozens of restaurant reviews she had written for the *Statesman* had not gotten her anywhere nearer a permanent job offer than she had been when Tari first scored that first assignment for her. She felt that if she could only get that one job, she would be complete. Then she would never have to consider the possibility that her parents had been right, that she should be using her law degree instead of wasting away her days trying to get Harvard alums to send more money to their already richly endowed school.

She sat at the creaky desk in the corner of the room where the computer was. She pulled up her resume on the screen and printed it. She pulled a stack of clips together and put everything in a brown envelope that she addressed to a magazine in New York. She had done this so many times before with the same disappointing result, but she would never give up.

CHAPTER
9

Tari read the e-mail again and sucked her teeth in disgust. It was from John Weston, jerk extraordinaire and the *Statesman*'s best writer, with two Pulitzers under his belt. He had been put on the MetroBank story, and she would be sharing a byline with him. She was seething but not in the least bit shocked. Yes, the story was big, but she could handle it on her own, for crying out loud. She was no intern. Those jerks in the front offices just had to go and put a man on it. She could just see Weston rubbing his hands gleefully. He'd steal her story, make it his own, get all the praise, and in a few weeks, everyone would forget that she'd been the one to break it.

The tone of his e-mail was condescending: *Just send me all you've got so far and I'll begin the lead-all for tomorrow's front page.* She ground her teeth and squeezed a stress ball Rebecca had given her as a gag gift.

She'd hoped that at this point in her career she could be trusted to see this story all the way through. She did not doubt for a nanosecond that she could do it on her own. No, she didn't have the contacts in the city's business world that John Weston had, and she didn't have a single Pulitzer to her name, but she knew how to pick up a phone and get people to call her back. She had been doing this for eight years, but they were treating her as if she were still a rookie. She squeezed the blue ball again.

She felt eyes on her and looked up to see Weston and her editor approaching. A part of her wanted to get up, take her belongings, and walk out of the office, leaving them standing there empty-handed. For good. But she sat quietly, waiting.

Weston was friendly enough, but she knew it was only because he wanted her story. The man was a pompous bore, and few people liked him. Normally he would not even acknowledge Tari when they crossed paths in the hallway, and as he smiled at her she was surprised to see that he had ugly, uneven teeth. But that did not stop Joe Martone from stuttering and genuflecting, as if Weston were some kind of god.

"I've got some friends, old Princeton buddies, at Metro-Bank, so I'll make a few calls. And Bill Boggs's and my kids go to the same school," Weston was saying, his droll voice, patrician accent, and overconfident attitude leaking all over Tari. She almost lost her lunch as Joe grinned humbly at Weston, thanking him for goodness knew what. How she despised the pretentious, arrogant creature standing in front of her. He never once looked her in the eye, though he was talking to her.

"So, Terry," Weston said, looking past Tari, who did not bother to correct him on the pronunciation of her name. "You'll send me an e-mail of the comment you got from Boggs today." It was an order, not quite a request.

She didn't answer. Instead, she began typing gibberish on her keyboard. Maybe it would look like she was sending him an e-mail. But she'd already decided that she would put off sending it until maybe a couple of minutes before deadline. Let him sweat through his hand-me-down Turnbull & Asser shirt.

"Tari, you did send him that e-mail, right?" Martone asked when Weston had slithered away from her desk.

Tari sighed and tilted her head to the side. "I don't like this, Joe. I really don't like this."

"You think I like it?" Joe asked, his hairy hands pointing to his chest. "These guys up there in the offices are really coming down on me. This is a big story. It's out of my hands and yours. I'm just doing what they tell me to do. Don't give me a hard time, okay?" Martone walked away, shaking his head and muttering to himself.

She didn't expect Joe to fight on her behalf. He was one of the more henpecked editors in the building and was terrified of the paper's executive editor, Steven Bluesteed. She could see Joe overdramatizing the whole thing, believing that his job depended on how the MetroBank story turned out and making everybody—her especially—miserable just so he would not tee off the powers that be.

This would not be easy, she thought as she began to write the sidebar to Weston's lead, a lead story that belonged to her, no doubt about it, and should have her byline only on it. She thought that her interview with the managing accountant for Framus LLC, the auditing firm that handled MetroBank's books, would get more attention from the bigwigs in the newsroom. The man had basically told her that his bosses ordered him to use a light hand when dealing with MetroBank because the bank was the firm's biggest customer. She could not believe Joe could not convince Bluesteed that this story should lead the paper. She began to suspect that there was probably an effort underway to slowly marginalize her and probably take her off the story completely. But that suspicion only strengthened her resolve to make this story shine. She ignored the instant messages that started to pop up on her screen the minute Martone walked away.

"What are they doing to you over there, sister?" Sarah

Fells, a health care reporter who also got the star treatment, wanted to know. Tari did not reply. Sarah barely ever spoke to her, and Tari was not in the mood to build fake friendships now.

"I'm really too busy now to think about that," she wrote to other colleagues who wanted to know whether she was going to fight the fact that Weston had essentially been given her story. They were throwing fuel on her, Tari knew. They knew about her temper and they wanted to see her make a scene, but she stayed cool and kept working.

Mariska Lunes asked in a bored, condescending tone, "Are you okay over there?"

Tari barely lifted her head to answer Mariska. The woman was annoying, annoying. Besides, she had real work to do. She didn't want to waste her afternoon blabbering away with Mariska.

"If I were you, I'd go to Bluesteed's office and fight this. There's no reason why you shouldn't get the lead on this. It's so unfair, Tari. So unfair," Mariska purred.

"It is. But that's life," Tari said evenly, her fingers flying over her keyboard furiously. "I'm a team player," she added for good measure. Mariska nodded something and turned back to her Internet surfing.

It was smarter to not get too involved with office gossip or politics, even when it involved her, she had learned over the years. The office was so cutthroat and competitive that she literally trusted no one. Besides Roger and one other writer in the Arts section, Tari could safely say that she had no real friends at work—colleagues, sure, but no real friends. But she wanted it that way. She knew how to take care of herself.

She wrote her sidebar as if it were the most important story she had ever written, ignoring the noise and constant telephone ringing as deadline neared. She kept all the great comments she had garnered during the day from Bill Boggs, disgruntled former executives from MetroBank, and other banking executives. She ignored repeated e-mails from Weston asking her for phone numbers and names of Metro-Bank executives. She smiled deviously. She would help him—but first she would finish her story. Two hours later, she had a polished, one-thousand-word story sent to Joe Martone's inbox. She took her time and answered Weston's e-mails. He didn't bother to thank her; it was a half hour before deadline.

She leaned back in her chair and sipped on cold coffee.

What a day, she thought: *I lost control of my story. I still don't have a bass player. . . .*

Her mind wandered back to the Good Life. Boy, he had sure looked good in that suit, though he was a bit over-dressed for a gig. She wondered how long he had played bass and why he never played in church. How could she find out who he was and ask him to be her bass player? The obvious implications were not lost on her. She knew she was attracted to him, but more important than that was the fact that she actually needed him. From their encounter in the church parking lot on Sunday, she knew he probably was not into her, and that wasn't a problem; she could get over that. She was no spoiled little princess who thought that all men owed her their undying love and attention. But she needed a bass player—and he played bass.

She checked her e-mail to see if Martone had any questions or issues so far with her story, and there was nothing but junk in her inbox.

Now on to the next problem, she thought. She reluctantly picked up the phone and dialed Violet Mathers's home number. Violet knew more than half of the members of the church, especially those who were male and single. Violet was forty-two, never married, and actively looking. She spent her days and nights in the church, leading the singles group, singing in the choir, and serving as full-time accountant. If anyone would know the bass player's name, it would be Violet.

"Girl, you must be talking about Shawn Phillips," Violet said excitedly after hearing a description. "Yes, girl. He is fine, isn't he? He's divorced, though. I hear he's got an ex-wife down in Providence." *I didn't ask for all that information,* Tari wanted to say, but she stuck that fact somewhere easily accessible in her mind anyway.

"So, he's a musician?"

"No. Well, I don't know what he does in his spare time. But he works for KPMG. He's pretty high up over there."

Tari was confused. "Oh, I heard that he was a musician on the side," she lied.

"He might be. I see him talking with the guys who play in the band all the time. But I don't know, girl. Hey, you want me to introduce you guys on Sunday? I'll set it up if you want me to." Violet was also notorious for playing matchmaker; maybe she thought it would bring some good relationship karma her way.

"Oh, no, not at all," Tari said. Last thing she wanted was Violet involved in her business. "I'm looking for a bass player for my quartet, that's all. I thought he played."

"Oh, I see," Violet said. "Girl, when you gonna start using your talent for the Lord?"

Tari rolled her eyes. It always ended up that way with Violet. "Thanks for your help, girl. But I've gotta go. My editor's breathing down my neck."

Tari turned around to look into Joe Martone's dark blue eyes.

"You need to rewrite the top of your story," he said, his eyes dancing and his shoulders tense.

"What? Why?" Tari asked, dismayed by the look on Joe's face.

"Bluesteed loves it, Tari. They want to lead the paper with it!"

"What? Are you kidding?" Tari's mouth was open.

"Yeah," Martone said. "Weston still hasn't turned his in yet. You're leading on A1, kiddo. Start rewriting. Punch it up a bit."

"Oh, my God," Tari said, her face breaking into a grin. "Thanks, Joe."

"Don't thank me, I'm not the one who wrote it," Martone said, pointing her to her keyboard.

Tari looked up and whispered a word of thanks and started typing furiously. Her story was back in her hands.

CHAPTER
10

That night sleep came and went intermittently. She turned over in her head every single word she had written, doing a mental spell check, worrying over possible factual errors, all the things that she knew the copy editors could handle.

And it was this tossing and turning in bed that led her to it again. Her hand inadvertently touched that same spot. Darn! Her eyes, temporarily forgetting their mission to remain closed, opened wide. She had almost forgotten about the doctor's appointment the following morning. It was only then she briefly allowed the scariest thought to enter her mind, but she quickly swept it out.

Focus, Tari, she told herself, willing sleep to rescue her. She ran her fingers over the lump several times. It felt hard and slippery under her fingers. Her eyes opened again. Maybe it was her imagination, but it seemed bigger since the last time she touched it. She told herself that it was the dark of night, the stress, the insomnia that was skewing her tactile sense. She had other things to worry about. Sleep.

Her mind swung back and forth from breast to story. She worried that the copy editors' headline would not do the story justice. What if they made an error? Maybe she should call over there and just check with them one more time. She stared at the ceiling, then the clock on her night table, and then at the phone. It was one A.M. They would think her insane if she called that late. She shut her eyes. Sleep.

The next morning Tari looked up at the dimpled, white ceiling of examining room Number 11 at the Pilgrim Health Associates office in West Roxbury. The center was like a minihospital, and Tari hated it. From the minute she'd parked in front of the building, she encountered sick people: on crutches, in wheelchairs, on the arms of loved ones, some exiting the building with little white bags bulging with prescription drugs. Pregnant women pushing crying babies in strollers waddled into the reception area, their faces droopy and exhausted. It was a sick scene, and Tari wanted no part of it. But there she was anyway.

Her doctor's tiny hands massaged her breast, and she worried that her nipples would harden. She concentrated on the white clock with the black ticking hands, counting seconds. The woman, a petite Ghanaian probably not much older than Tari, spoke with a British accent. It occurred to Tari that in two years she had only seen the woman twice. Those little postcards the office sent reminding her to fastidiously adhere to yearly physicals, gynecological appointments, and the like usually went unread and into the recycling with the rest of the junk mail. That unnerving procession of sick people outside the medical building had only confirmed to her that she had a low tolerance for sick people, doctors, or anything that could contradict what she thought of herself: that she was at the peak of good health. The only doctor she saw four times a year was her dentist. Twice for cleaning and twice for her laser whitening fix.

"Well, I think I'm going to have to send you down for a mammogram and a biopsy of this," the doctor said with no emotion in her voice.

Tari turned to look at her, searching the woman's eyes for

any hint of what she might be thinking. "You mean right now? Why? Did you feel something bad?" A warmth rose in Tari's chest and she sat up slowly, the crinkly paper under her naked back making a crackling noise.

The doctor maintained her impenetrable calm demeanor. "Since you have a history of benign cysts, I think we should find out what this one is all about. At this point I can't speculate at all. I'd advise you not to worry until the results come back."

Tari stared at the doctor for a minute. "But it's not serious, right?"

"At this point, Tari, I can't say that it is or it isn't."

The doctor smiled and touched Tari on the arm before she left the room.

The following hour crawled by, but it wasn't the anxiety over the test results that annoyed her. She put those concerns low on her list of priorities, subconsciously willing the scenario to be more an inconvenience than a potential tragedy. *I mean, how much time do I have to waste here?* Two of her precious hours had already been sucked up, she thought, looking blankly at her cell phone. There were calls to make, e-mails to catch up on. Who knew what else would unfold with MetroBank today? This was the last place she wanted to be. *History of benign cysts, give me a break.* Why did the doctor have to be so calm yet so sympathetic? What was this extreme kindness all about? She replayed every word said in the examining room. Why did she have to get this done now?

She tapped her feet impatiently and put away the cell phone as she watched the TV screen idly. Regis and Kelly were making the other women in the waiting room laugh. Tari looked away; Kelly Ripa had to be one the perkiest women alive. *Like, calm down, girl, everybody can see you're cute already!*

They sat in a semicircle of chairs around the thirteen-inch TV and a table full of *People, US, In Touch* and other celebrity garbage. They were all wearing hospital gowns that were too big. Tari quickly glanced at the women's rapt faces and wondered whether they truly were paying attention to Regis. None of them regarded the other. There was no small talk. Nah, Regis was not that good. Tari wondered whether they were waiting for test results, too. Were they worried, their minds stuck in that limbo of cancer or no cancer? They all looked to be in their late forties and older, and she felt self-conscious, like an impostor. She wondered whether they questioned what someone her age was doing there. People always told her that she looked much younger than her age, and she did with her hair pulled back in a ponytail and the big hospital gown that swallowed up her petite frame. But the other women seemed wrapped up in their gowns and cares; they didn't seem to even be aware of her.

Besides the gossip magazines, the waiting-room table also held literature on breast cancer. The brochure pictures featured women with graying hair or obviously mature faces, all smiling. *I don't belong here,* Tari thought, and that warmth rose in her chest. *I just so want to leave this awful place.*

When her name was finally called, she almost jumped out of the chair, following the nurse into a room full of heavy machinery. She tried to smile as the woman made small talk. "Nice day out there, huh?"

Tari wanted her to just get on with the biopsy, but there was no shutting up for the blue-scrubbed woman. "Yes, it's gorgeous." She signed consent forms, answered questions, and then lay back on yet another crinkly sheet of paper atop the exam room table. "Don't worry, hon," the woman said. "You won't feel any pain."

Tari grimaced. As much as she appreciated the woman's efforts to comfort her, she knew that was not technically true. Yes, the lidocaine would take care of the pain at the site of the biopsy, but there was no drug that could drown out the sound and the impact. She steeled herself. When the radiologist entered the room, Tari was already wound up tightly. "Relax, honey," the nurse said, grinning. Tari didn't smile back. She wondered if they knew that by telling her to relax, they were automatically inducing the exact opposite reaction.

She breathed out as the radiologist stuck out her hand for a sturdy handshake. The woman was businesslike and was probably in a bad mood. She explained the procedure quickly, without a tinge of gentleness in her voice. "Okay, let's get started," the radiologist growled, instructing the nurse to pinpoint the area of the lump.

Tari clenched her fist as the radiologist took the first sample of tissue. The machine made a sound like a stapler, an industrial-size stapler, and Tari could feel its impact. Kachunk! Kachunk! Each time, she clenched her fist tighter. The radiologist took six samples. When she finally relaxed her hands, she could feel a tiny sliver of blood running down her chest. The nurse quickly dabbed it away and bandaged the area. "You okay, honey?" she asked.

Hot tears burned the back of Tari's eyes, but she fought them back. It had been ten years since she had last done this, but this time it seemed more horrible. Still, there was no way in hell she would allow herself to cry. *I'm a butt kicker*, she told herself. *No tears.*

"Am I done now?" she asked the nurse weakly.

But there was one more step. Another nurse shepherded her into another room where she would have a mammogram. This one was young and talkative.

"Wow, we have the same birthday." The blond nurse peered at Tari's chart. "February the seventeenth. But I was born in *1979.*" Because the nurse said this with absolutely no guile, Tari allowed herself to smile kindly at her. Then she allowed her breasts to be squished and pressed into the mammography machine. The machine was brutal, reminding her of an inexperienced teenage boy who'd eagerly manhandled her breast in high school and left her thinking that this sex thing was certainly not as fun as it looked on TV. She was bent sideways, uncomfortable. But she did not complain. *I'm a butt-kicking kind of sista. . . .*

"You're pretty young to be over here," the nurse said.

"Yeah, I've had lumps before. They were just cysts, you know. Lumpy breasts." Tari shrugged.

The nurse's big brown eyes met hers, and they were serious. "Hey, can you tell anything yet?" Tari asked, knowing full well that the nurse could not reveal anything to her.

The nurse looked around the room and whispered, "I'm not supposed to do this, but since we have the same birthday I'll tell you. They're concerned because your lump is pretty hard. Normally, that's a bad sign. But it's also moving around, and that's a good sign. So you have one positive and one negative. But this one's not a regular cyst. It's solid—no fluid in it." The nurse looked around to see if anyone had heard her violate the rules of her job.

Fear did a gallop through Tari's heart. Not a regular cyst?

"But it's not cancer, right?" she asked the nurse, whose face told her that she already regretted saying so much.

"We can't tell that until we get the biopsy results back in three days. But you're young. I'm sure it's nothing. Don't worry about it," the nurse said.

But it was too late. Tari thanked her and got dressed.

It was another sunglasses-mandatory, UV rays–advisory type of day, but Tari was oblivious. The news announcer on NPR was telling of yet another attack on US soldiers in Iraq. Normally, this would get Tari's blood boiling and get her talking to her radio, but she did not even hear what was coming through the speakers. The words that kept echoing through her mind left her oblivious to everything else. *Not a regular cyst. They're worried.*

The budding trees on the West Roxbury parkway and the blooming daffodils in the overly landscaped front yards of the suburb's large homes did not catch her eye, nor did they remind her of her plans to start a garden this spring. All she could think of was the look on the nurse's face, that serious look. The woman had said not to worry, but Tari was not convinced. She reached for her cell phone on the passenger seat.

Thankfully, Melinda was not with a patient. She was quiet as Tari poured out her fears.

"Now, Tari. I don't want you to think you have anything until those test results come back. Do you hear me?" Melinda said in her most motherly voice. "I want you to go to work and concentrate on your story. You'd better pray to God that He gives you the strength to concentrate on the things you can control and gives you the strength to deal with what's not in your hands. But don't go making yourself crazy over this, because you don't know anything yet."

There were few times in her adult life that she felt this, but she wanted to keep talking to Melinda just to hear that strong voice assuring her that everything would be all right. But her sister had an appointment with a bipolar manic-depressive husband and an alcoholic wife in just a few minutes. Tari was so worried about herself that she did not make the obvious crack on Melinda's interesting roster of patients.

Melinda made all the sense in the world. Tari had no idea what she was worrying about. If she were to find out three days from now that she had wasted days worrying about nothing, she would only be angry with herself.

She turned up the volume of the stereo and switched to the local talk station. MetroBank was the topic of the day. As she listened to a news commentator excoriate the bank's executives, her mood changed. She laughed as the host mentioned her name.

"We've got to thank our lucky stars that we have gutsy reporters like Tari Shields out there who are willing to expose these guys for the thieves and cheats that they are," the host was saying, and the caller on the line agreed with him. "This is an example of great journalism," the caller said.

Tari slapped the steering wheel. "Yes!" This was what she had been wanting for so long. A big story that would show all her bosses and her smug colleagues what she was capable of and that would change something in the community. And it was happening. She stepped on the gas, eager to get back to work.

It was almost noon when she entered the office, and Joe was sitting at her desk. "Where've you been?" he asked. "I've been waiting for you over an hour!"

"Joe, I had a doctor's appointment. I told you that," she snapped back. She had learned over the years that to be polite with Joe or many of the men in the newsroom was to lose a significant amount of their respect. They were rude and brash and they could only relate to being treated the same way. Anything else was viewed as weakness.

"Well, you have to do TV now," he said.

"What? Now?" Tari's hand flew to her head in dismay. If she had known she was going to be on the NE News Channel, New England's twenty-four-hour news network, she would at least have blown out her hair.

Joe pointed her in the direction of the small studio in the newsroom where the news channel broadcast live a few hours of the day. It wasn't the first time she would do the TV part of her job, but usually she had enough warning to at least make sure her hair was done the day before.

She quickly took her seat in front of the camera after retouching her makeup. The news anchor was a young woman, probably younger than Tari, and friendly. But Tari was finding it difficult to keep a smile on her face. To her relief, the woman asked softball questions that had already been answered in the story that ran in the paper. Thank goodness, she thought, aware of the pile of e-mail and phone messages awaiting her. She was certain there would be some new update that she just wasn't aware of. Thankfully, the TV segment was short.

As she walked back to her desk, she felt the Bluesteed energy field approaching. Steven Bluesteed was a short, intense man with a bad temper and a terrible smoking habit. He reeked of cigarettes and authority, and Tari hated being near him. He made everybody, including her, nervous and afraid.

"Tari, good work," he said in his gruff voice, and she thought she saw the beginnings of a smile at the corners of his tight mouth. "Great stuff, great stuff. Keep it coming." He patted her on the shoulder without even breaking his stride.

Tari was so taken aback by the rare compliment and words of encouragement that she stood frozen, her mouth open.

Another reporter who had heard the exchange said, "Well, that's one for the record books. You should have gotten that on tape."

Tari shrugged and headed back to her chair. What a week this was turning out to be. She got on the phone again, calling her contacts to get more dirt on MetroBank. The CEO was still holding out, pointing fingers at other executives who in secret were saying that he knew all along about the corruption problems at the company he had been running for twenty years, and Tari was determined to see him fall. The man, Donald Meehan, was not immovable, she thought as she scanned her e-mails. But there was nothing new, no sign that he would make any statement that didn't deny any wrongdoing on his part. She had never met the man, but from his picture she assumed he was one of those blue-blooded, arrogant types who thought he would never have to pay for any mistake he'd ever made, because all his life, someone else had always paid.

All Tari wanted was one piece of proof, someone reliable who would come forward with something she could use to get this guy to admit he was as crooked as his henchmen. As she frantically dialed, begging people to talk to her, she forgot about the scary morning at the doctor's.

CHAPTER
11

Melinda listened to her patients bicker, keeping one eye on the clock. *Thank God, they'll be out of here in five minutes*, she thought. *These people don't need marriage counseling*, she thought. *They need a restraining order against each other.*

"We'll pick this up next week," she said, interrupting the husband's rant about his wife's housecleaning habits—or lack thereof.

She resisted the urge to call Tari again as she drove home through the rush-hour traffic. It would only worry her sister, and that was the last thing she wanted to do. Melinda wished she felt as sure and reassuring as she'd tried to be for Tari on the phone. But she was worried sick; she just couldn't help it. She had to see how Tari was holding up. She dialed Tari's number at work and got her voice mail. She tried her cell phone.

Tari sounded stressed. "What's up, Melinda? I'm on deadline."

"Oh, sorry. I didn't think of that. Just wanted to know how you were holding up."

"I'm fine. I gotta finish this story, okay?"

Melinda hung up and sighed. *Well, if she's not worried, then I probably shouldn't be*, she thought. Then, *Tari is fine. She's not my overweight, ex-smoker secretary. Last thing I need is something else to worry about.*

She called home to make sure Michael had picked up the kids and they were doing their homework. Taylor answered the phone.

"What are you doing, honey bunny?" Melinda asked.

"Watching *Dora the Explorer.*"

"Did you and Daddy read?"

"Not yet."

Melinda gritted her teeth. "Put him on the phone, baby."

Michael came to the phone. "I know. I know," he said. "Jared's doing his homework. And I'll read with her as soon as her show is over."

"But—"

"Melinda, it's her favorite show. Give the kid a break!"

"Fine. Just make sure you read to her, that's all. I'm meeting my women's group today. I'll be home around six-thirty or seven."

"Can you pick something up for dinner?" he asked.

"We have veggie lasagna in the freezer." Thanks to caterer Baker's Best, she kept a supply of their food in the freezer for the days when she couldn't get home in time to cook dinner. At least that way, the kids could be fooled into thinking it was a home-cooked meal. If she left it up to Michael he'd most likely order them pizza or KFC.

She pulled into the church parking lot and took a deep breath as she parked. *Why am I even a part of this?* she wondered as she walked toward the sanctuary. It was her women's group, a kind of support group for women like her—married with children and lots of religion. They were supposed to support and strengthen one another and do great works for the church. Most times they managed to do great things for the church and intentionally or unintentionally make one another feel inadequate and insecure. This group was the ultimate sorority. All the single women looked up to them with a fiery envy, especially the single or divorced moms who stood no chance of ever becoming members; the unspoken rule was that you had to have a husband. Tari always made fun of them, and at first Melinda thought her sister was just jealous. But the more time she spent with some of these women, the more she realized that some of them really believed their own hype: that they were somehow superior to other women who didn't have the total package, or at least their definition of that. It was sad, Melinda thought, because she could not think of a single one of them who had a perfect marriage or who did not sometimes envy the freedom that single women had: the ability to just pick up and go whenever and wherever without having to consult with anyone else or worrying about hurting some man's feelings or putting a child in danger. *They want our lives and we want theirs*, she thought. *None of us is completely happy.*

Melinda walked in and everyone turned to greet her; she was always late and they poured sympathy all over her. She grabbed a cookie and a cup of coffee, making a mental note to start exercising this weekend.

"Sorry, I'm late, traffic was absolutely awful," she said, sitting in the circle of chairs.

Her one true ally in the group, Lucy, looked at her and raised her eyebrows. She and Lucy joked about the other women sometimes, thinking that they were somehow above all the self-congratulating that always went on at these meetings. It was no coincidence that she and Lucy had the most demanding jobs and therefore were seen as renegades, not quite members of the club.

The leader of the group, Stephanie Strong, began to speak about their latest endeavor. It would be a women's conference, meant to empower the women of the church. Melinda tried her best to listen as Stephanie spoke about the topics and panel speakers she wanted for the conference, the singers, the caterer for the luncheon. Melinda and Lucy exchanged looks frequently, trying not to laugh.

Stephanie was the most self-righteous of the group and therefore the de facto leader. She home-schooled her kids, made many of their clothes with her own hands, did hours of research on what they should eat, where they should play, and other mundane things that most normal parents would leave to chance. She felt that both public and private school curricula were too liberal and ungodly for her tastes, and not only that, she believed that the schools did not do a good enough job of instilling ethnic and masculine pride into her black sons. This was her maternal platform, and so she always found a way to insert her child-rearing doctrine into every conversation. It had gotten to the point where the other women almost apologized for sending their kids outside of the home to be educated. As expected, Stephanie recommended a panel on Home-Schooling: Why It's the Responsibility of Christian Parents. Lucy coughed and Melinda shot her a warning look.

Melinda found herself signing up for chores she knew she had no business signing up for. *Why in the world am I doing this?* she wondered as she agreed to lead two panels on Mental Coping Strategies for Today's Black Christian Woman. *I must be a masochist,* she thought. *I shouldn't be leading this panel; I should be signing up for it.*

"Sister Melinda, you're just such a blessing to us all, the way you give your time," Stephanie said, smiling, as she signed Melinda's name to the list of duties. Melinda nodded. *Yeah, whatever.*

After the meeting, she waited for Lucy in the foyer.

"Girl, didn't I tell you she was gonna do that home-schooling thing again?"

"Lucy, you're bad." Melinda giggled. Lucy had been her friend for over a decade. They'd met in this very lobby, when they both served as greeters for the church. Lucy was a lawyer married to a lawyer who, like Melinda, tried to do it all. Their kids were about the same age and went to the same school. But unlike Melinda's kids, Lucy's kids were dropped off and picked up by the full-time, live-in nanny who pretty much ran Lucy's household while she and her husband put in 150 hours a week between them at their respective firms. Melinda liked Lucy because she was irreverent and carefree, despite her staggering work schedule. Instead of feeling guilty about everything, she let it slide off her back. "Girl, I don't want to be home with my kids. I'd rather be working," Lucy always said.

"You better be careful, she's gonna get on you for having a nanny," Melinda joked.

"She better not step to me," Lucy said. "I'll lay it on her—in the name of Jesus, of course."

They laughed as they walked out to their cars.

"So, how are you?" Lucy asked.

"Too blessed to be stressed. I think," Melinda said. "But my sister's got issues."

"What is it this time?"

"She found a lump in her breast."

"Really? Has she had it checked out?"

"Not yet. She doesn't care much, though. You know Tari. Work first, everything else after."

"Oh, Melinda. I hope it's nothing," Lucy said, adding quickly, "I'm sure it's nothing. Tari's so young and healthy."

"I know. That's what I keep telling myself," Melinda said.

"Well, I'll say a prayer for her," Lucy said as they went to their cars.

"Thanks, girl," Melinda said, waving good-bye.

When she got home it was almost seven-thirty, and surprisingly enough the kids had already eaten and were in their pajamas. She played with Taylor for a while before sending her upstairs to her room. Jared was already in his room, pretending to read. She knew as soon as she turned her back he'd turn on the television.

"Good night, baby," she told him.

"Good night, Mom."

"Love you," she said.

He mumbled something back. At thirteen, Jared was no longer the affectionate little boy she used to cuddle with every night. These days, he wanted her as far away from his physical body as possible. She was almost getting used to the rejection, but it still hurt sometimes.

She ran down the stairs. "You couldn't wait for us to eat together?" she asked Michael, who sat in front of the TV watching ESPN.

He looked at her and smiled slyly. "We'll eat together; they're going to bed early."

"Homework is done?"

"Chill out, Melinda," Michael said, following her to the kitchen. "I think you need to stop hanging out with Stephanie and her groupies. You're starting to scare me."

She sighed. "Yeah, it's scary to want the best for our kids."

"Don't start, okay? I wanted us to have a nice dinner together. Alone."

She turned to him. "Why?"

He shrugged and smiled. *Oh, he wants to have sex.* Well, she was too tired for that. She'd been up since five A.M. All she wanted was a long bath and a full eight hours of sleep.

She sat at the dinner table and began to eat. He sat across from her. "So how was your day?" he asked.

"Stressful," she said.

"Can I do something?" he asked suggestively.

She didn't answer, and she noticed the disappointment on his face. Guilt seeped into her heart. "Maybe after I read to Taylor and take a bath," she said.

"Never mind," he said.

"No, I want to," she said.

"No, you don't," he said.

She wanted to scream, *Sure, make me feel bad about working all day and then being too tired to have sex!*

They finished dinner in silence. She went upstairs to check on Taylor, who was already dozing off with her dolls scattered around on her bed. "Baby, don't you want your story?"

Melinda's heart melted as Taylor nodded and fell into her arms. Moments like these made her hate women like Stephanie Strong who got to stay home all day with their kids, who had moments like these all day, every day. She held her daughter close and began to read. She kept reading long after Taylor had fallen asleep just to make the feeling last as long as she could.

By nine-thirty, she was in bed and Michael was still downstairs watching ESPN. She'd softened up a bit and decided that if he came up, she'd let him have some. She tried to wait, thinking about Tari and praying that her sister would be okay, but sleep overtook her good intentions, and by the time Michael made it upstairs she was out.

CHAPTER
12

She would kill Violet. That's what she would do. That silly, silly, silly woman. She had warned her not to do this. *I can't believe her!* Tari played the message for the sixth time. His voice was deep, and Tari noticed that he had a faint, lilting accent.

"Hello. This is Shawn Phillips. Sister Violet told me that you might be looking for a bass player for your band. She gave me your number. Anyway, if you're still looking, give me a call."

Man! That Violet was freaking incorrigible and presumptuous, Tari thought. How could she have given out her phone number without her permission? It wasn't that hearing his voice hadn't immediately taken some of the edge off her rough day. It was that Violet had had something to do with it. Ugh. That woman! She could just imagine Violet telling all her busybody friends in the choir and singles group that she'd hooked up Tari with Shawn. The thought made her want to hit something. But she played the message again. Maybe she should give him a call. It was no big deal. It was all business anyway. What was she worrying about? It wasn't as if she'd thrown herself at him. Yet.

She began to dial and could almost hear her heart thumping. She almost hung up after the third ring. She searched in vain for the voice she used when she talked with her sources, her professional, no-nonsense voice, but all that came out was the high-pitched, squeaky tone she'd worked so hard to lose over the years.

"Hi, er, Shawn. I'm glad I caught you. This is Tari Shields." She rolled her eyes when her voice, unsure and perky, echoed in her ear.

"Oh, hey!" he said, sounding as if they were old friends.

Was this the same man who had seemingly scolded her just this past Sunday for leaving her car window open?

"You know, I don't think I know you," he said. "Violet tried to describe you, but I just don't think I've ever seen you."

Tari rolled her eyes. What did he mean by that? She wondered if he'd remember if she mentioned all the times they had locked eyes in the parking lot, in the sanctuary in the middle of the sermon, and the time they sat right next to each other and his knees kept brushing against hers. Yeah! He hadn't seen her at all.

"Well, it's a big church," she said dryly, hoping her voice wouldn't betray her sarcasm. *Sure, I'll play along with this game, Shawn Phillips.*

"So, you're a jazz singer," he said.

She explained to him that she'd only been performing on the local scene for a few years and that she did it mostly because she loved to sing, not for the money, because most times she did not get paid. She always told this to her musicians, warning them that they would never become rich from performing with her—and that she was only using her limited contacts and word of mouth to get gigs. She found herself telling Shawn that this was more than just a hobby. Singing was a passion she'd had since she was a child, and she was finally living her dream.

Shawn said he could identify. Tari was pleased to hear that he too had a deep love for jazz and that he sometimes left work in the early afternoon to perform hour-long gigs around town. She was surprised to hear that he'd played with contemporary recording artists like Stefon Harris and Walter Beasley and that he even knew Manny, her band leader.

"Wow, if I'd known that I'd have let him recruit you," she joked.

"I haven't seen Manny in years, though," he said.

Shawn was thirty-four years old, born in Barbados but had lived in Boston since he emigrated with his parents at age fifteen. Tari noted that he spoke in great detail about his work and his house in Hyde Park that he was renovating all by himself, but quickly glossed over his divorce, mentioning that his ex-wife had left a lot of her things in his basement. *Just in your basement?* she wondered silently.

"How long have you been divorced?" She put her hand over her mouth, but it was too late to stop the question. *What was I thinking?* she fretted. *This is supposed to be a business call, not a getting-to-know-you conversation.*

"About two years," he said without missing a beat. There was a short silence, and she almost ended the conversation there and then.

"So what's it like being a reporter?" he asked.

She soon forgot about her gaffe and the conversation returned to its easy, comfortable place. She smiled at the passion in his voice as he talked about his work as the director of new technology at KPMG, laughing as he described himself as a computer nerd, although the way Tari remembered him, a dark-skinned, muscular, 6'2" vision of near perfection, she knew that he was being modest.

Two hours later, Tari realized that she was hungry and that dinnertime had long passed. She looked for an opening to end the call but was reluctant. She strained to remember the last time she'd had a conversation like this with a man. The "audition" was what she used to call it back in her dating days. She tried to remember her old rules: careful not to reveal too much about her personal life and don't appear too interested. But then she stopped herself; this was not what this was about. This man was to be her bass player, not a potential date. She didn't want him to get the wrong idea. She didn't want to come off as one of the girls who used the church for their husband-hunting safaris. She only wanted a bass player, and she was glad that she had found someone who at least loved music and seemed highly qualified.

So what if he could make her laugh?

"You like to kickbox? Wow. I'd better watch my back."

Later she found herself replaying the conversation in her head as she ate a dinner of reheated clam chowder with oyster crackers and watched CNN. *How come Aaron Brown always looks and sounds drunk?* She was more than a little excited about the lunch date with Shawn at the Good Life later next week. *The right thing to do,* she told herself, *is to ask Manny to come along.* But she couldn't deny that she wanted him to herself. She called Manny anyway.

"Shawn Phillips? That name sounds familiar," Manny said, background television noise forcing him to yell. Why couldn't he just turn the thing down? Tari sighed.

"So, you wanna have lunch with us? Just to get to know him?"

"Nah, I don't have time for all that. You can talk to him. If he's good as you say he is, tell him to come down and rehearse with us on Saturday."

Tari mouthed a silent yes.

One problem solved, she told herself as the eleven o'clock

news made a loud, flashy entrance. She had no doubt then that Shawn would play for her.

Her hand went to her right breast. She would not worry. Not until she was certain that she had something to worry about; that was what Melinda said. But sleep was hard to reach that night.

CHAPTER

13

Melinda was doing her best not to nod off as Stephanie Strong went on and on about the women's conference.

"Ladies, we really need to reach as many of our sisters as we can this year. So many of them have just given up on marriage. We have to pray that they will not lose their faith. . . ." Stephanie's overly made-up face was tense with passion, and her manicured hands were moving a mile a minute as she talked.

Melinda looked at Stephanie and wondered if she too should get rid of her perm and go natural. Stephanie, who wore her hair in long dreads, said many times that a black mother sent her daughters the wrong message each time she used that "hair crack" on her beautiful nappy hair. *But how would I look with dreads?* Melinda bit her nails and tried to concentrate on Stephanie's pep talk to no avail. She'd noticed that Lucy had ditched her halfway through the meeting, claiming that she had to get home early for some fake-sounding reason. "Traitor!" she'd whispered as Lucy walked out of the sanctuary.

"So, like I was saying, we really need everyone to be committed—fully committed—to the tasks they've signed on for. Now, Melinda, I haven't heard anything from you since you agreed to lead the panels on mental health."

Did I just hear my name? Melinda's head jerked up. "I'm sorry, what?"

Stephanie's judging eyes looked through Melinda. "Are you okay?"

"I'm just tired. Long day at work." And it had been. She wanted to be home now with her kids, but here she was playing superwoman again with a bunch of women who had the luxury of staying home all day looking forward to these insipid gatherings.

"So, can we talk about the panels sometime soon?" Stephanie insisted.

"Sure," Melinda said, worried that she really hadn't given any thought to the stupid panels.

"If you can't do it, I will," said Rita Rich, also a stay-at-home mom, who as far as Melinda knew had no training to lead a panel on mental health. "I may not be a psychologist, but I'm anointed by God," Rita said.

Lord help us, Melinda thought. "I'll do it," she said firmly.

As the meeting broke up, Melinda wearily picked herself up from the folding chair and hoped that A) the kids would still be up when she got home and B) that Michael wouldn't want sex.

Stephanie came up to her, smiling broadly. "Melinda, sister! You sure you okay?" Stephanie, tall and pretty, always looked good, and that just added to the list of things that made Melinda hate her just a bit.

"I'm fine," Melinda said. "A lot going on."

"Well, sis. I'll keep you in my prayers. Remember there's no job out there that's worth the time you can spend with your family."

Melinda gritted her teeth.

"And as women of God," Stephanie continued, digging

her grave even deeper, "we shouldn't care so much for the material trappings of life, especially if it's gonna kill us to get them." She said this while eyeing Melinda's Prada bag.

Now she had gone and done it, Melinda thought.

"You know, Stephanie," Melinda said, slinging her bag over her shoulders. What she wanted to say was, *Seems to me that it's always the bored housewives who have enough time on their hands to come up with the nonsense that just came out of your mouth.* But what she did say was, "You really should be careful that you don't offend people with the things you say sometimes. Okay?"

Stephanie stepped back. "I didn't—"

"Good night," Melinda smiled sweetly. "Guess I'll go home to my gorgeous home and family now."

"But we haven't talked about the panel."

"I don't think I'll be doing the panels," Melinda said, turning around to face Stephanie. "As you said, nothing's worth more than spending time with my family."

Idiot! Melinda thought as she walked out the building. She knew that some of the women had overheard her and would probably be replaying the exchange over and over again for weeks, probably months, to come. *But let them*, she thought. She had no time for this, and she certainly didn't need some self-righteous supermom lecturing her about her life choices. *That's it*, she fumed. *I quit. I quit this stupid group.*

When she got home, Taylor was already asleep and Jared was again pretending to read *Native Son.* "How's the book?" she asked him, sitting at the foot of his bed.

"Good," he mumbled.

"Just good?"

"Pretty good," he sighed.

"You'll appreciate it more when you get older." She smiled. "I thought it was boring when I read it the first time, too."

"I don't think it's boring." He looked at her.

"Really?"

"No. I like it. Bigger Thomas is kinda real."

"Oh," she said, surprised. "I . . . I'm so glad you like it, then."

"Can I go back to reading now?" Jared asked.

"Sure, sweetheart." She stood up and watched his eyes travel over the page. He really was reading the book! "Good night," she said from his doorway.

He mumbled good night but did not look up from *Native Son*.

She ran downstairs to where Michael sat watching television. "Honey, Jared's really into that book."

"Yeah, I got it for him," Michael said.

"You did? I thought it was assigned reading for school."

"Nope."

She stood staring at her husband. Had he actually done something right? She couldn't believe it. "So, you wanna come upstairs?" she asked him. All of a sudden she wasn't as tired anymore. Michael's spurt of responsibility was making her horny, He looked at her and read the look in her eyes. "I'll be up in a minute," he said.

"Sure, play hard to get," she joked as she walked up the stairs. Seconds later she heard his footsteps behind her.

She giggled and undressed quickly as he walked into the room. "Hey, slow down," he said.

"It's been a while," she said, grabbing at his shirt.

"It's only been a week."

"That's a while."

"What's going on with you tonight?" He pushed her onto the bed.

"Just happy to be home, baby," she said and kissed him hard. Then they were entangled on the bed and Melinda forgot about her long day, the women's group, and all of her worries. This was one of the few times that she really appreciated her marriage; after all these years, the sex between her and Michael was still dynamite. She had to remember to keep her voice down because Jared was still up. Whoa! Michael was picking her up and switching positions like he used to when she was much younger, lighter, and more flexible. "Oh, God," she moaned as she climaxed. When she fell back on the pillows she was sweaty and out of breath. "Wow, baby. We're hot. We're like a couple of teenagers," she giggled.

"That's right," he said. "I'm the best."

"I said 'we,' Michael."

"Uh-huh."

She shook her head, smiling. That husband of hers could be trifling, but deep down he was a good man. A good, sexy man who gave her all the good loving she ever needed.

CHAPTER
14

Tari's and Roger Levine's failed relationship was old but juicy news in the *Boston Statesman*'s newsroom. Tari had never been good at hiding her feelings; neither was Roger, so the entire staff had known the cause, effect, and implications of every fight, and even when they eventually made up. The breakup, therefore, had been traumatic not only for the two of them but for the entire newsroom. Their public skirmishes made them the workplace spectacle for several months. Management finally stepped in and threatened them both with suspension if they did not stop the antics. This was after Tari had yelled within earshot of the entire office, "Well, screw you, too, you skinny bastard!" It was an experience that now deeply embarrassed her and one she hoped never to repeat. But their colleagues missed the drama and still spoke of them and their memorable fights nostalgically, as if they were legends.

According to the gossip mill, Roger was now happily dating a beautiful, young advertising executive that his mother had handpicked for him. Tari was genuinely happy for Roger, though she sometimes missed his dry sense of humor, his crazy hair that always needed cutting, and his long, brown eyelashes. But she knew that their relationship never would

have worked. She just didn't have the patience to be anybody's little woman. And work always got in the way when
they were together. With this MetroBank story taking off
now, Roger would have been beside himself with jealousy.
He never could hide the fact that he hated it when she was
in the spotlight and he wasn't.

She read the e-mail from him congratulating her on taking up daily residence on the front page. Tari hoped that he
meant it and decided to give him the benefit of the doubt.
One of the reasons that she was more than happy to switch
to business news from local politics was that she and Roger
would no longer be in direct competition.

She tried to shake memories of their relationship out of
her head as she hit the send button on an e-mail thanking
him. It wasn't that she still had feelings for Roger. It was
that there had been no one in between to fully get him out
of her system. That was the last time she'd had sex, and
that was not a thought she liked to linger on. Roger had
been the last man she kissed. Two years ago! Then a picture of Shawn entered her head, and it embarrassed her that
her heart rate quickened. This was getting out of hand, she
told herself. He had been all she was able to think of since
that phone call. She chuckled. *This is so pathetic, girl*, a voice
in her head mocked. *Get a grip.*

Roger bounced another e-mail back to her, saying that
they should have drinks, "orange juice for you," sometime
soon. She didn't reply, but she thought, *no way.* She would
not get caught up in this little drama ever again.

Her phone rang as she reread an e-mail from Steven
Bluesteed, again lauding her stellar efforts on bringing Metro-
Bank's crooked executives to their knees.

It was her doctor's office. A mix of terror and relief seized
her. The biopsy results were finally in, the nurse said.

"That's great!" Tari said and glanced over to Mariska's
desk to make sure she was not eavesdropping.

This is actually a good thing, she thought even as her heart raced. *The sooner I know, the better.* She wanted her mind to be stress-free for her lunch with Shawn on Friday. But the nurse's request gave her pause.

"Why do you need me to come in? Can't you just give me the results over the phone?"

They didn't do it that way, the nurse said gently.

Tari remembered the young nurse's words: *a positive and a negative. They're worried because it's solid, not a regular cyst.*

"Well, I'm pretty busy here at work. You're going to have to give them to me now," she said in her bitchiest tone.

The nurse sighed. "Sorry, we can't do that, ma'am."

Fine! She decided not to argue with the nurse anymore. *Who knows? It doesn't mean anything that they want me to come in for the results.* Maybe they had changed the rules. HMOs were getting sued all over the place by money-hungry people. They were just being careful. She'd told the nurse she would stop by the doctor's office during lunch, but she couldn't wait. She ducked out of the office minutes later.

She tried to keep her mind clear as she drove toward West Roxbury, taking deep breaths, in and out through the nose, remembering the way Dee taught her in yoga class. She said the Prayer of Serenity a few times.

But she was shaking when she pulled into the medical building's parking lot. When Tari went into the examining room, she was surprised that the nurse took her vital signs. "Am I having a checkup?" The nurse had a Jamaican accent and wore her hair in a short afro. Tari would remember that face, downward looking, among the many details she would remember about that day. "It's just routine," the nurse said, not meeting Tari's eyes.

Just routine. Okay, then. Tari thought of shopping, what she would wear to lunch with Shawn, what she would write in the lead of her story this evening. The attorney general was beginning to outline his investigation. *I still have a few min-*

utes to pretend that this ridiculous thing is not happening, she told
herself, swinging her legs over the edge of the exam room
table. Her doctor entered the room a few minutes later with
Tari's medical chart in one hand and a pen in the other. She
sighed before she sat opposite Tari on a small plastic chair.

Before Tari could ask any questions, the doctor began to
talk. "Well, your test results came back, Tari, and your
tumor is malignant. I'm sorry."

Tari's right hand flew to her chest, and she leaned forward, her eyes widening.

"Excuse me?" she asked, almost choking.

"I'm sorry, Tari. We found cancer."

The words felt like hot oil leaping up from a frying pan
onto her skin, quick-hitting and stinging. "But how? I'm
only thirty."

The doctor nodded. "There've been younger—"

"Are you sure?" Tari asked, her journalistic skepticism
kicking in. "Let me see the report." She reached out and
the doctor handed her the chart.

Tari could barely understand the words she was reading,
but they looked like cancer: invasive ductal carcinoma and
ductal carcinoma in situ, right breast 1.5 cm. That sounded
like cancer to her. She suddenly felt numb.

She handed the chart back to the doctor, who stood looking at her steadily.

"If you think you'll have trouble sleeping, you might
want to—"

"What do I do now?" Tari asked calmly, trying to stem a
wave of sorrow that made her lips tremble.

"I've already talked to surgery." The doctor was kind but
pragmatic. "We'll need to set up a date to have the tumor
removed, and then we'll go from there. Are you going to
need anything? Would you like to call a family member?"

Tari shook her head, looking across the room to avoid the

doctor's searching eyes. "Am I going to have chemo? Is my hair going to fall out?"

The doctor stood in the center of the room and said nothing for a minute.

"Tari, I'm really sorry. We'll have to decide on postsurgery treatment options later. But you're a young woman, in good health. That will help. I will have the surgeon call you soon."

The doctor sighed again as if this whole exercise was more difficult for her than the patient. "Will you need a family member to drive you home?"

Tari shook her head, her mouth still open. It felt like several minutes of silence went by before she realized that the doctor was still standing there.

"Do you have any more questions I can answer, Tari?" the woman asked.

"No," Tari whispered.

"You'll get through this. It's not like the old days," the doctor said and patted her arm.

Tari thanked her as she left the room.

Usually, she couldn't wait to get out of those stuffy little examining rooms. But today she sat erect on the paper sheet, afraid to move, afraid to think, afraid to leave that little room. She knew she was going out not quite the person she had entered it. She had cancer.

CHAPTER
15

She was now among the walking wounded—the brittle elderly, the colicky infants, the harried middle-aged, and the stressed-out mothers. She had joined their daily-pill-popping, weekly-doctor-visiting ranks, and she'd probably never make her way out. There would be months, maybe years of sickness ahead of her. She just knew it. She'd read books, articles, about how breast cancer could devastate. She felt the invincibility of youth and health flickering, as if storm clouds were unleashing torrents on the fire that kept her alive. Tears crowded her eyes, then overflowed down her cheeks as she walked to the car, which resembled a big champagne-colored blob in the sunlight. She blinked hard and reached for her keys. Her legs felt like tree stumps as she heaved herself into the truck. She felt small, weak, defeated, and afraid.

"Melinda, I have cancer," Tari said and began to sob loudly into the cell phone, bowing her head over the steering wheel.

"No, you don't!" her sister screeched. "You're playing around, right?"

"No, I'm not. I'm at the doctor's office."

"Tari, don't move. I'll be right there."

"But—"

Melinda had already hung up and was on her way.

Tari wept, her sorrow in full view of anyone who cared to stop and observe. She cried because she was afraid that she would die. She cried because she was afraid of what her parents would do when they heard the news. She cried because she had tried so hard over the last few years, stopped drinking, tried to alleviate her stress, ate right and exercised, yet she still got it. She cried because God apparently was still punishing her for the mistakes she had made in the past. She cried because though she knew she could count on Melinda and Rebecca to be there for her through this, she really was on her own. No husband, no boyfriend to lend a shoulder to cry on or to hold her late into the night. She cried and the tears wouldn't stop.

A while later, still sobbing, she heard tapping on her window, and she looked into her big sister's face.

"Tari," Melinda said firmly, taking her face in her hand after she had moved aside a mountain of Kleenex from the passenger seat. "I know you're upset right now. But I want you to stop crying like this, okay?"

Tari nodded and swallowed, sniffing.

"Okay. You have cancer. That's what the doctor says. But that's all you have, a disease. Not a death sentence."

Tari shook her head, and tears started to stream from her burning eyes once more.

"Listen to me, Tari," Melinda said, her voice steely, her eyes red. "We're going to deal with this, do you hear me? We'll get it out, we'll pray it out. We'll do what we have to do. But this is not going to kill you, okay? Now let's say a word of thanks to God."

"What?" Tari said, her voice hoarse.

"You heard me, let's thank God that we found this thing early and that you're already healed."

"Melinda, I don't think. . . ."

"Tari, bow your head with me right now. I don't want to hear anything more from you until we pray, okay?"

Tari bowed her head as Melinda prayed loudly, powerfully. Tari wasn't sure if she even believed the words her sister was saying. Did it even matter? God couldn't possibly be listening.

She sighed and opened her eyes minutes later. She felt clearer headed.

"What do you want to do now?" Melinda asked.

"Get a strong drink," Tari said dejectedly.

"Good. You still have your sense of humor. Do you want me to drive you home? I'll send Michael to pick up your car."

Tari shook her head. "I can drive myself. I'm going back to work."

"Are you sure?" Melinda was surprised but relieved that Tari wanted to go back to work instead of spending the afternoon moping at home, but the psychotherapist in her worried that she would not allow herself time to grieve over her diagnosis.

"I'll be fine," Tari assured her, straightening up in her seat. "I've gotta work on this story. Cancer doesn't change that." She bit her lip and stared off resolutely into the distance of parked cars.

The two were silent as Melinda tried to process all the questions that were swirling through her mind. Cancer? Tari?

"What exactly did the doctor say? Really? Is she still in there?" Melinda asked, looking toward the building. She wanted to hear it for herself.

Tari shook her head. "Here, I have the results printed out."

Melinda read the report, shaking her head. "This is so unreal, girl. This is so unreal. Tari, what about Mom? You want me to tell her?"

Tari sighed. This was a question she had been too afraid to ask herself even before the test results came back. Coletta did not do well with tragedy. Tari remembered Coletta's collapse and hospitalization after Jeffrey's minor car accident his senior year. Jeffrey had spent one night in the hospital with a sprained ankle and some bruises; Coletta spent two nights with an IV in her arm under heavy sedation.

"I'm not going to tell her yet. I'll wait and see what happens." *Maybe they'll find out that they have my medical records mixed up with someone else's,* Tari thought.

Melinda searched her sister's face. "She won't be happy about that."

"I know, but in a way, I think she's going to make this worse for me. If I tell her . . . Who knows how she's going to take it?"

Melinda sighed. "You have to tell her at some point. I don't mind doing it. So just say the word and I'll call her."

Tari nodded. Melinda was probably the one who should do it, she thought. A part of her was ashamed to have to deliver this news to Coletta. For as long as she could remember she'd wanted to show her parents that she could be as smart, as big, and as capable as Melinda. She'd never succeeded. It was why they worried so much about her, always asking whether she was okay "in that big house all by yourself." Tari always found herself exasperated, reminding Coletta, "I'm not a baby, I can take care of myself, Mom. I can stand on my own two feet!" Now what would Coletta think when she dropped this bombshell? She grimaced at the thought.

"I can't think about Mom now. It's just too much."

"Okay," Melinda said softly. "You sure you want to go back to work? We could go get coffee or ice cream or shoes or just talk. Anything to make you feel better."

Tari shook her head. A mixture of anger, rage, and defiance grabbed at her throat. The parking lot, full of the sick and weak, at that instant became physically unbearable. "Mel, I need to go now, okay? Thanks for coming down."

Work was where she wanted to be, had to be right now.

Melinda watched Tari drive away in a haze of undigested tears and false bravado. She finally released her own tears as Tari's truck disappeared onto the parkway. She followed close behind. "What the hell is going on, God?" she yelled in the quiet of her car. "Why is this happening?"

She wiped her eyes and tried to concentrate on the road. It just wasn't enough, she thought. It wasn't enough that she prayed so much for that girl. Cancer? The girl didn't even have a boyfriend, never mind a husband and kids. What kind of life could she have after having a disease like that?

Mom! Melinda put a hand over her mouth as if trying to shut off the impulse to run to her mother for a wise ear or comforting words. *How is Mom going to take this?* Melinda bit her lower lip. She had made light of it, but it would not be an easy task, no matter who did the telling.

It was just so wrong, so unfair, she thought as she headed back downtown. Just when she was thinking that it was probably time for her to start getting things right in her own life. Maybe take one more stab at talking to Michael about getting his life on track and to stop playing around, start being a good father instead of just a present father. And this time if he didn't straighten up . . .

But she couldn't very well concentrate on her own problems now. Her sister needed her, and the girl had nobody else to turn to.

Why didn't she? Why couldn't she? Melinda sighed heavily. Tari always had to do things her own way. She knew their family history, yet she was still singing in those smoky bars, getting that nasty stuff in her body. They'd never met their grandmother because she'd died of the disease when Coletta was barely out of her teens, and their aunt had had a bout with breast cancer, too. But reason told Melinda that their great-aunt Erica had smoked every day of her eighty-seven years and was still as healthy as a young mango tree back on the island. But still . . . Somebody, something was to blame for this, Melinda thought.

"This is just so crazy," she whispered. "With everything I have going on right now. This is just so crazy."

It didn't help that Michael was on the golf course, annoyed that she was interrupting his game, when she called his cell phone seeking a little comfort.

"Babe, I'm so sorry," he said distractedly. "How's Tari holding up?"

As if by instinct, she reached up and cupped one breast in her hand. She squeezed it awkwardly. She felt nothing. She touched the other one, letting her fingers sink into the flesh, from the top, where she could feel her sternum, to the base of her breast, where it was just fatty flesh held up by her C-cup bra. Again nothing. Guilt shamed her. It seemed selfish to be thinking of herself, her breasts, now; her little sister was terrified, and all she could do was focus on herself and on her own fear about what would happen if it had been her. Who would take care of Taylor and Jared? If she were not around, would Michael finally grow up and lead his family? The question chilled her because she realized that she did not know the answer. And not knowing was almost more terrifying than feeling something ominous and threatening in her breast.

When something tragic happens that shakes the very core of your world you expect the rest of the world, the universe really, to take notice or at least to acknowledge that your life has been jolted, altered forever. What counts for normal annoyances, like red lights, impatient drivers, potholes, ambulances, jaywalkers, can seem amplified by millions of degrees. Minor grievances are no longer so, because you have a serious beef with the natural order of things, and you feel that surely the tide should shift entirely in your favor from this moment forth. After all, things cannot possibly get any worse.

So Tari, her mind dulled into contemplativeness, was shocked by the rudeness of drivers, the foolishness of the schoolchildren who took their lives into their hands as they raced across Blue Hill Avenue, daring the traffic to slow for them. She noticed the young men on the corner barely out of their teens, idle and angry, and she felt mournful that their lives appeared so meaningless from where she sat. She longed for the health that they obviously had and took for granted. A Mercedes SUV full of young white boys blew by her, hip-hop blasting from the windows, their eyes full of wonder as they beheld the "hood" that they heard so much about in their music. It angered her that her neighborhood was a source of entertainment for them.

The streets had not changed since she last drove over them barely two hours before, but they were paved with a different reality. She was seeing more and thinking more, certainly more aware of what was around her. Those asphalt-covered paths to everyday life began to figure into her mortality. Was it nobler to die of cancer at thirty than to die on the street at thirty, her life cut short by a bullet wound or a knife? She remembered seeing blood pouring down that same street several years before when a young boy had been shot by another young boy. Then, it was common to see such deaths as a societal problem, something much bigger than that sixteen-year-old whose blood stuck to the white lines of the crosswalk at Washington and Erie. She wasn't one of those people, her father had said back then, so not to worry. And that hadn't been difficult for her to believe. She didn't do drugs or know anyone who did; she certainly did not fall into the "wrong crowd." Of course she would have a long, successful life, like normal people who weren't part of societal problems, who did well in school, went to work and even to church. But here she was facing death just like one of those poor, desperate people you saw on the news, idling on the streets, or read about in those studies coming out of Human Rights Watch or the Civil Rights Project. Young, black, and dying. Wasn't she supposed to have been different? It was so unfair.

When she pulled into her parking space at the paper, introspection gave way to panic. What would happen if she told? What if she never told? What if someone found out? Would they take her off the story? Would she be well enough to keep working? She sat in her car and pondered what she should do. It was too early, she knew. Maybe she wouldn't need chemotherapy and this evil thing would just go away with surgery. No one would have to know then. She could just go on with life as it was now. She heard footsteps approaching, and she looked up.

"Are you all right? Your eyes are all red." She could see from the concern on Roger's face that he knew she'd been crying.

"I'm fine." She reached into her bag and pulled out some Visine.

"What's wrong with your eyes, then?" Roger asked skeptically.

She wanted to hit him for his nosiness. "Nothing. Just allergies." He didn't believe her but she didn't care. She put her head back and squeezed the bottle.

"Do you need help with that?"

"No, thanks, Roger." Tari bristled. This was the worst time he could come up to her and try to make small talk, she thought.

He stood there awkwardly as she drenched her other eye with the clear liquid.

"I wanted to tell you the other day, that, um . . ."

She turned to look at him and blinked to let the Visine rinse her eyes. His eyes didn't seem as blue as she remembered them, and his hair was way too long.

"I asked Sharon to marry me and she said yes."

When Tari didn't say anything, Roger continued. "I just wanted you to hear it from me. You know how people gossip around here."

Tari sighed. Roger's engagement was old news to her, but somehow hearing it from him, now, hurt. "That's great news, Roger. Congratulations."

"Do you mean that?" His eyes were pleading for her approval.

"Of course I mean it." And she was surprised that even with all the turmoil going through her head, she did not snap at his insecurity. *Sure,* she thought, *I have frigging cancer, and you're worried about whether I'm happy about your impending marriage to Ms. Perfectly Healthy Advertising Executive?* But she managed to smile reassuringly. She did mean it deep, deep down inside. But her happiness for him could only go so far. "You look happy. Nervous but happy."

He sighed and ran his hand through his mile-high hair. "Yeah. I know it's what I want, but marriage is so . . ."

"Come on, Roger," Tari said. "You've been wanting to get married forever. From what I hear, this Sharon person is a real catch." *And will you go away now, please?*

Roger seemed to quickly forget about Tari's red eyes as his eyes lit up and he began to talk about his fiancée. Tari wanted to hit him. Couldn't he take a hint?

"Roger, I really need to get inside . . . MetroBank. . . ."

As she walked into the building, she steadied herself and checked her emotions. *Stay calm and act normal.* She would tell no one. The only people who would know would be her family and Rebecca, no one else.

She surveyed the rows of desks, heard phones trilling,

fingers clacking at keyboards, voices yelling into receivers. This was not the place or the time to be sick, she thought. She would gain absolutely nothing by telling anyone about this. She could just see the results: the doubts about her ability to perform, the pity and concern in their eyes every single day. That would not do. Right now she was the hottest reporter in the city of Boston, and she intended to keep it that way. It was just cancer. She could get through this. No one had to be the wiser.

CHAPTER
16

On condiment night Tari fed her inner child. It was one of the pure joys of living alone, better than letting the dishes pile up or leaving discarded shoes in disarray on the living room floor. There would be no one telling her to clean up the mess or stop stuffing her face with junk. She felt deliciously sneaky in her clandestine affair with super-chunky peanut butter and anything in a jar made by Smuckers.

This is a disgusting habit that you just have to quit, she would tell herself as she sat in front of the TV, a *Newsweek* in one hand, a spoonful of strawberry jam in the other. She would sometimes eat the stuff until the sugar made her dizzy and disoriented. It was the equivalent of a crush, a sweet one. So deep was this love for empty calories, Tari dedicated the yellow shelf on the wall above her kitchen counter to para-phernalia pertaining to condiments. There was a maple cream jar from a small family farm in Putney, Vermont, blueberry jam from Hediard in Paris, a marmalade she had picked up at a funky shop in Picadilly Circus, and a Smucker's raspberry jam from 1949, a Christmas present from an editor.

Rebecca, who didn't know that her presence intruded on

Tari's ritual, shook her head at the display of empty glass jars on the shelf and grabbed some ice out of the freezer.

She wanted to know whether Tari felt up to having lunch with a strange man under the circumstances.

"I'm not under any circumstances," Tari yelled from the living room.

Rebecca sighed and walked back to the living room. She lowered herself onto Tari's beige faux-suede couch, sipped on the overbrewed iced green tea, and made a face. Tari had only rolled her eyes when Rebecca informed her that green tea should only be brewed for no longer than a minute or so. "Yes, Miss Food Expert," her eyes had said.

The tea had been a gift from Melinda, who preached its power as an antioxidant. Plus, it was better than coffee, Melinda had lectured Tari, in one of her now-daily pep talks.

"Becks, I just want to feel normal," Tari said, her eyes on the television. "Is that so bad? Geez. It's not like it's a date."

"I understand that," Rebecca said gently. "But you have to face . . . face it. And it just doesn't seem like you're doing that."

"I don't know if I'm ready." Tari closed her eyes. She didn't want to talk about or think about cancer.

"Well, for one thing, you could stop being sarcastic. And angry at everything. That might help."

Tari sighed. "I'm not angry. I'm stressed. And I'm just . . . just questioning why."

Rebecca shifted in the soft couch. "Remember after 9/11 when we had this big argument about God and I told you that your God was bogus for allowing something like that to happen?"

Tari remembered the conversation well. She and Rebecca didn't speak for a week afterward.

"Your argument was," Rebecca continued, leaning forward to face Tari, "that God doesn't want to harm any of His children, right? And that sometimes when bad things happen, it's only so that good things eventually come from them, right?"

Tari looked at her, wondering if she should engage her. Rebecca was using her lawyerly voice, Tari noted, the one that meant they were on the way to an argument.

"I don't think that's exactly what I said. But that makes sense." *Maybe it's better to just agree with her,* Tari decided. *Yup. Whatever you say, Counsel.*

But Rebecca obviously wanted a dustup. "So, you're actually saying now that God allowed something terrible to happen to you and you want to know why. But you said just a few years ago that it wasn't for us humans to question God, because His ways are not our ways, right?"

"Rebecca, were you tape-recording me?" Tari was forcing herself to inject some humor into the conversation, though she just wanted to change the subject. She hardly remembered what she said two months ago, never mind five years ago.

"No. I remember those things because I'm always trying to understand where your faith comes from."

Tari rolled her eyes. "That's only because you either ask me so many questions I feel like a research project or we can't talk for five minutes without getting into an argument." She leaned back into the soft cushions. This girl was starting to make her crazy.

Rebecca ignored the jab. "All I'm saying is that if you use the same argument that you used back in 2001, then you shouldn't be angry. You should be accepting this. In fact, you should be grateful that things are not worse."

"I know that," Tari said testily. "And I'm getting there." At the heart of it, she really was ashamed that an agnostic would be the one to try to set her straight on her faith. "What is this anyway, Becks? Are you trying to discredit what I said five years ago, or are you trying to get me to admit that God makes bad things happen?"

"I'm not trying to do either." Rebecca's expression grew defensive. "I'm mad, too, Tari." She pointed to her chest. "But I'm not angry with God because I'm not sure if he or she or it is responsible for this. I'm just angry because you have to go through this. I'm not angry at anything or anyone. I'm just angry."

"I just wish this weren't happening," Tari said and leaned her head way back on the couch so she was looking up at the ceiling. "I mean, I did nothing, absolutely nothing to deserve this. Geez. I take care of myself, Becks. You know that. I just don't get it. I could see if I were fifty or sixty. Or fat. Or a smoker. I'm not ready for this crap."

Rebecca had no words that could comfort her.

"I just keep thinking that the doctor will call and say it was all a mistake. That they mixed up someone else's medical record with mine." Tari shook her head and laughed. "It can't be God doing this, Becks. It has to be something else. Maybe something I did that I'm being punished for."

Rebecca looked at her incredulously. "Like what? Out of all the people who do terrible things every day, I can't imagine what you could have done to deserve this, Tari."

Tari sighed. "I know. But there has to be a reason."

"Only if you're looking at it from your Christian point of view. The way I see it, is life is cruel and unfair and we have very little control over what happens to us, good or bad."

Tari shook her head. "I don't know about that. I mean, even though I do have this thing. I know deep down that God will give me the strength to get through it. And that's having some control, right?"

Rebecca shrugged.

"If I just resigned myself to having bad luck and no control over the outcome of my life, then I should just accept this and not fight it. But if I believe and if I act like everything's going to be okay, then I have to be okay."

"That seems to be the way you deal with things," Rebecca said wryly.

"Well, it works for me. I believe that ultimately God knows the answer to why all of this is happening," Tari said.

"Well, just don't ignore the facts."

Tari bit her bottom lip. She was tired of breaking down, and it seemed that had been happening way too often these days. She was either finding herself dissolving into tears in the morning while she put on her makeup, in the shower, in the car. It was sickening. She wanted to be like her old self. Even if that wasn't possible now, couldn't she at least pretend?

It was Thursday evening and they would usually have headed out for a book reading or lecture, or dinner, hoping to find a good discussion or something interesting and worth listening to somewhere in the city. But Rebecca had wanted to stay in to talk. *Trust her to get all philosophical about this*, Tari complained inside.

But maybe Rebecca had a point. Her home was a place of comfort, where she escaped to from work, bad relationships, overbearing Melinda and Coletta. The warm tones of paint on her walls soothed her, the beige and brown furniture calmed her. She looked at her large book collection and marveled that she had read every single one of the hundreds on the four five-foot bookcases that lined her living room walls. It satisfied her that she'd had that same clock since college, a $9.99 steal she'd bought from a Duane Reade in Greenwich Village during freshman year. The familiarity of her home, her long, carpeted staircase and her sparely furnished bedroom, made her feel insulated from everything—scary diagnoses, uniformed nurses, cold doctors, and prying coworkers.

"Okay, to follow through on your argument, then," Rebecca said after several minutes of listening to meaningless jokes on *Will & Grace*, "you couldn't have avoided it no matter what you did."

"What?" Tari asked, lost for a minute.

"I said that if God is all powerful and He already had a plan for your life before you were even born—that's what the Bible says, right?—then you couldn't have not gotten cancer." Rebecca looked at Tari as if daring her to contradict her point.

"But, Becks, I'm not even sure if it works that way." Tari sighed. She couldn't explain what she wanted to say. It would be so simple for her to just say that yes, cancer is what God wants me to have, so there. But that couldn't possibly be right; she did not believe that in her soul. She was a Christian, for goodness' sake. Things like cancer happened to unbelievers who lived messed-up lives and who needed some trauma to shock them into seeing the error of their ways. She was no sinner! No one could convince her that this was from God. Not the God for whom she had given up drinking, smoking, sex, and partying. Not the God who got 10 percent and then some of her salary.

"Well, I'm sorry, but I think you're wrong. I've been reading the Bible, too," Rebecca said.

Tari looked at Rebecca. This was news to her. On the one hand, she was touched that Rebecca was going to all this trouble to get a better understanding of her faith. But on the other, she was angry that Rebecca took such an academic interest in the whole thing. She couldn't throw it back in her face and attach the same attitude toward Hinduism. For one thing, Rebecca would be the first to back her up.

"To say I'm a Hindu would be like saying I'm a human being. Hindus just don't have all the issues other religions seem to have. All Hinduism asks is that you treat yourself and other people well," Rebecca joked whenever she had an audience. She wore a bindi on her forehead but only to attract attention, she said, because she did not have a religious bone in her body.

"So, how far have you read into the Bible?" Tari asked, not wanting to dwell on the topic of cancer any longer.

"I'm up to Leviticus," Rebecca said excitedly. "But I've started the New Testament, too. That stuff is fascinating. You know, Jesus sounds like a really cool guy."

Tari's head tilted to the side and she sighed audibly. She was uncomfortable with that kind of talk. In the household where she grew up, taking the Lord's name in vain was a sin, a big one, a violation of one of the Ten. But Rebecca didn't know. *Forgive her, Father,* Tari thought.

"I'm glad you're taking an interest," she said.

Rebecca let the patronizing tone slide. "I just wish I had read all of this stuff before."

"Why?" Tari asked reluctantly, wanting to turn up the volume of the television as *Will & Grace*'s credits rolled up the screen. What was on next?

"Because I understand you so much better now. All that guilt . . ."

"What guilt?"

"Well, you just seem to take a lot of that stuff literally," Rebecca said, directing her gaze toward the television, knowing that she was now treading on dangerous ground. "You know, all the Thou Shalt Nots, the retribution, wages of sin. . . ."

Tari's body tensed and she looked squarely at Rebecca. "Now, Becks, that's why I don't like to talk about religion with you. I don't know what you think you understand. But whatever it is, just keep it to yourself, okay?" Tari's dark eyes were flashing, and the legs that were pulled up under her were now down, her feet on the floor. "Let's just not talk about this anymore. When you're done reading the Bible cover to cover, maybe we can talk then. But you've got a long way to go before you understand what my faith is all about and why I think what I think."

Rebecca nodded but did not look away from the TV. The two of them watched *The Apprentice* in silence for several minutes.

"Sorry, I didn't mean to upset you, Tari," Rebecca said finally. "I don't want to make you feel worse."

Tari didn't answer. She fully agreed, and her stony expression said as much. The last thing she needed was more stress. For Rebecca to use an occasion like this to attack her was just plain insensitive.

When Rebecca announced she was leaving, Tari only nodded. But as she heard her friend's footsteps on the footpath outside, despair and loneliness came over her. "Becks, I'll give you a ride home," she called out from the open front door.

Rebecca raised an arm. "That's okay. I'll take the T. It's still early."

Tari turned off the TV in exasperation as she sank down on the couch again. That girl! She wished there were someone else to call as restlessness crawled through her. She wished Rebecca had stayed longer. The void of the large, lovely house made her feel small, like a dust mite on the carpet. What was she doing in this big, old house anyway,? she thought. Why couldn't she have stayed in her condo? It had been like a trophy for her, the house. She was barely thirty but she owned real estate—in Boston. But now this trophy felt like a concrete necklace around her neck. It was as if Rebecca had taken all its warmth with her. She felt alone, tired, and afraid. She looked out of her window and onto the quiet street. What was the cancer doing in her body right now? she wondered. Was it growing, mutating further, infecting other parts of her, traveling through her blood, sucking the life out of her healthy cells one by one?

She took a huge gulp of green tea as if that could somehow wash it away.

It was almost ten. Melinda would be in bed by now, with her family safely tucked in. She hadn't told her baby brother Jeffrey yet. She did not plan to tell her parents if she could get away with it. At least not until she absolutely had to. Rebecca was probably sitting on the Red Line headed toward Cambridge.

What now? She was wide awake and she wanted to talk to somebody who would tell her that everything was going to be just fine. She did not want to be alone. But there was no one she could call. She grabbed her laptop from where it sat in a corner on the living-room floor and went on-line and stayed in that spot on the couch scrolling through pages and pages on eBay, unable to sleep, unwilling to think, until the sun came up.

CHAPTER
17

Melinda lay in bed, wide awake, as Michael snored beside her, dread keeping her company. She recognized the feeling. It was the same one she'd felt fifteen years ago when Tari had woken her up bawling her eyes out one night. "Melinda, I think I'm pregnant. Mom's gonna kill me." Melinda remembered being angry at first; how could Tari have had sex, unprotected sex even, after everything they'd been taught? Didn't she know it was wrong? Hell, didn't she fear Coletta and God enough not to do it? She'd tried to be calm and rational about it but she was scared, too. If Tari turned up pregnant it would somehow be her fault. She was the oldest, Coletta's deputy, really. She was supposed to keep Tari in line when her mother couldn't. Tari had crawled into Melinda's bed and they'd stayed up together the whole night, not saying anything, both terrified out of their minds.

The next day they'd gone to Osco Drug, riding the number 66 bus all the way out to Brighton so they wouldn't run into anyone they knew, and bought an EPT pregnancy test. Tari couldn't stop crying, and Melinda remembered grabbing her shoulders and commanding her to calm down. It wasn't like Melinda had had a plan back then. She'd been so mad at Tari for even putting herself in that situation. When did her little sister start having sex? Why wasn't she consulted before Tari decided to do this? She didn't know what she would have done if Tari's test had come back positive. But it was what she did: act as if she had all the answers. The test was negative, but it took another two weeks before Tari's period showed up, putting their fears to rest. It was probably the only two weeks that had gone by in their entire lives that they didn't fight.

The one good thing that had come out of it was that Tari began to trust her more and see her less as an adversary or Coletta's muscle. Tari had even told her that the boy, who also went to their church, had been her first. Melinda had vowed never to tell and had kept her word. But the whole incident had made her look at her little sister with a bit more respect. Tari had had sex. Before her!

Those days seemed so long ago, though. This time it was different; it wasn't just a matter of being pregnant or not, this seemed more real, scarier, Melinda thought. Tari was being strong, but it had to be all a front, Melinda decided. The poor thing was probably crying herself to sleep every night in that big old house all by herself. She looked at the phone on the nightstand. No. She wouldn't call over there. Tari's pride would be hurt. She didn't want anyone to feel sorry for her. But still . . . Melinda almost picked up the phone.

How do I solve this problem for her? she wondered. This time there was no test to exonerate them from the danger. And Melinda felt that her hands were truly tied. It was not a feeling she was used to, and it saddened her to the point that she could not fall asleep.

CHAPTER
18

avi was waiting at the coffee table in their one-bedroom
apartment when Rebecca walked through the door,
red-eyed.

"How is she?" Ravi asked, concern in his eyes.

Rebecca sighed. "Tari is being Tari. She said she didn't
want to talk about it. So we talked about religion and then
she got upset with me." She sank down in the chair next to
Ravi and he ran his hand through her hair.

"How are you, then?"

"I don't know. I still can't believe this is happening sometimes. But then Tari's attitude . . . I don't know. It's like
she's so detached from the whole thing. She's acting as if it's
nothing. Like she couldn't die." Rebecca's voice shook.

"Babe, Tari is not going to die. You know that."

Rebecca nodded. "She just won't let me help her."

"Tari is who she is. You just have to give her space, that's
all. Be there for her when she needs you, but don't push."

Rebecca, too, had not slept well since Tari told her of her
diagnosis. She had spent a few dazed minutes looking at the
phone in her office after Tari had called her with the news.
How in the world could this have happened to her friend?
She had always admired Tari's fit body and the fact that she

was so good at yoga and at kickboxing. Tari was healthy. How in the world? Then, she, too had done the instant breast self-exam and was continuing to do them almost nightly now.

She decided to look for answers in the Bible, and all she'd found so far were engrossing stories that left her with even more questions. Ravi had laughed at her sudden interest in Christianity, but Rebecca was undeterred. She wanted to study, to find out more. Maybe it would help her to find the right way to get through this, to help her find the words to help Tari through this.

"So what does that mean for our trip to Trinidad in August?" Ravi asked almost apologetically.

Rebecca shook her head. "I'll have to see. I can't leave her to face all this stuff by herself."

Ravi nodded, but there was disappointment in his eyes. "What if Tari hadn't gotten sick, would you still want to go? I know we've been through this before, but . . ."

Rebecca sighed. "I don't know, Ravi. I just can't leave her now. And no, I don't want to deal with my parents now."

"You're going to have to deal with them at some point." She escaped to the bathroom, her solitary refuge in the tiny apartment.

Ravi had been trying, she knew. But he was becoming impatient with her moodiness. She knew she was depressed; she didn't need a doctor to tell her that, but she wasn't sure why. Maybe it had something to do with Tari. Maybe it was because she felt stuck in a job that made her want to scream and throw things most days. Maybe she wanted to be able to put her finger on a decision and just keep it there until the thing happened.

She had never told anyone else the lie. It wasn't something that she was proud of, and to share it with someone, especially Ravi, would only add to its ridiculous existence. When her parents called, she placated them with loose, vague comments, like "work is stressful but okay." And that was it. The sort of statements that could apply to any job, fund-raising for the law school or an afternoon drawing up contracts for a Fortune 500 company. What she never included in those vague statements were the specifics, and her parents never dug deep, making it easier for the lie to get comfortable. It was what they wanted to hear anyway.

She had to go home; there was no way around it. If they came here they would see her bohemian life, and before she could even make up an excuse as to why she could not take them on a tour of her downtown office, they would see right through her. But going home posed other problems. She would have to get Ravi and his parents in on the lie.

And she felt a bit silly even thinking the thought. This type of thing happened to ditzy girls, those who had so much pride that they made up stories and thrust themselves into wild situations just to make their run-of-the-mill lives seem interesting. She by no means was one of those girls. She was serious, grounded, and even proud to be a bit boring. This dilemma was a trivial, trivial, silly thing that she had brought on herself. Especially now with Tari facing something so real, so serious.

Rebecca knew that the solution was simple. Come clean and be an adult. Tell them, *Hey, I quit the firm after four months. I couldn't take it anymore. I felt that people were making fun of my accent. I didn't fit in with the rest of the young associates with their designer clothes, weekend ski trips, and outings to trendy bars. I just couldn't take it one more day. I feel more comfortable at the university; everybody there at least dresses like me. The work is boring but at least I can breathe over there, and I have more time to write restaurant reviews. Sorry I wasted your money. But I don't want to practice law.*

"What's on your mind?" Ravi pulled at her curly hair, later in bed when she could not sleep.

"Just stuff, you know. Tari, the wedding, and all that."

CHAPTER
19

The morning flew by through a flurry of telephone calls, e-mails and instant messages, and questions from all directions. By the time lunchtime neared, it occurred to Tari that she'd not even thought of cancer once that Friday morning. And when the thought entered her mind, she exiled it to a place where it would not ruin her façade of normalcy.

She did not know what to do with the diagnosis yet. She had cried, lost precious sleep over it, mourned the collapse of the wall she had so carefully constructed around her body that she thought healthy living had deemed indestructible. She clenched her teeth, angry that all the cancer had to do was roar at her defenses and they just came tumbling down, like the wall of Jericho. *God grant me the serenity . . .* She focused on the things that she could do something about right now.

The MetroBank story had gone international, spreading swiftly and putting her byline in newspapers across the globe. Someone, Joe, she suspected, had dumped a *Wall Street Journal*, *New York Times*, a *Financial Times*, and an *Economist* on her desk, and she noticed that all those papers were leading with some variation of the story she'd broken.

That was the first sight that had greeted her when she walked into the office. It helped train her focus on the controllable present. It got her competitive juices flowing. She could easily forget that she'd not had a decent night's sleep since that awful day. She could ignore the messages from her mother, who was calling to check up on her. She could put off calling the surgeon's office for a consultation. Instead, she had immediately gotten on the phone, trying to mine her sources for more dirt so she could continue to be first to feed this frenzy she had created. She continued to work all morning in that reality, unconsciously ignoring the other unwelcome one that she knew wouldn't continue to lie still and accept this lower rung in her priorities.

She recognized the bright red flash on her screen and the short screech she'd programmed into her PC as her cue to leave for lunch. Before thinking about how nervous she was, she grabbed her hobo leather bag and ran toward the exit. Joe Martone called after her, "Tari, where are you going?" She hastened her footsteps, grabbing her keys out of her bag, knowing that if she turned back and acknowledged Joe she would be chained to her desk for the rest of the day.

She pulled out her makeup case with one hand as she pulled out into traffic. It was a warm day, and she lowered the windows, letting the spring air calm her. As much as it bothered her to see other women do it, she used the red lights to dab some powder on her cheeks, nose, and forehead and to retouch her lipstick. She wet her index finger with saliva and ran it over her eyelashes. A driver behind her leaned on his horn, and she gunned the gas into the intersection.

The slowness of the traffic once she got onto I-93 north finally gave her enough pause to really consider what she was doing. *Why did I wear this?* She panicked, critically eyeing the lime green V-neck cashmere sweater and black cotton pencil skirt with slightly painful black slingbacks. Her legs were bare. She hated pantyhose and would endure the cold wind whipping against her skin before she would allow any form of nylon to touch her legs. She worried what he would think. Of that. Of her. Shawn seemed like the kind of guy who noticed things, and she could just see him appraising her and rating her a five or a four. *Maybe I should have worn all black*, she fretted. From what she had seen of him, he was a pretty smooth dresser himself. And that had bothered her in a way. She had never been attracted to pretty boys who were obsessed with their looks. Her kind of man had a soft heart and rough hands. He would know what to wear to a nice restaurant, but he would not disrupt the room with his outrageous sense of style. He would notice that she was wearing a new dress, but not that it was in Diane von Furstenberg's 2005 spring line.

She shook her head to let her hair fall onto her shoulders so it would look carelessly sexy, blew the air out of her mouth, and rolled her eyes. What was she thinking? She checked herself, stoically. She needed a new bass player, and here she was trying to turn this guy whom she barely knew into the perfect man. *Get your head out of the clouds, girl,* she chided herself. This lunch was a business transaction, and with all that she was facing, she did not need to add another layer of uncertainty to her life right now.

She turned off Storrow Drive and took the Central Square exit. She snorted at the runners and walkers along the Charles River who were slowing traffic as they ambled through the intersection at River Street. The thumping anticipation about meeting Shawn began to abate as she parked in front of the restaurant. She suddenly felt silly, as she often did when she worked herself into a frenzy over an event only to have the actual occasion turn out to be anticlimactic. Maybe Rebecca was right. This wasn't the right time for this. What if she did need chemotherapy and her hair fell out? Would she even be able to sing then? Did it even make sense for her to get a bass player? Maybe this was God's way of telling her that she needed to quit singing. She sighed, slowly getting her things together. *We'll just have to see,* she thought as she opened the door and stepped onto the curb.

As she walked into the dimly lit restaurant, her confidence stuttered and she almost turned back toward the safety of the car. Her body suddenly felt heavy and exhausted. She stopped and held on to the edge of a chair at one of the many empty tables. *What am I doing here?* she asked herself again. *I am sick. Sick!* But then she looked off in the distance and saw him sitting there. She took a deep breath.

The Good Life was as down home as a speakeasy, dark as a Southern night despite the luminosity of the day outside. A young but woeful-looking bartender, probably a student with a burdensome student loan, read a thick book at the bar. It was quiet except for a few lunchtime diners.

Shawn stood, smiling as their eyes met. He seemed taller, bigger, and more handsome in his business-casual garb. Tari's heart raced with each step that drew her closer to him. *Oh, my God,* she thought. *I have a crush on a man. I have a crush on a man!*

He held out his hand and she shook it firmly, business-like. "That's quite a grip you've got there, young lady." His smile shone even brighter up close.

She sat primly, hoping that her smile was as porcelain as his. *Yes!* she thought, *he has calluses!*

"Gee, do you moonlight as a carpenter? What's up with the calluses?" she joked, hoping to break the tension that hovered over the table.

"Actually, I do some woodworking for pleasure. But some of the calluses are from the bass."

"Oh, of course," Tari said, embarrassed that she'd failed to pick up that very obvious factor.

The waitress came and they ordered.

"So, that's quite a story you've got going there in the paper," Shawn said, sipping his water and not taking his eyes off hers. The intensity in his stare made her uncomfortable. He didn't just look at her. She felt that he was looking through her. Or maybe it was all her imagination. Maybe it was her own desires that were fogging up her perceptions.

She nodded brightly but reminded herself that she was not there to talk about her work, tempting as it was to expound on the finer points of banking and financial fraud.

"Well, I'm just glad that tip came my way. It's exposing a lot of bad things that have been covered up for too long."

"How do you find the time or the energy to sing with all of this going on?"

She sighed. He didn't know that she had just been given one more brick to add onto her burdens.

"Well, I love to sing, and it's what keeps me sane." *Ugh*, she thought after the words made their exit. *Now he's going to think I'm crazy.* She tried to save face. "If I don't sing, then I can't do my day job well. They kind of feed off each other. But it's really a hobby, I guess. Well, it's more than that, but for now that's the best way to describe it. I guess." She shrugged. *What am I saying?* She cringed.

He nodded. "I know what you mean. Bass is more than just a hobby for me. I've played since I was a kid. But I had to give it up for a while." He paused. "My marriage took me in a totally different direction than where I'd planned to go . . ." He paused again, as if choosing his words. "But I think I'm like you in that I need to have that balance of professional and personal fulfillment. You can't have just one and be complete."

Tari nodded as Shawn spoke but tried to fill in the blanks in her head. From what Violet had told her, his marriage had been long over and his wife lived in Rhode Island. The fact that he raised the issue so soon in their conversation raised a flag. *Is he trying to tell me something?* she wondered. *That he's available? Still stuck on his ex? At least we're getting along,* she thought, relieved. She then realized that the entire purpose of the lunch had not even come up. But he wouldn't let her cut in.

"So, are you divorced, involved?" he asked, an inert smile on his face.

She found herself blushing. "Neither. Too busy." *Now, why in the world did I feel the need to explain my marital status?* she thought.

"I see," he said.

See what? But she didn't ask. Instead she steered the conversation back to music, and soon they were talking without the self-consciousness getting in the way about financing their CD collections, their shared addictions to Amazon.com and *Meet the Press.*

"Oh, Shawn," she said, absently putting her hand on his in the overfamiliar way she tended to have with people who made her feel at ease. "I almost forgot." She quickly pulled her hand away when she realized what she had done.

She cleared her throat and straightened her back as if that could right the slip in gesture. "You know, my friend and I saw you play here the other day, and I'm just going to come right out and ask you to play for me. Okay? You don't have to say yes, of course."

He laughed. "Wow, you're direct. I thought you were trying to soften me up first with nice conversation and then you'd ask me to go up and play something when the quartet came on."

"Ah." She smiled. "I don't beat around the bush."

"I like that." He flashed his pearly whites once more.

"So, will you have an answer for me today?"

He threw his head back and laughed. "No, I'll have an answer for you after I have a chance to think about it."

Okay, she thought, amused. *He won't let me push him around, and that's a good thing.* But she had a feeling. His eyes said that much. "Okay, I can wait," she said, then took a sip of water.

The conversation flowed smoothly as they finished their meal, and more tables filled with diners and folks waiting for the quartet who used the lunchtime hour for rehearsal to take the stage. Tari found herself laughing at his jokes, which were on the head-scratching side. He was smart, but not consumed by his intelligence. That was refreshing in a city where it was so common to meet men who were well educated and only wanted to talk about how well educated they and their friends were and how they only could be attracted to well-educated women. Shawn's humble and self-deprecating sensibilities made it easy for her to open up to him, and she found herself explaining to him the ups and downs of her relationships with Melinda and her mother. "It's like we get along but we don't get along; we're close but we're not that close," was how she described her relationship with her sister. As if to make her feel better, he joked about being thirty-four and divorced, saying that these days most of his friends had never even been married yet. "I feel like an old man around them sometimes." She could sense from his joking that a part of him took his divorce as a personal failure, and that touched her. She wanted to ask whether he would marry again but didn't for fear of sounding too forward.

The hour that she had planned to spend at lunch quickly turned into two. It was Shawn who gently reminded her that time was getting away from them.

"Oh, goodness!" Tari wailed, looking at her watch. "My editor's going to kill me!" She grabbed her bag. "Shawn,

I'm so sorry. But I have to fly. Thanks for lunch. Oh, and thanks for . . . thinking about playing for me. I really appreciate it."

His mouth opened, but he could not get in a word as Tari busied herself with trying to exit the restaurant.

"Call me, day or night, when you make a decision," she said as she buttoned her raincoat. She would later regret sounding so desperate, but at that moment all she could think of was the mountain of phone messages, e-mails, and the big, fat deadline that waited for her back at the office.

"Well, it was nice seeing you," he said, looking at the frantic woman in front of him ready to bolt out of the restaurant. "Drive carefully," he added with a half-confused, half-amused look on his face.

"Uh-huh," Tari replied and hightailed it out of the restaurant.

She tore through Central Square, down River Street, and made it to Storrow Drive in two minutes.

"You're bad, girl," she said out loud as she merged onto the parkway, heading straight from the on-ramp into the left lane, keeping one eye on the rearview mirror for the diligent Cambridge police. "Outta my way, folks. I'm in a hurry!" She weaved her truck in and out of traffic, heading for I-93 south. "A two-hour lunch! What was I thinking? I hope they didn't give my story to that jerk!" She pounded on the horn as a Saturn dallied in front of her. The chastened driver quickly swerved into the middle lane.

Ten minutes later she pulled into the *Statesman*'s parking lot. She ran into the building, walking once she entered the newsroom. Joe was sitting in her chair.

"Tell me you were out getting me something on Metro-Bank." The look of sarcasm on Joe Martone's face made Tari want to tell the man a thing or two.

"Joe, I told you that I had some personal things to take care of. Now, I'm gonna give you your story, the one we talked about this morning. And you'll get it at six P.M. That's my deadline, right? Or did that change while I was gone?" She tried to hide her irritation.

"Where in the world were you?" Joe demanded, getting up from Tari's chair and letting her take her place behind her computer screen.

"Joe, I'm going to start working now. If I answer all your questions about what I do with my personal time, I won't have enough time to give you a story by deadline, will I?" Tari said as if she were speaking to a child.

"Tari, I don't have to tell you how big this is. I've got a bunch of readers calling asking me if they should take their money out of MetroBank. I've got Bluesteed breathing down my neck every second. He wants to know what you've got. Don't keep me out of the loop."

"Joe!" Tari said. "Listen, I will send you a top of my story as soon as I have it written. But you have to get out of my hair so that I can write it. Okay? Just leave me alone . . . for a bit. I need to check my messages."

Joe Martone looked at his star reporter for the moment and shook his head. "I wouldn't take this from you if you weren't—"

"Go away," Tari flicked her fingers. "And relax," she said to Joe's back.

Mariska turned her way as soon as Joe disappeared. "That must have been some lunch date," she said, barely smiling but clearly angling for information.

"Really, it wasn't," Tari said, grabbing her telephone receiver and dialing madly. The last person in the world she would confide in was Mariska Lunes. But there was a smile on her face as she remembered the meeting with Shawn.

CHAPTER
20

It was nine o'clock when Joe Martone wearily walked over to Tari's desk. "You can go home now."

"What about the copy desk? Do they have any questions for me?" Tari asked, still wired from five cups of coffee.

Martone shook his head, his shoulders slumped, and walked away, no doubt haggard from his long day and dreading facing a wife who yelled at him constantly about missing dinner with his family.

Tari yelled good night after her tired boss. She, too, was exhausted, but she was still high from the raves the top editors were sending her way about her latest installment in the MetroBank saga. An hour-long interview with the state attorney general had given her some great quotes for her piece, which would again be on the front page. She was in heaven. "I'm gonna celebrate by ordering in from Shanti tonight," she wrote to Rebecca in an e-mail. "Can you believe it? I have a bass player. A fine one who does woodworking and tells funny jokes. And I'm on A1 again tomorrow. Ah, God has a sense of humor. I was just about to say my life is perfect."

She hit the send button and called the Indian restaurant

to order a shrimp vindaloo with brown rice and steamed vegetables.

A half hour later she switched on all the downstairs lights in her home. She hungrily plopped down on the couch with the food, turning on Fox News for a good laugh at the over-the-top, hysterical delivery of their crack news desk. Fair and balanced? Yeah, they had jokes!

The blinking Caller ID box distracted her, and she reached for the phone. The voice-mail access recording said that she had three messages. The first took away her appetite.

"Tari, this is Joanie Williams. I'm a patient coordinator in your doctor's office. We wanted to schedule your surgery for next Wednesday at eight. We need you to come in for pre-operative testing on Monday at eleven if you can. The surgeon wants to move as quickly as possible on this, so call me as soon as you can if you have a problem with either of those times or dates."

The second message bore no better news.

"Hi, Tari. I'm Dr. Susan Blakely. I'm your surgeon and I'll be doing your partial mastectomy. I'm hoping we can meet on Monday and talk about your treatment some more. I'll be going out of town soon for a while, so I'd really like to get your surgery done as soon as possible. Anyway, my nurse will call you. But I hope to see you on Monday and we can talk more."

The third message was her mother.

"Tari, how you doing? Child, I've been having some bad dreams about you lately. Call me, okay? I hope you're not sick and you're taking care of yourself. Call me. I love you."

You have no more messages.

It was 10:55 P.M. Her parents would be asleep now.

The tail end of the 10 o'clock news flashed before her unseeing eyes. She barely had the energy to be angry. Her mind told her that anger was what she should be feeling.

No one had even asked her whether she wanted to have surgery or what kind of surgery, for that matter. But it seemed that her HMO had already made all the decisions. Who were these people? she wondered, looking at the handset of the phone. Those people who didn't even know her but had made all these plans: Preoperative testing on Monday. Surgery, a partial mastectomy, on Wednesday. At eight!

She chuckled sardonically. That surgeon *had* to go out of town. Maybe she had a spa vacation that she really could not afford to miss, and Tari's breast was just one thing she had to get out of the way before running off to the Berkshires for a deep sea-salt rub. The nerve of those people, Tari fumed. And when was it decided that she'd have a partial mastectomy and not a lumpectomy? Just how much of her breast were they planning to take from her? She put the half-eaten food away.

Well, sorry, Doctor, Tari decided. *It's not going to happen this way. I'm in the middle of the biggest story of my career, and now is not a good time for surgery. We're just going to have to come up with a time that works for both of us, that's all. I need more information, more control over this,* she thought. She tapped her bare feet on the wood floors. The nerve of those people!

After a long, hot shower, Tari settled onto the pillows with a cup of chamomile tea. She had stopped bargaining with sleep, scolding it to hurry up and come. So she waited for fatigue to force her body into rest. Most nights she could wrestle cancer out of her consciousness and focus on MetroBank instead. But not tonight.

For the first time in her life, her goal was to not face this problem the way she had tackled others. There would be no head-on, grab it by the horns, scream at it until it cowers in submission attitude. But those phone messages could not be ignored. They, those faceless people with their plans and appointments, wanted to take the thing out as soon as possible.

She jumped up and paced before her queen-sized bed. How would she explain this to Joe?

Without thinking of the late hour, she dialed Rebecca's number.

"Tari, what do you want?" Rebecca answered the phone groggily.

"Sorry to wake you, Becks. But I was just thinking—well, I wasn't really thinking." The words flew out of Tari's mouth and she was breathless. "I won't be able to hide this. I mean, they want me to have surgery next week. Next week, Becks! What am I going to tell Joe? I can't just tell him I'm taking vacation!" Tari stopped to catch a breath.

Rebecca sighed. "Tari, didn't I tell you that it's better to just tell your work so you don't have to drive yourself crazy trying to hide this?"

"But, Becks, you don't know what those people are like!"

"Tari, you don't know how they're going to react. But it's going to be harder for you to hide it than to deal with it out in the open." Again, Rebecca was making sense, and Tari knew it and hated it.

But she persisted. "How do you know?"

"Tari, did you read any of the information I gave you from the American Cancer Society?" Rebecca asked.

Tari paused. "I really haven't had time. MetroBank is taking up all—"

"Tari, I hope you know that acting like you don't have cancer won't make it go away."

"Becks, I don't need this right now, okay? I really need some support here."

"Tari, stop pacing the floor."

"What?"

"I said stop pacing the floor and stop breathing so hard.

You're driving me nuts." Rebecca could not hide her impatience any longer, and her rising voice signaled as much. "I'm not going to tell you what to do. And I'm not going to talk to you until you read all the information I gave you and until you start doing some research on your own. Those doctors aren't going to tell you everything. You're going to have to do some of this on your own. You sound ignorant, foolish, and selfish. The last thing you need to be worrying about is your editor. You have a serious disease, and you need to start thinking about how you're going to deal with it!"

Tari made a sound of disbelief at how her normally calm and even-tempered friend was speaking to her.

"Don't say anything else," Rebecca snapped. "I'm going back to sleep."

Tari heard a click on the other end of the phone.

"What is wrong with her?" Tari said out loud. She stood, confused, in the middle of the dark bedroom. Her eyes were wide open and sleep was the last thing on her mind. It was almost two A.M.

She walked down the stairs to the living room, switching the lights on ahead of her, and picked up the heavy package of literature that Rebecca had left on her rarely used mahogany dining table.

There were several little booklets and pamphlets inside. The largest book, *A Breast Cancer Journey: Your Personal Guidebook*, was over 400 pages. Smaller ones included *Understanding Radiation Therapy* and *Understanding Chemotherapy*. Tari decided to start with the booklet that was smaller and less intimidating to look at, *Life After Cancer Treatment*.

CHAPTER
21

The sun had come up, tearing through the windows of her bedroom, and Tari was still reading. As if in a daze, she carried the 427-page book with her to the bathroom, her fingers marking page 138, and then to the kitchen, where she made her morning cup of green tea. She read until eight A.M., till her eyes burned and her head ached from staring at those pages for six hours straight.

She looked outside. It was a beautiful Saturday. The Phams next door were on their knees in the dirt getting their garden ready for hydrangeas. Her garden was barren. It was time to pick up a few potted plants from the Home Depot and plop them down in the front so that her house would blend in with the more diligently landscaped ones on the street. She hoped the Phams would again take pity this year and trim her hedges and some of the weeds that cropped up in her yard.

She waved to the older couple, and they said hello cheerfully. Tari had always loved the Ashmont Hill neighborhood. For years she had looked on the historic homes as if they were castles in a fairy tale. Sometimes she still could not believe she lived in a neighborhood that Abraham Lincoln had visited, that had been home to prominent Boston families and three past presidents of Harvard, and that was older than the city of Boston itself.

Most people now thought of Dorchester as part of the triumvirate—together with Roxbury and Mattapan—that made up black Boston, but it was so much more than that. Dorchester was full of a rich and beautiful history that was still evident in its Greek Revival, Queen Anne, and Colonial homes built in the nineteenth century and still standing proud today. She couldn't see herself living anywhere else.

She walked away from the window and surveyed the kitchen. The plan that had begun to form in her mind in the early hours of the morning was beginning to take shape.

The phone rang, and it was Melinda.

"I was just about to call you, girl," Tari said as she began to clean out her refrigerator.

"Everything okay? You want me to come over?" Melinda sounded worried. Since the diagnosis she called Tari three or four times a day, each time asking, motherly concern in her voice, "Are you okay? Are you sure?"

"Nah. Nothing like that. Do you still have that book on vegetarian eating? The one with the recipes?"

Melinda had flirted with being a vegetarian for a while but had given up after she grew tired of cooking two sets of meals for herself and for her omnivorous family.

"Why? You thinking of becoming a vegetarian?"

"Yup. I'm chucking the ground chuck, the cheese. Oh, my Lord," she wailed. "How am I going to make it without my Roquefort on wheat and sesame crackers?" Tari stood dismayed in the middle of the kitchen, holding the package of smelly cheese.

"Tari, you are so doing the right thing," Melinda said. "The antibiotics they feed those animals, girl. You don't know what those chemicals are doing to your body. Throw out the stinky cheese, girl!"

They giggled. "Okay. I'm really doing this." Tari sighed. "I'm doing this for real. The cheese goes." She dumped the cheese in the trash bag together with her 2 percent milk, Healthy Choice sliced ham, and a pack of four-month-old Italian sausage.

"Wow, that wasn't too bad," she said, looking at the bag. "I guess I don't eat that much meat after all."

"So you won't miss it much, then," Melinda said.

Tari agreed. "Yeah, we'll see what happens the next time I go to a restaurant. I hope I'll have the willpower to say no to meat."

"Well, I called you for a reason, too," Melinda said. Her tone put Tari on alert.

"Yeaaah?" Tari said slowly, still searching through her kitchen for any offending animal products.

"Well, a colleague of mine runs this support group with the YWCA. It's for women of color who have breast cancer or who have been affected by the disease. It's called Spirit-Wise Sisters."

"And?" She knew what was coming next.

"Well," Melinda said, already sensing resistance in Tari's voice, "I didn't sign you up or anything, so don't go getting all upset. But I'm going to e-mail you the address and times that they meet. It's up to you if you go or not. But I've read about research studies that say women with cancer who have some kind of support network tend do better."

"I'm not going to a support group, Melinda," Tari said firmly. She imagined a group of middle-aged women seated on the floor in a circle, holding hands, wearing scarves on their heads, and talking softly about what it means to go through life with one breast, or worse, no breasts.

"I knew you'd say that. And I know what you're think-ing, but you're wrong. Do you think you're the only hot young chick who has cancer? You might be surprised to find that's not the case. All I'm saying is you don't have to suffer alone. Not that you're alone. You have me. Us. But do what you want. You always do anyway."

"I'm not suffering," Tari said defiantly. "I'm gonna fight this thing with everything I've got, and I'll beat it. But I'm not doing it your way."

Melinda sighed. It was no use trying to persuade Tari to do anything when she was in this mood. "It's not about doing it my way, Tari. Why do you have to be so stubborn? I'm just trying to show you that there are a lot of resources out there in case you—"

"I know. I know. Okay? Thanks for the tip. But I don't think I'm the support-group type."

"Fine," Melinda said tightly. "So what are you up to today?"

"Grocery shopping, then I'm reading this book from the American Cancer Society."

"That's great. Educating yourself is—" Melinda stopped as she heard Tari sigh on the other end. "I'll go grocery shopping with you," she offered, almost pleading.

"Nah, that's okay. You'll only end up trying to counsel me, and I need to clear my head. I haven't slept all night."

"Tari, you need your rest. Especially now."

"See what I mean?" Tari said.

Later, Tari walked into the Whole Foods Market in Brookline and was immediately bewildered. She held Melinda's vegetarian recipe book like a pastor walking onto a pulpit, Bible in hand. But she felt unsure. Compared to the Super Stop & Shop, this place was small and crowded, and certainly not as brightly lit. She tried to put her finger on what was so different about this supermarket. Maybe it was the pretentious décor and the fake cheeriness of the staff. Or probably the colorful flyers everywhere advertising yoga instruction, Ayurvedic medicine, and panchakarma cleansing.

The shoppers themselves were different enough from

the folks in her neighborhood. She judged them to be the type of people who read the *Globe* and the *Times* on Sundays, who didn't own but rented on Nantucket, who encouraged their kids to think of BU as their safety school, and who walked around with a 300-foot yacht-load of liberal guilt on their shoulders. So pretentious, she thought. She somehow felt that she was betraying a part of herself by being in this fancy-schmancy grocery store, with its clear-skinned, straight-toothed, green-aproned young staff who probably drove to their jobs in their dad's old Volvos.

But she soon forgot about her class convictions as the wide selection of food drew her in. Organic, pesticide-free tomatoes, apple juice, orange juice, blueberries, and strawberries went into her shopping cart. She scooped up unsalted nuts, Norwegian salmon, a few pounds of shrimp, fresh coriander, parsley, celery. Then it was on to cereals. She grabbed a couple boxes of kashi, not knowing then that it would take her about a month to get used to the nontaste of it.

She couldn't resist the bath and beauty care products aisle. She grabbed some organic soaps, lotions, and deodorant free of glycol and aluminum chlorohydrate. On a particularly stressful day she would find that her new deodorant was safer but that it needed to be used very, very liberally.

As her cart filled up, Tari began to think that she would never go back to her mega–grocery store. For too many years she had eaten recklessly, without considering what was going into her body, she thought as she grabbed a carton of soy milk. She considered all of the pesticides in the vegetables, hormones in the cheese and other dairy products, antibiotics in the meat, and it occurred to her that all of those things could have caused her cancer. But then she thought of all of the people she knew who had much worse eating habits than she and who probably would never get any kind of cancer. It just didn't make sense. *But at least,* she thought, *just doing this makes me feel better already.* She began to feel more empowered, like she was starting to gain some control.

Before she hit the checkout line she grabbed one more thing from the refrigerated section, a container of wheat grass juice. She'd read it about it in some magazine somewhere. It looked ominous, so it had to be good, right? She sniffed it and her stomach lurched. Then she did a double take when she saw the total of her grocery bill on the cash register: $153.27, twice what she normally shelled out for a week's worth of food. This was going to be the fight of her life.

CHAPTER
22

Melinda sang along with the Nancy Wilson CD as she vacuumed her carpeted staircase. Taylor, wanting to imitate her mom, performed her best rendition of "Twinkle, Twinkle Little Star" over the blaring stereo.

It was Saturday morning in the Jones household, one of Melinda's favorite times. Her family was all hers, with no interruptions from homework, television, or her office. Once a month she had a woman from a cleaning service come in to give the house a nice, thorough scrub, but in between she liked the therapeutic benefits of housework. It gave her tangible insurance that she was the woman of this house.

"Mom, we're out of Tide," Jared called from downstairs.

"No, we're not," she yelled back and told her son where to find a new carton. She shook her head, thinking that boy of hers would try anything, use any ruse, to get out of doing his chores.

She looked up as Michael walked out of the bathroom clothed in his golf shirt and wearing golf shoes. She sighed.

"Michael, I was hoping that we could all do something together today," she said calmly. "Remember last week when I said we should take the kids to the movies or the museum?"

Michael shoved his hand into his pockets. "Who said we can't go? I'll be back late this afternoon. We'll catch a six o'clock show."

"But that means they won't get in bed till nine or ten." Melinda could hear the whine in her voice, and it irritated her that she had to beg her husband to spend time with his family, that she and the kids were competing with golf and losing badly.

Michael sighed deeply. "I'll try to make it back a couple of hours earlier, then."

He walked down the steps, carefully stepping over the vacuum cleaner to kiss her lightly on the cheek. She made her best effort not to turn away.

"I'll see you later, babe," he called out.

She didn't answer. Instead, she turned the vacuum cleaner back on and moved the machine from step to step, singing as best as she could. She was no Tari, whose voice could bring water to the meanest man's eyes, but she could hold a tune. She missed the days when she and Tari sang in church while her mother played piano and Jeffrey played guitar. She'd had such high hopes then. It had never occurred to her then that she could ever be unhappy.

She had been the prettiest girl in the church and in high school, too, and no one could have told her then that she wouldn't end up with everything she ever wanted. She thought back to all of those teenage boys who had written her love letters, made pledges to marry her. But her perfect Prince Charming would not be among them. Her dreams had always wandered to the bad boys who wore their hair in high-top fades, blasted Big Daddy Kane and EPMD on their Walkmans, and used street slang.

But Coletta Shields had noticed this and guarded her

daughter like a mama grizzly bear. "Those boys will just mess up your future. Wait for a good one to come along."

The good ones would have been West Indian boys with good heads on their shoulders who loved God, served in the church, cleaned up the As in school, and had dreams of hard-to-get-into colleges and boring but upwardly mobile professions. To Melinda, they all seemed the same with their sensible haircuts, straight-backed gait, and glaring lack of street wisdom. So despite Coletta's admonishments, she had not waited too long.

Michael Jones had fallen into her life by error. If she had followed her mother's advice, their paths would never have crossed.

She met him on the street, of all places. She was out pasting flyers for revival week on lampposts and store windows. He was shy, and she had been touched at the obvious effort it took for him to ask her name. She had given him her phone number, knowing full well that according to Coletta's definition he was not one of the good ones worth waiting for. There were hints of a gangster lean in his walk, and he used double negatives in his speech. Above all that, Coletta always warned: *Don't ever talk to a man who approaches you on the street.* But Michael had kind eyes, and he lacked the craggy edges of the other neighborhood boys; he did not call her "baby" or try to get fresh with her until she was ready.

Four years later and pregnant, she dropped out of college. Michael had been more than happy to marry her. He was working in Waltham then, in an entry-level job at IBM while taking a few courses at UMass, and was eager to show the world that he had become a man, worthy of a woman like Melinda. He found a one-bedroom with an eat-in kitchen in Hyde Park for the two of them. Things went well for a while until Melinda delivered Jared and began to get restless. She began to see her friends achieving, accomplishing things. Girls she had gone to school with, had been smarter than, had done homework for, they all seemed to be surpassing her, with their jobs downtown and their adventurous lives in big cities like New York, Chicago, Miami. Some had married those boring boys whom she had rejected and were now living in suburbs like Stoughton, Randolph, even Milton. And there she was, stuck in an apartment, working part time as a file clerk for Prudential, three courses short of a degree in psychology.

By the time Jared was old enough to say bye-bye, she was back in school to finish up her last year. Then it was on to grad school and the doctorate program. Melinda never stopped. She studied, worked, nurtured, built, and all the while Michael shrank back further and further. She was too busy to notice. She thought that by now she would be sitting pretty professionally and financially. And she never paused to consider the fate of her marriage in all of this dreaming.

And she was sitting pretty in many ways. She had her lovely house, a fixer-upper on Fort Hill in Roxbury that she had transformed into the envy of many of her neighbors. Both of her children were in private school, and if she took the view of an outsider, her marriage was tranquil, even ideal in some ways. It was working like a fifteen-year-old Toyota. Running well, as well as only a fifteen-year-old car could.

To say Michael had disappointed her would be an understatement. There were so many dreams in the beginning. He, too, had wanted a doctorate. He had wanted to teach engineering at the university level, maybe at UMass or Northeastern. He had wanted more for a long time. But once he got laid off from IBM, he languished in her everlooming shadow.

And at first, Melinda had understood. He had worked his behind off in those early years when she stayed home pregnant with Jared. So she said, "No. Go ahead and take a year off, honey. I'm making enough to carry us for the time being."

Now she regretted those words. She longed to see her man busy again, passionate about teaching, about studying, about something other than golf. She wanted him to feel ashamed when he saw her haggard and irritable, weighed down by her patients' troubles and by her own. She wanted sympathy. She wanted him to write the checks for the gas company, for the electric bill and their cell phone carrier. She wanted him to remember to buy milk and veggie chicken patties and to take Jared fishing or even to the golf course once in a while. She wanted him to start being a man, her man, again so she'd have something to brag about.

Every day, every night now she fought the wrenching urges that took hold of her. Thoughts would turn into an almost physical desire that nearly forced her to her closet. She already pictured what she would take with her, the outfit she would wear to the airport. She saw every fine detail of the small flat she would occupy in Paris, maybe in the Fifth Arrondissement. She imagined teal walls, white-tile bathroom in the old European style, wood floors, quiet, quiet all the time. Then guilt would force its way into her daydream and she would find a way to include the kids. Somewhere.

But she wasn't going anywhere. Especially now. Even if she did work up the courage to go against her will, against her marriage vows, her better judgment, God, she now faced a real obstacle. Her little sister needed her, and so all those silly dreams of breaking free from her life would just have to return to the back of her mind, deep, deep down in her mental archives. Her hand went to her breast again. Nothing.

So, she cleaned her house, sang her songs, praised God, loved her children, and took on the responsibility before her. As the old hymn promised, she would exchange this cross for a crown. Someday.

CHAPTER
23

When Tari took the stage she looked over her audience. It was the same crowd of graduate students, yuppies, and a few older couples sprinkled throughout, but they looked different—a bit friendlier. She waved to a couple of her colleagues from work seated in the front row. *Oh, this is going to be a good one*, she thought.

She began her first set with one of her songs, "New to Me." She had written the words to one of Manny's tunes a year before. It had been an optimistic time, as she'd just lost ten pounds on the South Beach Diet and gone out on one promising date with a short but cute doctor. She'd decided that he had to be the one. Nice hands, smart, kind, and romantic. The song had been so easy to write. Three blissful dates later, he dropped the bomb: he was married, and of course, unhappy. She sent him packing, and the ten pounds came running back to her hips two weeks later. But she still loved the song. And the South Beach Diet book had long disappeared under a stack of other books in her living room.

But she felt good tonight. Something about the low lights, the sweet smell of alcohol, the chatty, friendly audience, and her new Giuseppe Zanotti shoes sent her soaring.

Even Manny seemed to be in a light mood as his fingers rattled over the piano keys. This night was one where nothing else mattered. One to take a hiatus from life's ugliness and only see pretty, perfect things, like cute, happy, young couples, wide-eyed college students with sky blue futures ahead. "You make me wanna do bad things," she sang and then laughed out loud in the middle of the song. Manny shook his head and rolled his eyes at her playfully. She'd parted her hair down the middle and wore it straight as a bone, and it flowed past her shoulders. The fake eyelashes that had seemed a good idea while she was getting dressed felt sticky and itchy, but that just made her want to laugh even more. "And being bad is so new to me."

One person kept clapping long after the others had stopped, and she strained her eyes in vain to see the back of the room. Her skinny new high heels trembled as she walked off the stage, and audience members patted her, shook her hand, smiled, and complimented her on the way to the dressing room. Then she felt a tap on her back.

"Hey, you've got a beautiful voice."

She whirled around.

"Shawn!" Tari's hands flew to her hair self-consciously. The wild and sudden thumping in her chest was so powerful she hoped it was not visible or, worse, audible. "What are you doing here?"

"I came to see you. Thought it would help me decide whether I wanted to play for you or not." He was smiling the megawatt smile that had never left her thoughts since their lunch date.

"Well . . . I'm so surprised," Tari said, laughing and smoothing her hair again. She scolded herself to calm down and to stop giggling like a teenager backstage at a Justin Timberlake concert.

"And . . . I wanted to give you something," he said. He put his hand in his pocket and opened his palm to reveal a small but perfectly crafted varnished wooden microphone. "I had this laying around my workshop," he said.

She opened her mouth but no words came. "I don't know what to say, Shawn."

"You can say thanks," he said as she handled the index-finger-sized wooden microphone.

"It's beautiful. Wow. You made this?"

He nodded. "I also do parties, bar mitzvahs . . ."

She laughed. "So, have you been here before?"

He shook his head as he surveyed the place. "I actually don't do nightspots. I stopped going out a long time ago."

She didn't quite know what to say to that because she knew what his statement implied. They were both Christians, and places like Rico's were not the typical places a Christian found himself on a Saturday night.

"I wouldn't be here if it weren't—"

"Tari, come on. I wasn't implying that you shouldn't sing here. I know how this business works. You have to get out there if you ever expect to have any success."

She appreciated his kindness, but a part of her still felt guilty. *He shouldn't be making excuses for me,* she thought.

"So when do you go on for your second set?" he asked.

They found a table near the stage and sat and talked. She observed him, took him in, trying to find out more about him by just looking. His casual manner, the way his body so overwhelmed the chair that it seemed to shrink under his long, muscular frame, made her feel secure. She could almost feel herself all safe and wrapped up in his powerful arms. *Mind out of the gutter, girl;* she tried to focus.

"Why are you always telling jokes?" she asked after he once again had her laughing out loud, drawing attention from other tables.

"Because you have an amazing smile and I love to hear you laugh," Shawn said.

Tari blushed. "So, have you made your decision yet?"

she said, trying to regain control of the situation. This flirting was too much. Too much, she thought.

Shawn nodded. "I have. I'll do it."

She wasn't surprised, but it seemed appropriate to act that way.

"You will?" When their eyes met, she felt the kind of warm feeling that inspired her to write silly songs, and she immediately looked away.

"Yes, I will," Shawn said, but he didn't take his eyes off her.

"Thanks, Shawn. I'm really glad you're going to be doing this for me." She cleared her throat. "For us. The band. 'Cause these guys up there"—she nodded to her band, who were preparing for the second set—"are like brothers to me."

"I know what you mean. I'm still close to guys I used to jam with back in high school," he said.

"Are you going to stay for the second set?"

"Sure. I really want to hear you do that Dianne Reeves song you've been threatening me with."

She hit him on the arm playfully.

Her stiletto heels seemed to have gained height and lost width as she took the stage again. She was nervous. The crowd was thicker, and all eyes were turned toward her now that that the distraction of dinner had ended, and the room seemed quieter than usual. Where was he? She couldn't see him, but she could feel his dark eyes boring into her. *Oh, please, God, don't make me mess up tonight!*

She began the set with "Better Days." It was one of her favorite songs, and she remembered telling Dianne Reeves how much she loved it at the JVC Jazz Festival in Newport in 1999. Maybe it was because she was trying so hard to impress Shawn, but Tari's voice captivated the audience, and they held their beers and wineglasses, transfixed. But this show was not for them. She wanted him to know that she was good, that she was worthy. She experimented with the songs Manny had carefully arranged for her, challenging the band to follow her meandering vocal highs and lows; she closed her eyes and lost herself, oblivious to the crowd and the glare in Manny's eyes.

When she finally opened her eyes, the crowd stood, whistled, cheered. She looked at them as if someone had replaced her audience with aliens. But the applause filled up that place in her soul that craved validation. It solidified for her that maybe she was not wasting her time after all.

"Good job," Manny said as they bowed. "But warn me next time you plan to go off like that."

As she left the stage, Rico came up to her, complimenting her on her second set.

"That's my girl. You're gonna be big someday. Like Patti LaBelle," he said. She smiled genially but wondered, Patti LaBelle? The woman was an R&B and soul singer. A flaming diva! The last person Tari would compare herself to. But Rico was sixty-three years old. It was probably the first name that came into his mind when he thought of a great black singer. She shook hands with some members of the audience who came up to her, also offering compliments and asking her whether she had a CD.

"That's the next step," she said.

She made her way through the crowd to where Shawn was standing.

"So what did you think?" she asked.

He shrugged. "Not bad," he teased.

"You're such a comedian," she said. "Hey, do you want to go get a late snack at the South Street Diner?" she asked, then almost slapped herself for being so forward.

"Can't," he said. "I have to be up early tomorrow. You know, eight o'clock service. I'm filling in for Brian, the bassist."

"Oh, you are? I hope I'll be able to get up early to hear

you," she said, hoping again that she did not sound too eager.

He smiled. "You've got a real gift."

"Thanks," she said. "I think we'll work really well together."

She bit her lip hard as she watched him disappear into the exit sign. *What did I just do? Twice!* Twice she had put him on the spot, throwing her interest in his face like an eager beaver. *Aaack!* She chided herself. *Never, ever ask a man out, under any circumstances.* It was a credo she lived by, but Shawn's casual, easy manner made it so easy to forget her self-imposed rules. Now she had to make up for her unacceptable behavior. It was time to play hard to get.

CHAPTER
24

Late again. Tari groaned as she looked at the clock. She had exactly thirty minutes to get dressed and get herself to the ten o'clock service before all the good seats were taken. Otherwise she'd be stuck in the back rows with those who were nursing hangovers and sleeping off the sins of the previous night. She stumbled out of the bed, eyes half closed, feeling her way to the bathroom. The bright sunlight from the clear-as-ice day did not filter through the thick, heavy drapes over her windows—her weapon against the unwelcome natural alarm clock of daylight saving time.

"Oh, noooooo!" She pounded the tiles in the shower stall as the cascading water flushed the sleep from her body. She had missed Shawn at the eight o'clock service. *Now he's going to think I'm self-centered.* "Aaargh!" And she wouldn't get her chance to play it cool with him, to show him that she wasn't as interested in him as he thought.

But it had been difficult to fall asleep. The clock had read 3:30 A.M., but she was wide awake. Her body was still jumpy from the performance, thoughts of Shawn still fleeting through her mind as she worried about what he really thought of her. *Does he truly believe I'm talented? When he said he loved to see me smile, what exactly did he mean by that? Do I smile too much? Is he as into me as I think I'm into him?* And then, amid all of those thoughts, *Oh, my God! Do I have to tell him I have cancer? What will he think? Will he still like me?*

Maybe I should consider those sleeping pills the doctor suggested, Tari thought, as she dried herself quickly. But then she saw herself living through a groggy, languid daze as her MetroBank story slipped from her fingers into the hands of a more lucid coworker.

"No way," she said out loud, not realizing that she was talking to herself. "We'll get this sleep thing together. Just need a plan. Maybe some more vitamins."

She briefly wondered as she slapped moisturizer over her skin whether there was anything new on her story, but she decided that she would worry about that after church.

If she had had a chance to turn on the television she would have seen that the national news shows were mentioning her scoop as they talked about the chicanery that was taking place at MetroBank. She would have seen that the state senator who was the chief of the Senate Finance Committee was calling for stronger penalties for white-collar crimes like embezzlement and accounting fraud.

But Tari was slashing through her closet, grabbing the first thing that didn't need ironing, a black skirt and a pink shirt. She threw on some black suede pumps that pinched her little toe, pulled her hair back in a ponytail, and fastened a string of pearls around her neck. She grabbed her makeup bag as she headed out of the house. She'd have to do her face at the red lights.

The church parking lot was full at 10:09 A.M. Tari drove her 4Runner around the block, keeping an eye out for a parking space. She saw one, a tight one, between an Escalade and a Corolla. She took a deep breath and put her parallel parking skills to work. Six minutes later, and feeling a tad sweaty, she was out of the car and running across the street to the church building. She looked back at her truck, sand-wiched between the two others, and hoped the driver of the Escalade would be gentle when he or she was backing out.

It took a few minutes to settle down and get into the mood of the service, so flustered she was from rushing all morning. She was embarrassed to find herself writing out a check for her tithe and offering while the buckets were being passed.

At least it would be the bishop who would deliver the sermon and not some junior pastor. People came from as far as New Hampshire to hear Bishop Ferdinand preach. He was in such high demand across the country that he only preached at home about twice a month. Tari could listen to him for hours and hours without growing tired or bored or insulted. He was not like other preachers who talked down or regurgitated sermons they stole from greats like Vernon McGee, or who tried to emulate the pastors du jour like T. D. Jakes. Bishop Ferdinand was himself. He was so real that he made many people uncomfortable, and Tari admired this about him: the fact that he was not afraid to be human.

In her childhood church she'd always regarded her pas-tor, her father, as a figure so self-righteous and holy, one who could hear things directly from God, and who was able to pronounce damnation on her, even though she was only a child. He seemed so out of reach to her, a mere human on a much lower rung of the stairway to heaven. One of the Bible verses that never ceased to give her incentive to say her prayers at night was: "The wages of sin is death."

She had never heard Bishop Ferdinand threaten the con-gregation with fire and brimstone. Her mother would wrin-kle her face in disapproval at the bishop's teaching method. "You can't sugarcoat the Gospel," Coletta would say. But Tari'd had enough of the tongue-lashings of a Pentecostal church and home, so this was the place for her.

After the sermon, Bishop Ferdinand did a strange thing. Instead of beckoning sinners and backsliders to come to the altar, he made a special request.

"I feel that there are people in here today who are struggling with questions, with sickness, with family issues. I just feel that there is a great need for deliverance today. And if that includes you, I'd like you to just come up to the altar right now. If you need to be healed, come on up. If your marriage is not working, come on up. You're struggling with revealing some bad news to your husband, your wife, your parents, come on up."

The altar overflowed and the aisles filled with people who answered the call, walking up to where dozens of church elders stood waiting to pray for them. Tari took a furtive glance and noticed that there were young women like her, some she knew, young and old men, even younger students, who were making their way up to the altar. And in a way she was jealous of their courage, because she could not move.

She was rooted to her chair, her head bowed. She felt the pull. It was not just an emotional thing; she felt a physical urge in her body. *Go,* said her limbs, her organs, her heart, and her mind. But she sat, holding on to her seat as if for dear life. She had not answered an altar call in years, and it terrified her, the thought of going up there and letting the whole world see her reaching out for help. She stayed in her seat.

As she drove home, she felt unsettled, as if she had unfinished business with God and with herself. *I should have gone, I should have gone,* her mind said. Besides Melinda, she had not had anyone pray for her since the diagnosis. She herself could barely look up to heaven. She felt so betrayed by God that she had not given herself a second to even talk to Him since that day the doctor said those words that shook her world.

She looked in the rearview mirror and saw the outline of the church building. There would be one last service for the day, and she had a few minutes before it started. She made a U-turn in the middle of Blue Hill Avenue and headed back toward the church.

People were still milling about the emptying parking lot. She walked in, straight to the front, where some of the elders remained talking in small groups. She noticed Melinda's women's group friends were clustered around in groups, chatting, gossiping. She avoided their eyes and took a deep breath. She was never one to push herself to get involved in the whole church hierarchy thing, and she felt uncomfortable just being there in the front with the church brass.

She knew there were many women who joined the church years after she had who were now deacons, who sat in the front row and looked down on people like her who weren't involved in ministry. But she never wanted to be one of them; she'd had enough of that growing up.

She held her head high as she walked past the high-and-mighty and made a beeline for the assistant pastor. She knew his name though they had never met, and she decided to take the approach she did in interviews. *Stick out the hand and start talking.*

"Hi, Pastor Terry, I'm Tari Shields," she said, smiling. He shook her hand warmly.

"How are you, Sister Shields. I know about you but I've never met you. We're so glad we have a tithing member who works for the media," Pastor Terry said.

Tari was taken aback; she had no idea that she "was known about" by the church leadership. Probably because of Melinda, she thought.

"This is a church; people talk." Pastor Terry laughed, sensing her discomfort.

Tari nodded understandingly.

"Um . . . well. I just wanted to. I need some help. Some

prayer. I have this issue I'm dealing with," she said, looking around at the dozen or so people who might or might not have been paying attention to them.

"Do you want to go somewhere quiet, maybe outside?"

Tari followed the young-looking man out a side door that led to the pastors' parking area. She felt comfortable with Pastor Terry. She knew that he was not much older than she was, in his mid to late thirties, but he was very mature and wise for his age. His wife was the children's pastor, and they had four children. They reminded her very much of Melinda and Michael—the idealized version.

"So, what's going on, sister?" he asked as they stood in the now-quiet parking lot.

She sighed, wondering where to start. Then her lips began to quiver and the tears came. Pastor Terry did nothing. He was used to seeing church members in crisis and knew enough to let them express their pain.

"I have cancer. Breast cancer," Tari whispered, looking down at the black asphalt, her voice cracking. "And I need to talk to my mom. But I can't. I can't tell her that I have this. I don't know what she'll do. And my job. I worked so hard for everything. And my story is just starting to develop . . . and I have to just . . ."

Pastor Terry took a handkerchief out of his pocket and handed it to her.

She shook her head and reached into her pocketbook for her own. She wiped her eyes and nose and breathed in deeply. She felt ashamed for breaking down and looked around to see if anyone had seen her crying. "I'm sorry to break down like this."

"It's okay," he said gently. "How long have you known?"

"A few days," she said, wondering why that mattered.

"Have you prayed about it?"

"Well . . . yes. Um . . . I'm still trying to sort a lot of things out."

"With your anger toward God?"

She didn't answer. Up until that point, Tari had not been able to articulate to God just how she felt about being stricken with this disease. She had wanted to ask why. But she knew that there was no satisfactory answer and, besides, God was not usually forthcoming with His reasons.

"Sister Tari, I'm going to pray for you right now. But you have to realize that you cannot do this on your own. When things like that come our way, sometimes it's God's way of drawing us nearer to Him. You'll know it because sooner or later there won't be anywhere for you to turn but to Him. But in the meantime, while you're still in that stage where you're mad and you don't know what to do, I'm going to pray that God will give you guidance and clarity. You're not going to die, and you should believe that right now. God has blessed you. Just look at the life you have. You're educated and you have a wonderful job where you reach so many people with your work. And you're alive and healthy. You made it here today on your own two feet, didn't you? See, I don't have to know a lot about you to know that you're a blessed young woman. Take a look at some of the women you'll see on Blue Hill Avenue, women who've been through divorce, prison, drug overdoses, abuse, violence—and some of them were in service this morning. They made it, and they're still struggling every day on less than half of what you've got going for you. Sister, you have to believe God that you are not going to die. God is making His will manifest in you, but He can't do it if you don't trust Him. So I'm going to pray that you will begin to let go of yourself, your fear, and your anger. Let Him guide you and let Him take care of you. As for your mother, don't worry about telling her. Just put it all in God's hands. Remember, if He takes care to see that the sparrow is fed and cared for, then what do you, made in His own image, have to worry about? Are you understanding what I'm trying to say to you?" Pastor Terry asked.

Tari nodded, but tears were streaming down her face because each word that came out of the young pastor's mouth was like a balm on her scarred heart. She would never forget those words: "You're not going to die. You're blessed. Just look at the life you have."

CHAPTER
25

Before she even kicked off her uncomfortable shoes, she picked up the phone and dialed.

"Tari, I was just thinking about you." Her mother's voice tugged at her heart, and she knew that this would probably be the hardest thing she would ever have to do in her lifetime.

"Mommy, I need to tell you something, so go sit down."

She heard the intake of breath, and her fist clenched.

"You're okay?" her mother asked, her voice full of worry.

Tari paused. She had practiced in the car, but the little speech she had planned to give to soften the blow had slipped through her mind, so she blurted it out. Three words.

"What?" Coletta Shields shrieked.

Tari closed her eyes tightly and bit her lips so she would not cry again.

"What did you say to me, child?" her mother said, even louder this time.

"It's true," Tari whispered. "I'm having surgery on Wednesday."

"No, Tari. No!"

Tari heard a sound as if the phone had been dropped, and

a few seconds later her father came on the line, his voice hoarse.

"What's going on, Tari?" he asked. William Shields had never been an emotional man; in some ways he was the exact opposite of his wife. Tari had always run to him for refuge and advice when she was younger, preferring his coolheadedness to her mother's outsize moods and impulsive actions.

"Daddy, I have breast cancer," she said.

She heard him sigh.

"Is Mom okay?"

"She's . . . she's . . . she'll be fine. She's crying. How are you taking it? Did they see how bad it is? Has it spread?"

"I'm doing okay. I'm having surgery on Wednesday. No, they don't know yet if it's spread," she said quickly, biting her lower lip.

"Wednesday?" She could hear him making plans. "Well, we'll be there. We'll fly up on Tuesday." Her father sounded resigned, and that saddened Tari even more. There she was, causing havoc in the family again.

"Daddy, you guys shouldn't come for that. I haven't met with the surgeon yet. It may be just a one-hour thing," Tari pleaded. She feared that seeing her family all around her might make her feel sicker than she wanted to.

"Don't argue, okay?" her father said, sounding distracted and weary. "I'll call you back. I need to go. Your mother needs to calm down. Does Jeffrey know yet?"

"No, I'm going to call him and tell him." She had been neglecting to make that same call to her little brother, who was in divinity school in North Carolina.

"No, I'll tell him," her father said. She was relieved that he offered. He and Jeffrey were very close, and it would probably be better for Jeffrey to hear it from him.

She hung up the phone feeling guilty, as if she had committed a crime against her family. *It is so like me to be the one causing all the controversy*, she thought. Again. She was the one always telling tales and starting fights when she, Melinda, and Jeffrey were kids. Her parents always had to keep both eyes on her and keep her on a short leash because she was always giving other people a piece of her mind. They were always apologizing for something she had said but hadn't meant. Something she had done and wouldn't apologize for. Why couldn't she have been the good, quiet one like Jeffrey, or the super-achiever, goody-two-shoes like Melinda?

The phone rang again.

"Yes, Mom," she said as her mother called her name.

"How did you get that thing? My God, child. You're just a baby. How could God let this happen to my child?" And Coletta Shields was weeping hysterically again.

"Mom, stop," Tari said. "Stop, please. You're upsetting me."

Coletta sniffled.

"Mom, it's going to be fine. This is America, okay? Not the islands, where the doctors still use equipment from the nineteenth century. They have all kinds of drugs for this stuff. It's not like the old days. I'm gonna be fine. So stop making me feel worse." Tari hoped that throwing the guilt on Coletta would somehow calm her.

"I didn't mean to make you feel worse, Tari. I'm sorry. I just . . ."

Tari sighed as her mother broke down again. She had expected this. Her mother just did not take bad news well.

"Mom, why don't you go get some water or something."

"I'm drinking some water right now," Coletta Shields sobbed.

Tari resisted the urge to laugh at the way her mother sounded. *Drama queen*, she wanted to say.

"Well, go lie down or something. But don't worry about me. I'm fine. Okay?"

There was no answer from the other end.

"So, I'll see you guys on Tuesday, okay? Let me know what time to pick you guys up from the airport."

When Tari ended the phone call with her parents, she called Melinda immediately. It was an invariable routine. Every time either of them talked with the parents, they had to call each other to decompress.

"So, how was she?" Melinda asked.

"Oh, what you would expect," Tari said.

"Histrionics and then some, huh?"

"Oh, yeah." Tari giggled. "You know, it actually felt good trying to calm her down. I mean, I forgot about how I was feeling 'cause I was trying so hard to make her feel better."

Melinda sighed. "Well, that's not necessarily a good thing, Tari. It's your health that's at stake, not hers."

"I know. But it just felt good to know that even though I may have cancer, at least I'm not as crazy as she is. Sheesh!"

They laughed; "crazy woman" was what they called Coletta behind her back.

"By the way, they're staying with me when they get here," Melinda said firmly. "I already told that husband of mine."

"Ha!" Tari scoffed. "You think that woman's gonna leave me alone for a second?"

"I'm serious, Tari," Melinda said. "I know how you like your privacy. I'm not going to have her adding any stress to your life right now. I don't care if I have to chain her to the radiator in the spare room."

"Well, we'll see. But she's gonna fight you."

"And I'll win," Melinda said.

Tari scoffed. She doubted that Melinda would get her way, and if she did it would come at a huge price; someone could end up not speaking to somebody else. Coletta would not give in easily. At least, Tari thought, the family drama that was about to unfold would provide some entertainment amid all the craziness.

* * *

Melinda busied herself with cooking Sunday dinner and tried to ignore the television, which was giving her a headache. She'd given up trying to understand why Michael couldn't watch basketball without the volume blaring. Today was not the day, she told herself. There were other battles much more worthy of fighting.

She herself couldn't wait for the big showdown with Coletta. It had been a while. The two of them had a tenuous relationship, but it was all under the surface. She did not go off half-cocked, yelling and screaming when Coletta got on her last nerve. She knew how to be civil. She'd learned to grin and bear what her mother dished out, only letting the frustration boil over when she absolutely could not tolerate it a second longer.

She remembered bringing Michael home that Sunday afternoon years before to meet them. Her father was disappointed, but as usual he did not let it show. He was polite and kind, if a little aloof. But Coletta had looked the skinny young man up and down as if he were the cheapest suit on a sale rack.

"Where your people from?" she'd asked after he had introduced himself nervously. Then: "What part of Alabama did you say? Speak up, I can't hear you."

Melinda had bitten her tongue, clenched her fists, and tensed her muscles, willing every cell in her body not to tell that woman to just shut up, just stop it already. *No one would be good enough for you anyway, so just accept it. This is the man I love!*

That day, she had gone from being the Shields family's great hope to its great disappointment. Coletta had had big plans for her oldest daughter. She saw her achieving great things that people the world over would take notice of, and the girl was letting this skinny, yellow boy from Alabama just devour her potential. Shy? He wasn't shy, Coletta had told her husband when they had settled in that night. "He's just trying to fool me into thinking he's not trying to get into her panties. They're all the same." Melinda had been standing outside her parents' bedroom door when those words came out of Coletta's mouth.

But Melinda, loser of many battles with her mother, had won the war. She had achieved, she did get written up in the *Globe* and the other papers. She had even been interviewed for a news story on Channel 7 a few years ago. And her son was a top student at his exclusive private school, and her baby girl was already showing signs of genius. It was Coletta's mistake to have given up on her so soon.

And there was nothing Melinda loved more than to have her mother in her home, under her roof, desperately searching for something to criticize but finding nothing. Nothing that could hurt Melinda, anyway. "Oh, the maid will get that when she comes next week," Melinda loved to say when Coletta would point out a speck of dust in some faraway crevice.

Melinda could just see Coletta making Tari's ordeal worse with her obscene motherly love that tended to barge in like an avalanche and make you forget that you were the one in pain. Her smothering kind of care that sometimes did nothing else but pile up on your original hurt.

Let her come here, Melinda thought, as she peered out her study to glance at her husband's reclining frame in front of the television. She was itching for someone to fight with.

CHAPTER

26

Rebecca suggested the all-veggie restaurant on Beacon Street near Fenway Park to make it easier for Tari to stick to her vegetarian diet. But Tari could not hide her trepidation as she inspected the menu. This vegetarian thing was growing more tired by the minute. She missed the belly-warming goodness of grilled chicken, sautéed chicken, fried chicken, chicken salad, oven-baked chicken, chicken nuggets. Aaargh! Just how many ways could you be imaginative with vegetables? There had to be a limit, and Tari felt that she was right up against it.

For Rebecca it was no great leap, because there had been no meat in her diet since childhood. One of her first acts of rebellion was eating a chicken dinner the second week after she arrived in the United States. The experience had been a letdown. Her first thought was, *I haven't been missing anything.*

The restaurant was almost empty that Monday afternoon, and their food came quickly.

"So the folks are coming tomorrow," Rebecca said, noting the bags under Tari's eyes and worrying that her friend might not be as honest about her worries as she was letting on.

"Yup. It's going to be pandemonium. Melinda's already knuckling up."

"Your mom is such a trip." Rebecca laughed.

"She is," Tari said. "She's just so . . . emotional. I'm scared she's gonna make this worse for me."

"Hmmm." Rebecca was chewing bean curd slowly, and Tari could almost see the wheels turning in her head.

"Hmmm. What?" Tari asked.

"Nothing," Rebecca said, poking at her stir-fried vegetables with chopsticks. "She has a right to be emotional. Same as you do."

"You should talk to my sister about this head-shrinking business. You'd be so good at it."

Rebecca rolled her eyes. "I'm just saying that if I'm her, with a daughter like you, I'd be emotional, too. And with what you're going through now, she must be even more of a mess."

"Girl, you don't know what Melinda and I have been through with this woman. She's a true mother hen. Melinda says she won't let her stay with me."

"Not even after your surgery?" Rebecca asked, her eyebrows rising.

Tari shook her head. "I'll be fine. Melinda's less than ten minutes away."

"But don't you want someone there with you? I'd planned to stay with you until you said your folks were coming in."

Rebecca frowned. Ravi had been so disappointed when she finally canceled their long-planned trip to Trinidad. Now she didn't know when he would meet her parents in the flesh, in a way further delaying their marriage. But she felt that she needed to be around Tari. Not only for Tari's sake but also for hers. She was so afraid that Tari was not dealing with this problem in the appropriate way and that one day the enormity of it all would hit and she would crash. Rebecca didn't want to face the thought of not being there when that happened. And now it seemed Tari was pushing her away.

"That's so not necessary, Becks. I had the preop thing today. They said I'll only be in the operating room for about three hours." Tari wrinkled her face at the metallic taste of tap water. She pushed the glass away.

"Three hours! That's like major surgery!" Rebecca gasped.

Tari shrugged. "It's not that major. I'm going home the same day. They have to take some lymph nodes out." She sipped the tepid water again. "Sheesh. You think they could give us some cold spring water up in here?" She looked around for the waitress.

"Tari, are you serious?"

Tari didn't answer. Instead she tried to catch the waitress's eye. She, too, had been surprised when the doctor slowly explained the surgery that morning. But she was not going to make a big deal out of it. *Let it go*, she told herself. *Just let them do what they have to do so you can go back to your life.*

The surgeon had popped into the examining room earlier that day to say hello while a physician's assistant took Tari's vital signs. Melinda had watched, itching to play a more active role, as Tari took a series of tests—two tubes of blood, one container of urine. Once they sat down to talk with Dr. Blakely, Melinda could not remain quiet anymore. "Please, shut up," Tari said after Melinda finished rattling off a list of questions before the doctor even began speaking.

Tari had liked the surgeon on sight. She was pretty, mid-forties, with beautiful brown hair and light brown eyes. Tari, a hair-color aficionado, had wanted to compliment the doctor on her shade but had thought it inappropriate, especially with grave-faced Melinda in the room.

She held on to her list of questions in her reporter's note-book, waiting for the right moment. The literature from the American Cancer Society had told her almost everything she needed to know, but she wanted the doctor to know that she'd been studying and researching cancer herself. She wanted to use the terminology to show Dr. Blakely that she was no fool and that she was in charge.

"I'm glad you have so many questions," Dr. Blakely had said, a bit amused by Tari's defensiveness. In typical practice, she took out a pen and piece of paper and began to sketch out a breast, showing Tari exactly where the tumor was and the size of it. Then she brought out a copy of Tari's mammogram film and pinned it up on the wall.

"See all this gray area here?" The doctor pointed with a pen as Tari looked at the film intently. "This is all breast tissue. It's pretty dense because you're young. Now, see this white area, right there?" She pointed to the spot under Tari's right nipple. "That's your cancer. See all those little white spots around it? That's the noninvasive carcinoma. They're cells that if left alone for a few years may become cancerous and invade your breast ducts the same way the large tumor already has."

Tari nodded silently, looking at the picture. Seeing the tumor, facing it, made her hate the thing. It looked so harmless, so white and ghostlike against the grayness of the rest of the shadowy image. But she knew it was insidious and deadly. She wanted it out of her.

"So, you're going to remove all of that stuff, too, right?" Tari asked. "Including the, uh . . . noninvasive stuff?"

"Of course they're going to remove everything," Melinda interjected, and Tari glared at her until she lowered her eyes apologetically.

"Right," the doctor said, ignoring the exchange between the two sisters. She began to draw another picture on her yellow pad. "We're going to remove the tumor and an area around it. That's what we call a margin. We're also going to do what is called a sentinel node biopsy. That will tell us whether your cancer has spread beyond the breast."

Tari had read about the lymph node surgery, but she was hoping she would not have to undergo it. From what she'd read, the operation would leave her right arm sensitive and painful for months ahead. That meant no strenuous activity until it was completely healed. No kickboxing class. She did not even want to consider at that point whether the cancer had spread to other parts of her body.

"So what are they saying?" Rebecca asked, bringing her back to the present and the unappetizing plate of stir-fried vegetables in front of her.

"Well, they're going to remove three or four nodes during the surgery and then test them. If they're negative, they'll stop. If they show signs of cancer, they'll remove six or seven more, and hopefully that will be all of them."

"Oh, my God, Tari," Rebecca said, putting down her fork. "So what will that mean, chemotherapy?"

"Oh, I have to have that anyway." Tari said this in a most offhand way, as if she were saying that she would have the Greek salad, dressing on the side, please.

"No way!" Rebecca's hand covered her mouth.

Tari nodded. According to the doctor, the younger the patient the more aggressive the treatment. She would face four months of intense chemotherapy and then six to seven weeks of radiation therapy on her right breast to zap any microscopic cancer cells that might have escaped.

Rebecca looked away, and Tari knew she was upset. "It's okay, Becks. You know, when I saw that tumor staring back at me from the mammogram film, I just kept thinking, 'let me at it, let me at it.' I'm gonna kill this thing, and I'll do what they tell me to do. It's just six, eight months out of my life. I'd rather suffer for that short amount of time than spend the rest of my life worrying about whether I could have done more. You know what I mean?"

Rebecca nodded and her voice grew heavy. "So, what about work? Are you going to take time off?"

"Heck no," Tari said emphatically. "Ugh! I can just see that smug John Weston getting his grubby hands all over my story. No way. I'm working till I drop."

Rebecca shook her head. "But do you think that's wise, Tari? Chemo makes people really sick."

"The doctor said they have all kinds of drugs today that make it easier to take. Girl, I'll do whatever I can to beat this. But I want to live my life, too. If I stay in the house waiting to feel better, I never will."

Rebecca shook her head and sighed. "You're crazy."

Tari smiled. "I know."

"So when are you going to tell your editor?"

Tari shrugged. "I'm not ready yet. I'm going to try to think up some crazy excuse as to why I need the next few days off." She paused. "I really want to tell Joe, but I don't think he can keep his mouth shut. It's not him I'm worried about. It's about those other vultures."

"Tari, it's just a story. Your health is more important," Rebecca said gently.

"It's not just a story. It's the biggest thing that's ever happened in my career," she said. "You know how long I've been writing about these boring small-time mergers, lay-offs, and lawsuits. In my eight years as a reporter, I've never had the chance to bring down a bank! It's bad enough I have to share it with Weston. I can't just walk away and hand it to him on a platter." She laughed, but there was a seriousness in her eyes that hinted at desperation. Rebecca saw it and looked down at her plate.

Neither of them said anything for a few moments.

"God sure has weird timing," Tari finally said. "This could have been such a great year."

Rebecca shrugged sadly. "You never know. Maybe something really great's going to happen on the other side of this."

CHAPTER
27

Coletta Shields had not slept since she arrived in Boston. The seven-hour plane ride from Dominica had been bumpy, and she could not find anything edible in her youngest daughter's refrigerator. Wheatgrass juice? Who did the girl take her for? A Rastafarian or something? Then that Melinda had to go and get on her nerves, trying to tell her that she shouldn't stay in Tari's house because she would stress her out even more. It had taken every ounce of her God-given grace to not throttle the girl as they stood in the airport. Her baby had cancer, and they were trying to tell her that she had to keep her distance. Those children of hers. Lord help her. The way they mistreated her, even in her old age.

God bless them, but they should know better than to try her like that. Jeffrey was the only one who wasn't rebellious. He had done exactly what his father told him to and gone off to study the Word in North Carolina. He would be a preacher, a great one, like his father. But those two girls never stopped testing the limits of her faith. She suspected it was a thorn in her flesh placed by the enemy to distract her from serving God the way she should. Just like the Apostle Paul. So when times like these arose, she rebuked

Satan, bound demonic forces, and told the enemy that he was a liar.

And this cancer thing, it was just another trick of that wily devil. That serpent would not claim her daughter if she had anything to say about it. He had tried before when the girl had gone off to New York to go to college. She came back with all these earrings in her ears and even in her nose. And those white boyfriends and rock music! But Tari had come to her senses. So why was this was happening now? Coletta wondered. The girl was living right, from what she could see. *Besides, God doesn't go giving folks cancer because they're sinners. If that were the case, we'd all be walking around sick and dying by the second.*

One thing Coletta did know was that she would be there at her daughter's side, and she didn't care who liked it or didn't like it.

"Will, you want some orange juice?" she asked her husband, who was watching television in Tari's living room.

"Keep your voice down, Coletta," he scolded. "Tari's sleeping."

Coletta rolled her eyes and handed her husband a tall glass of juice. She walked back to the kitchen, doubtful that she would find anything worth cooking for dinner. She glanced at the contents of the refrigerator skeptically. Everything was low-fat, low-carb, or vegetarian this or that. They even had fake eggs these days! She couldn't understand how these daughters of hers walked around with so little flesh on their bones and still complained about how fat they were. They couldn't pay her to eat this plastic food.

She scoffed as she poured herself some orange juice. That Melinda had shown herself at the airport, Coletta thought. Before she could even hug the girl, she was already barking out orders, telling her where she would stay. *I'm glad I set her straight*, Coletta thought. *Thinks she's so grown because she's got a doctor behind her name. But I'm still the mother in this family, and no snot-nosed daughter of mine will tell me what to do or where to go.*

Even after all these years, she was still praying every day that God would give her patience to deal with Melinda. That girl was always trying to get into it with her. As if it were her fault that she married that lazy husband of hers. Coletta could have told her from day one, matter of fact did tell her many a time, that country boy was no good for her. A good man would never let his wife go out and work while he stayed in the house doing nothing or walked around a golf course all day hitting a ball with a piece of iron. What kind of a man did that?

She got some vegetables together and looked at the organic label dubiously. She had to get herself to the store, else she'd starve to death in this house. She sighed.

And now she's stuck with him after I warned her not to marry him, and she wants to take it out on me, Coletta grumbled. *Even in my old age, those children of mine.* She sighed again as she ran water over some yellow squash. All she wanted to do was play with her granddaughter and grandson and tend to the flock of congregants in the church she and Will ran back home. But the devil was always sending something to get in the way.

Tari needed her. She had to be there. The girl was so skinny and tired looking. All of that makeup on her face and that brown color in her hair didn't hide anything from Coletta. All she saw was the same little girl who was always pulling on her dress, begging for her attention when she was four, five, six years old. *She still has that stubborn look in those big eyes she inherited from me,* Coletta thought. Big eyes that lacked a lot of the brightness that anyone who knew Tari had come to take for granted. The girl still didn't want to think she needed anybody to help her with anything. But Coletta knew better. God knew she was the same way, too. Always thinking she had everything all figured out. Well, she did. But Tari was still young. She had a long way to go. And Coletta was praying, praying, her baby daughter would get there.

Meanwhile, upstairs, a reflexive wince of pain interrupted Tari's Percocet-induced sleep. She grimaced and lifted the cover carefully to look again at the incision site covered in a clear plastic bandage near the base of her armpit. No red that she could see. This clear, Band-Aid-like thing had far surpassed her postsurgery expectations. There was no bulky, gauzy, bloody bandage to flinch from in disgust. No pus or strange bodily liquids were being expelled that she could discern. It occurred to her that she could continue to wear tiny tank tops in the summer without worrying about her scar showing. She peered at the bandage again. Yes! No major harm done. Then shame came over her for her vanity. *Tank tops should be the last thing on my mind.*

But she could not see the full length of the incision that was on the base of her right breast. It would have upset her, for it was long and claimed almost half her breast, as if someone had underlined it with a big C. The swelling from the surgery fooled her into thinking that her breast remained its rounded 34C. It even felt a bit bigger to her curious hand. She would only find out weeks later, after the wound healed, that the flesh would retreat and there would be an indentation, one that would require her to stuff her bra to make it appear even with her left breast.

Over the din of television, she heard Coletta puttering around downstairs in her kitchen. Melinda had underestimated their mother again. Tari chuckled as she remembered the scene at the airport when Coletta forcefully informed Melinda that she would not be telling her what to do. "Melinda, I'm not in the mood for your nonsense, okay?" Coletta had said dismissively as she held Tari to her tightly. "I'm here to be with Tari. So just keep your mouth shut. I have enough on my mind without having to deal with your nonsense."

Melinda had cowered, shocked that she could be so easily and summarily dismissed. Tari had only shrugged, to Melinda's chagrin. She was a kid again in that warm, safe place when Coletta held her. What privacy? All she'd felt in that airport terminal was warm comfort, deep and sweet smelling like the Anais Anais Coletta had worn since forever. All her sleepless nights disappeared in that first hug, where she allowed herself to be smothered in her mother's arms.

Now the noises downstairs encircled and conquered her aloneness. Her parents' lighthearted bickering took her back to her childhood days, when she'd felt invincible by virtue of only their presence. She'd been wrong. The last thing she wanted right now was to be alone.

It had been only hours since she'd awakened in the surgical recovery room as if from a bad dream, frightened at first until realizing where she was. She felt embarrassed now that she had cried like a baby when she came to and saw her parents, Melinda, and Jeffrey waiting for her. *Why in the world did I cry like that?* She looked at the clear surgical bandage again. *All clear.*

There was a light knock, and the bedroom door opened a crack. "Tari, you want your pain medicine?" Coletta asked softly from behind the door. Tari assented, her voice still hoarse from the breathing tube that had been placed in her throat during surgery. She allowed Coletta to fuss over her for those few minutes. They both needed it after the day they'd had.

Tari's fears that morning about going into the operating room had not quite dissolved despite the battalion of support that rode with her to Brigham & Women's hospital at six A.M. To Tari, the ride had seemed funereal, and Rebecca's attempts to keep the mood light with humor had fallen flat. Coletta was silent and so was her father. Melinda was unnaturally chirpy, patting Tari on the leg often. Jeffrey was sullen. She tried to keep her mind clear, concentrating on the empty streets, the blue sky, everything but what was about to happen.

She had seen the apprehension in Jeffrey's eyes, and it had tugged at her heart. It hadn't been hard for Melinda to convince him to stay with her and Michael. Her little brother had seemed uncomfortable around her since he arrived from school and then downright terrified the closer they got to the hospital. At one point, Tari found herself reassuring him that everything was going to be okay.

They had never been close, and she had taken stock of him through the rearview mirror. He was all grown up now, a senior at Davis Bible College. She noticed how much he and her father mirrored each other in looks, mannerisms. Jeffrey had been the "good one." The one who never talked back; the model son. Even before he left home for college, Tari knew that Jeffrey would be a serious, pious man just like her father, and she did not know how she felt about that. There was a part of her that wanted to see him go out into the world, make some mistakes, and live a little bit. But all she saw for him was an imminent marriage to a woman who would probably be another version of him, docile and unassuming, who would give him dutiful, obedient, Christian children. There was nothing really wrong with that, Tari thought, but then there was. She wanted to talk to him, really talk to him. But there hadn't been enough time.

There'd been so much to do before the surgery. After the signing of admitting forms and meetings with anesthesiologists and an upbeat Dr. Blakely, Tari found herself in a hospital gown and hospital socks atop a stretcher. Her legs were bare and freezing. She barely had time to concentrate on what was going on or even remember the breathing exercises that she thought would get her through the experience as she went from test to test. She closed her eyes as a young doctor injected ink into her breast and underarm to provide a road map for the surgeon. "That didn't hurt, did it?" the young man said. She scowled. Then another needle for the IV fluids. "Yes, that hurt," she told that nurse. And there was a fleeting panic when the nurse said to her family, "You can't go with her beyond this point."

Beyond *that point*, it was just her, the cancer, and her mortality. It occurred to her then that those people in front of her were her life, the only life she had—not her job, not her singing. Coletta had wept, but she had not. She swallowed her tears and stuck out her tongue at a smiling Melinda as the nurse wheeled her away into the brightly lit operating suite. "How do you feel?" Dr. Blakely asked as an army in blue scrubs connected wires, laid drapes, gathered surgical instruments, and moved heavy equipment. "Fine?" That was the last thing she remembered about surgery.

"I made some pumpkin soup, no meat. You think you can have some?" Coletta asked.

Tari shook her head. She had vomited the crackers and ginger ale that she had tried to ingest earlier and her stomach still felt queasy. "I'll try some ginger tea."

"Mom," Tari called out before her mother left the room. "Thanks for coming to take care of me."

Her mother rolled her eyes. "And what was I supposed to do? Stay down there and cry and worry?"

As soon as she could hear Coletta's heavy footsteps ascending the stairs, Tari picked up the phone on the night table.

"Hey, Joe," she said trying to sound awake and alert.

"Tari? I thought you were home sick today," a distracted Joe Martone said.

"I am. I just wanted to know if anything else broke on MetroBank." She felt that she was betraying her family and her own common sense, like an alcoholic sneaking a beer, but she could not help herself.

"Nah. Nothing much is going on. Hey, take tomorrow off, too, if you need it. You've been working hard, kid. You need a break. We'll take care of everything here."

"Uh. Okay, Joe. Actually, that's why I called. My doctor says I have some weird flulike virus. I'm on antibiotics and I don't think I should come in the rest of the week. I may be contagious." She coughed a few times to make it sound believable. She knew that this ruse would work with Joe, a notorious germ phobic.

"By all means, stay home, then," he said quickly.

"But, Joe, you gotta promise me," Tari said, lowering her voice. "If you hear anything, anything at all, call me at home. I can file from my laptop here, okay?"

Martone sighed. "Well, I'll see what I can do. But Weston's making calls. He's really chasing this thing down, too."

"That bastard!" Tari cried and winced as pain shot through her breast and down through her right arm. "Okay, Joe. I gotta go now. But I'll be in touch."

She settled back into the pillows. She'd let the Percocet do its thing. Another six to eight hours out, she figured, but nothing was worth this pain.

CHAPTER
28

Melinda pretended to be busy with getting the kids ready for the trip to the movies with their grandparents, but she was listening intently to the conversation that was going on downstairs between her parents and husband.

"One more year, then I'm going back to school. I can't wait. It's been so long," he was saying.

Melinda could imagine her father encouraging, nodding, and her mother observing dubiously. Her parents had developed only a tolerable relationship with Michael. The way she told it to them, it sounded good: he was only home until Taylor started elementary school, and then he would start to get his own life on track again. She tried to mask his laziness as if it were his own personal sacrifice for the good of their family, and she believed that she at least had her father convinced. *If only they knew*, she thought, shaking her head as she buttoned up Taylor's coat.

She almost laughed at the passion she heard in Michael's voice as he talked about teaching engineering someday. It was the same wistful tone he had used when driving her little brother Jeffrey to the airport so he could go back to his classes in North Carolina. *He's got them all fooled*. She wondered what her family would think if she told them Michael had turned down five job offers just in the last two years, saying that they were just not what he was looking for about now and that he wanted to finish up his degree before taking on just any job. Just any job, he had said, while she paid for his greens fees, health club memberships, and other trappings of his idle life. But she, Melinda, had done it. She had taken just "any job" while she completed her master's and her PhD. What made him so much less capable than she? What made him so special?

She walked down the stairs and dressed her face with her smile.

"Oh, my, my, my." Coletta's face lit up at the sight of her two grandkids.

The kids immediately began to argue about which movie they would see. Melinda spread her hands. "You sure you want them for the whole afternoon?"

"Oh, please, you and your sister were much, much worse." Coletta scooped up Taylor in her arms.

Once the good-byes were said and the house quieted down, Melinda decided to do something she hadn't done in a while. She stood over Michael's favorite spot, the leather recliner in the living room with the best view of the plasma screen television. "So, I overheard you talking to the folks," she said, trying to make her voice seem friendly and unthreatening.

"Yeah, they just wanted to know how things were going."

"Well, I was really glad to hear that you want to teach so badly. These days it's kinda hard to tell. . . . You never even talk to me about that stuff anymore."

Michael sighed. "There's nothing to talk about, Melinda."

"I think there is. I don't know what your plans are."

"My plans? I've had the same plan the last four years. To finish my degree and then find a teaching job."

She put her hands on her hips, not knowing what to say. Afraid to say that he didn't need to finish his degree before he found a job that paid some of the bills, that she was tired of feeling like the man of the house, of carrying the entire load while he inched toward his degree, one course per semester.

"What's on your mind, Melinda?" His voice told her that he knew she was thinking combative thoughts.

"I'm just tired, Michael, that's all. Tired of working so hard and feeling like I'm the only one around here who ever does anything."

Michael turned toward her, a harsh glint in his eyes. "You agreed to this, Melinda. You said you didn't mind if I took time off to go back to school. Matter of fact, you said it would be good for us and the kids—to have one of us home all the time."

"But that's just it, Michael. Taylor's still in day care two days a week when you go play golf or squash. And I still have to go pick them up after work most times . . ."

His jaw clenched. "Fine, I'll pick them up from now on. All you had to do was ask."

She stood there, wanting to say more but afraid of the anger that was threatening to explode inside of her and him.

"Is there anything else?" he asked gruffly, reaching for the remote.

She turned on her heel and walked up the stairs.

She looked in her closet, at the jeans, the white shirt, burgundy leather jacket. That was exactly what she would wear to flee this life of hers. Her outfit to freedom.

Chapter

29

Summer was hesitating, and the entire city was on edge with anticipation, eager to shed coats for sandals and shorts. But the nights were still too cool, hanging onto shards of a spring that had long overstayed its welcome.

The grand trees of Ashmont Hill were budding shyly, and they cast shadows in Tari's room. From outside her house you could see illumination from a window in a room upstairs. Not a television-blue burning bright and then brighter every few seconds. It was just a yellow light in the otherwise dark house at three A.M.

Tari could hear her father's snoring two doors down. The constant heave and hum comforted her, reminding her of the childhood sound that lulled her to sleep what seemed like eons ago in a faraway place but which in reality was just five minutes away.

They'd sold it when they moved back to Dominica, but she still drove by it from time to time when she felt nostalgic for the old days. She had driven by just days after the doctor had given her the news, just to feel connected to the person she used to be before this thing. Just to feel invincible—the way she'd felt when she lived under Coletta and Will Shields' roof at 27 Stephen Street. The pink house had done its part in bringing back memories to make her feel alive. Its new owners had taken good care of it, she noticed. It was still baby pink, her mother's choice, with white trim. And the hedges were sharply trimmed, the way her father had always kept them. Instead of her father's Buick, someone's Audi was sticking out of the garage. And it seemed that yet another neighbor had sold out, because there was a white child peering out of a window in number 29 next door. In her day, their family was among eight West Indian immigrants who had somehow all found their way to the same street.

She could almost see herself, ten or eleven years old, on a warm day playing in the yard, careful not to step over the line Coletta had drawn for her and Melinda not to cross. *Don't ever let me see you in the street!* The neighborhood was quieter now. She suspected that none of the kids she'd grown up with even lived nearby. The older folks did, however, and some of them would have recognized her had she bothered to step out of her truck, knock on their doors, and say, "Hello. Remember me? I'm the one who always baked rock-hard chocolate chip cookies and sang 'Amazing Grace' at the annual Stephen Street Summer Block Party."

Tari wondered why her parents had not asked to go back and visit their old house. Had they put it out of their minds for good? she wondered. Maybe they never felt as connected to it as she and Melinda did. She always suspected that they never wanted to be here, in this country, and that they were only working so hard, sticking it out, until she, Melinda, and Jeffrey were old enough to fend for themselves, and then they would make their escape.

They'd had a steady stream of their old friends through her house in the last week. Aunts, uncles, and church folks had come by bringing prayers, flowers, cards, and food she could not eat. No one had asked her whether or not she wanted all of these people in her house, in her business.

Coletta had taken over the show, and Tari just played along, too resigned to care.

She sighed and tried to get comfortable in her bed, propping up her sore right side with another pillow. She wasn't sleepy, and she steeled herself against the temptation that the orange prescription bottle offered. Those magic white tablets could put her to sleep and make all of her nagging pain and thoughts disappear in seconds. But they terrified her. Once this cancer episode was over, she hoped to never need one ever again.

She sat herself up slowly and grabbed the laptop from the night table. She adjusted the sports bra that kept her sore breast in place. Her hands became busy with the keyboard and keypad mouse as she embarked on her new late-night obsession. She read the pages of Breastcancer.org hungrily. She had gone through every word of the pathology report the doctor had handed her at her postoperative visit, looking up the foreign-looking words and acronyms on-line and comparing her results with the statistics. She typed in all the terms. Nuclear grade, ER and PR positive, histology grade, HER2-NEU. What did they all mean? What were her chances? The doctor had said her cancer was a Stage II, midsize, aggressive tumor, but it had not spread. Her lymph nodes and margins were clear. So what were her chances? She scoured the web site some more. Seventy-nine percent five-year survival rate. Okay—her brows furrowed—so if she made it to age thirty-five, she'd be a true survivor then? Cancer would not kill her at least until age thirty-five, and what then? Could she have children? She looked up the side effects of the drug Tamoxifen that would be the final stage of treatment, after chemo and radiation. The data on the Web site mirrored what the oncologist said. The chances of birth defects would be very high. *Okay, so no kids while I'm on this drug,* she thought. What about the chance that the cancer would come back even after all the chemo drugs, radiation, and Tamoxifen? She knew in her heart that she had the gene, BRCA1 or BRCA2, but she had adamantly refused genetic testing. The doctor's demeanor had terrified her when she laid out the risk: a 40 percent chance of recurrence if they found the gene. But Tari had shaken her head defiantly. "No way in hell," had been her response when Dr. Blakely quietly said to her, "A lot of women in your situation choose mastectomy because they don't want to have to face the fear of getting another cancer."

"So what are you saying?" Tari had asked impatiently. "If I have my breasts removed, does that mean I'll never get cancer again?" The doctor could not promise that, and Tari did not expect that the woman could guarantee something that really only was in the Creator's hands. "I'll take my chances," was how Tari had ended that conversation. There was no way she would give up her breasts for an extra 2 percent or 5 percent of insurance. "If this thing comes up again, I'll fight it with everything I have left," she told Melinda and Coletta as they left the doctor's office. They were silent, and she didn't care that they did not agree with her decision. But they were her breasts and not theirs. She wasn't ready yet to throw in the towel. She would keep her one and a half size 34Cs for now, thank you very much.

Tari obsessed over every page on the Web site, unsure of what she was looking for but looking anyway. Then she went to the American Cancer Society Web site to crosscheck. *Wait a minute!* She checked the figures again. This one said that she was looking at a 98 percent survival rate, based on a 2001 study. *What the heck?* She lost all sense of time and place, so immersed she was in the flood of information at her fingertips. She felt empowered from knowing all these facts, contradictory as they sometimes seemed. It was almost as if she had somehow gained some supernatural control over her own life with all this data.

So I won't die at thirty-five! Although, she thought, everything she ever wanted to do she should probably accomplish in the next five years. Thirty-five. She mentally began to write her own obituary. She imagined the picture that would run in the paper, the comments from her colleagues: "She was so young and beautiful and talented." Her editors would probably say, "She was one of our best writers. It's such a shame. She had a great future ahead of her." She laughed at her silliness but was saddened that such morbid thoughts had taken up daily residence in her mind. It was four A.M. before her eyes grew too weary to stay open. She turned off the computer and pulled the covers over her head, exhausted but unafraid.

CHAPTER
30

Tari frowned at the mirror. She didn't look unwell, but she didn't exactly look like a ray of sunshine after a rainy night either. She took a deep breath so that her breasts would rise and fall against the material of her light sweater. It was still a bit swollen, and the tight sports bra constricted her breathing. But it was better than her painful breast moving around with every step she took. She put on an extra layer of foundation to make up for the dullness in her skin and a bright lipstick to improve her mood. But so far the extra makeup wasn't doing its job. She picked up her briefcase and headed out the door. Maybe no one would notice.

Darn! She felt completely naked. It felt like all eyes were on her as she walked to her desk in the newsroom. As the day wore on, she grew even more paranoid. Did they notice that she had lost a few pounds in just that one week and that she seemed less lively, less quick to make a sarcastic comment or throw a verbal jab? she wondered.

What were they thinking? She walked slower, and the cup of coffee that had once seemed a permanent appendage to her right hand was no longer there. She was even mellower than after the breakup with Roger. Something had happened.

Her colleagues didn't know what it was, and they murmured. She strained to overhear their conversations, and Mariska was more than willing to provide her with the circulating rumors.

"Sweetie, I told him you had a virus, but they're saying you just weren't ready to handle a major story like MetroBank and you lost it. But I know better and you know better, so don't worry about it." Mariska's smile was faker than Beyonce's hair.

"What else are they saying?" Tari asked, disappointed in herself for even having this conversation with Mariska.

Mariska shrugged. "It's really tasteless, Tari. But I've been standing up for you." Mariska cleared her throat and leaned in close. "I think it was John Weston who said that you probably didn't want to do the work that such a big story required, so you faked being sick. He and Dan Silver were joking around, saying you were probably off somewhere getting your nails done."

Tari clutched the edge of her desk.

"But, Tari, I wouldn't worry about it. Those guys are always making sexist jokes like that. I told John he was a jerk," Mariska said, the same self-satisfied smile on her face. "You know, we women, especially women of color, have to stick together."

"Thanks, Mariska," Tari said dryly. "I should get some work done. But thanks for sticking up for me and not being part of the rumor mill. I really appreciate it."

Mariska, not reading the sarcasm in Tari's voice, smiled even wider. "Oh, no problem! I'm sure you'd do the same for me."

Uh, sure, I would, Tari thought grudgingly. She was on edge. She wanted to go over to John Weston's desk and tell him off. She wanted to smack Dan Silver. She thought she noticed people staring at her out of the corner of her eyes or whispering as they walked by her desk. It was maddening. *I am now officially the chip-on-the-shoulder-carrying, overly paranoid black woman of the workplace; all I need to do now is cry racism and file a discrimination suit to complete the profile.* She exchanged frantic e-mails with Rebecca.

"Why don't you just tell them? Tell your editor. Send out a mass e-mail and just tell everybody. You're going to drive yourself crazy with this," Rebecca wrote.

Tari shrugged off this suggestion and bit her fingernails as she waited for a call back from Bill Boggs. It had been hard to give work her full attention, but she struggled. After she heard what Weston had said, she was determined to retain control of her story. She would show him, all of them!

But she felt worn out; it was only five P.M. The four straight days in bed had left her groggy. And she suspected that the general anesthesia had not fully worked its way through her body, making her even sleepier. She downed large amounts of water, trying to dull her desire for coffee. She could almost hear the gossip mill buzzing every time she ran to the ladies room.

"Wow, you're really putting away the water today," Mariska said.

Tari didn't bother replying. Thankfully, the phone rang and Bill Boggs's gruff voice was on the other end. Boggs had become the star whistleblower in the MetroBank story, and the attorney general was threatening a gag order so that he would stop shooting off his mouth to the media. Tari herself was beginning to doubt whether his interests leaned toward exposing the bank's wrongs or keeping himself in the spotlight. She had heard that a New York publishing house had offered him a book deal.

"Tari, I'm so glad you're back," Boggs said. "I've been sitting on this for a week 'cause I wanted you to have it. I can't stand that smug Weston." She rolled her eyes. *Is this man jerking me around?* She just didn't fully trust Boggs anymore, so there was no way she would badmouth a colleague with him, even smarmy John Weston.

"Yeah? Talk to me, then."

"Donald Meehan's son's birthday party," Bill Boggs said triumphantly.

"What about it?" Tari asked, sipping water from a Poland Springs bottle.

"You know what he paid for that with?"

"Get to the point, Bill."

"He used MetroBank's money. Know why? He said that half the kids there were kids of MetroBank executives, so he expensed his kid's seventh birthday party."

Tari sat up in her chair. "Are you sure of this, Bill? And can you get me something other than your trusty word?"

"Oh, yeah. I got pictures of the party. And the expense report is in the files the attorney general subpoenaed."

Tari scratched her head. "So if the AG already has the files, then how come they haven't talked about this party yet? They're making all kinds of crazy allegations in the *Globe* and in the *Herald* about the paintings, the vacations—why not use this one?"

"Aha! Now you're talking like a veteran and not a rookie," Bill Boggs said, excitement building in his voice.

"Guess whose six-year-old daughter was at that same party? In the pictures, too."

Tari gasped. "No way, Bill! No way!"

"Yes way. Listen, if you want, I can messenger these pictures to you in a hurry. This will be on page one, right?"

"Oh, definitely, Bill. This is a huge one."

"Good, I want to see all these bastards go down." Boggs couldn't hide the contempt for his former employer in his voice. And Tari felt suckered into his hour of retribution. But what could she do? This was huge. She was shaking as

she walked over to Joe Martone's desk. She didn't know if it
was from exhaustion or from the excitement of being back
in the game.

"Joe, you won't believe what I've got," she said to her
editor, whose eyes almost popped out of his head when she
told him what she had learned.

She was almost crawling along with fatigue, but she finished the story an hour before deadline. The gossip that
had greeted her that morning now turned into grudging silence. She could feel the dagger looks of envy as Steven
Bluesteed complimented her again within earshot of John
Weston. And she brimmed with pride at the congratulatory
e-mails from some of the veteran reporters and editors. *Thank
you, Bill Boggs,* she thought as she glanced again at the picture
of the attorney general's daughter eating birthday cake with
the rest of the rich kids at Donald Meehan's lavish property
in Pride's Crossing.

It had been a victorious first day back, she thought with
satisfaction as she gathered her things to leave.

Roger Levine's immense shadow came over her desk.
"Are you okay?"

"Why? Shouldn't I be okay? Didn't I just make A1 again?"
she bragged good-naturedly.

He shrugged. "You just look really wiped out. And then
you were mysteriously out last week . . ."

"I wasn't mysteriously out," Tari interjected. "I had this
weird virus. I was on antibiotics. My doctor said it was contagious."

Roger looked at her a long time. "I hope that's all it is."

She rolled her eyes. "Of course that's all it is."

"Well, I'm here if you ever need to talk."

"Roger, come on. I'm fine. Okay?"

But minutes later when she sat in her car, she felt dizzy,

and she had to put her head down on the steering wheel to stop the spinning.

Dinner was ready when she walked into her house, and her parents sat bickering in front of the television.

"I'm home," she called out.

"Tari," Coletta cried. "Didn't President Bush go to Harvard? Your father says he only went to Yale. I'm telling the man that—"

"Mom, he went to both, I think." Tari rubbed her temples.

Her mother pondered this for a moment. "See, Will, I told you I was right."

Tari walked into the kitchen, shaking her head at her parents' Fred and Ethel act. At least her favorite meal, though meatless, was on the stove. Coletta had made vegetable rotis, using tofu instead of chicken. Tari stood over the stove and took a bite out of one and closed her eyes in pleasure. Oh, that mother of hers could be crazy, but that woman could cook!

"Mom, these are soooo good!" Tari called from the kitchen.

Coletta whispered to her husband, "See what I told you? And she wanted me to go and stay with Melinda. Those children don't know what's good for them." William Shields nodded. It was always easier to just agree with his wife.

Tari walked into her living room where her parents still sat watching the news roundup on CNN.

"I broke another big part of the story today."

Her father turned to face her. "That's good. Good," he said proudly. "Is it going to be on the front page?"

"Yup." Tari nodded, pleased to make her father proud.

"Tari, what about . . . You didn't tell them you needed time off like I told you to?" Coletta's eyes registered disappointment.

"Mom, I feel fine. I just got a little tired toward the end of the day. I can keep working."

"But what about when you start the chemotherapy?"

"I'll cross that bridge when I get to it," Tari said, walking back into the kitchen to escape her mother's probing eyes.

She did feel much better, she decided as the food began to give back some of her energy. So what if she'd been a little weak earlier? She'd go to bed a few hours early and that should take care of it.

Melinda reminded her about setting a wig shopping date as they chatted about their day on the phone. Tari had pushed the thoughts of chemotherapy far back into her mind, although in two weeks she would have no choice but to face it.

"I don't know, Melinda," Tari said doubtfully. "I was reading on-line that some women don't lose their hair. I may not lose mine. My hair's real nappy."

Melinda sighed. "But what if you do? Don't you want to be ready, just in case?"

"I'll think about it."

The thought of losing her beautiful hair still brought tears to Tari's eyes. It was her long-term investment that had yielded years and years of compliments and personal satisfaction. She thought back to the many years of deep conditioners, roller-sets, perms, coloring—so much cash, so much time. And now her twenty inches would just fall out of her head, leaving her head bald like a tree at the end of November. It was strong medicine to take.

"You know," Melinda said, as if reading her mind, "worrying about losing your hair is better than worrying about whether you're going to live or die. It will grow back."

"Melinda, please. Okay? Don't give me a lecture after the day I've had," Tari pleaded.

But Melinda persisted. "How are you going to explain it to your coworkers when or if your hair falls out?"

"Fine. I'll get a really good wig, then," Tari said. "I'll just say I'm giving my real hair a break for a while. They won't ask too many questions. They know black women have a lot of issues with their hair."

"Yeah, but you've never had any issues with your hair. You spend more money on it than I spend on my kids' school tuition," Melinda said.

Tari rolled her eyes. *Here we go again*, she thought. *She just had to go and criticize me.* "Well, if I had two kids in private school, maybe I wouldn't have beautiful hair. But since I don't, then I can do whatever the hell I want with my money. Right?"

"Saving for a rainy day is probably a better investment," Melinda said testily.

"You don't know how much I have in my savings, Melinda."

"It's not hard to guess from what you spend on clothes, your hair—"

"Listen, you're not my mother, okay? I work hard for my money, and you can't tell me how to spend it!"

"I'm just trying to talk sense—"

"No, you're sticking your nose in where it doesn't belong," Tari said, her voice rising. "I don't tell you and Michael how to spend your cash."

"You can't compare—"

"Melinda, I gotta go. Good night." Tari slammed the phone down.

She heard her mother's footsteps in the hallway and then a knock on her door.

"Tari, you all right? I heard you yelling."

"I'm fine, Mom. Telemarketers."

"Okay," Coletta said.

Tari let herself fall onto her bed. She laughed. *I'm not even going to stress out over her,* she thought. Waste of time. Total waste of time. They'd had this argument too many times before. The phone rang again.

"Tari, I'm sorry. I . . . We shouldn't be fighting now."

Tari sighed. Why was Melinda always turning everything into a big family drama, complete with accusations, recriminations, and then tearful apologies?

"I'm not mad. I'm not even thinking about you, Melinda," she said.

Melinda sniffed. "Fine. I just wanted to say I'm sorry. Have a good night."

"Good night," Tari said, rolling her eyes as she hung up the phone.

Another day, another fight with Melinda. What else was new? In a way, the fight made her feel good. At least the false niceness her illness had prompted between them seemed to have ended. Just because she was sick didn't mean they had to be all lovey-dovey. For crying out loud, Melinda was still her annoying, holier-than-thou self!

CHAPTER
31

The only people talking at the table were the ones who were too young to feel the tension that hovered over them like a fighter jet before it dropped its ordnance.

Coletta wrinkled her nose and asked again. "So, this fish . . . Where did you get it? Is it fresh caught? Did you buy it from the supermarket?"

Melinda was about to answer when she felt her husband kick her gently under the table.

"Tastes like it's been sitting in the refrigerator a few days," Coletta grumbled.

Melinda's mouth opened, and Michael kicked her again under the table.

"Mom, so everything's going well over at Tari's?" Michael asked gamely, wanting to steer the topic to something everyone agreed on.

Coletta shrugged. She hated it when her son-in-law called her Mom.

William Shields piped in. "She's a fighter. I know Tari's going to beat this. We've been praying with her every night. God's listening."

Melinda nodded. For as long as she could remember, her father had spent hours a day praying, early in the morning before he went to work and late into the night. She knew Tari's illness had a profound effect on him, but his way of dealing with it was to become contemplative and even quieter than usual. She noticed how he was aging well; his hair was now completely gray, but his dignified, distant manner made him seem still youngish. She loved her dad so much, though she felt so far away from him. All her life she had heard people say, "Pastor Shields is close to the heart of God." They would say this in a hushed, reverential manner, and so she and Tari would always be quiet in his presence, not wanting to disturb the peace that surrounded him or the God that lived so close to him. He was so opposite from her mother, who had an equally strong faith but was the kind who slammed you over the head with it until it hurt. Coletta sang with Aretha-like emotion, testified passionately. She said *hallelujah* and *amen* the loudest during the sermons. She was not only the pastor's wife but also the leader of the women's ministry, and the children's disciples, and all the outreach ministries in the small island church. She was respected, feared, and secretly despised by many of the women in the church. She had embarrassed Melinda and Tari enough times in their lives, and by the time they were teenagers, they had grown immune to Coletta's vainglorious manifestations of her faith. Their way to deal with it was to rebel in every way possible without bringing shame on their father's good name.

Melinda was surprised that her mother had kept it so together for Tari. She had expected daily wailings, probably a fainting spell or two. But her mother's calm impressed her. And it even eased the tension between them a bit, if Melinda was willing to let the occasional barb slide. Coletta had not even commented on Melinda's weight once since she had arrived. Maybe it was old age. Maybe at sixty, the woman was finally starting to mellow.

"Nobody answered my question about the fish," Coletta

demanded after a brief silence at Melinda's dining room table. "Is it fresh? Melinda?"

Melinda took in a deep breath. "Mom, I picked it up from the market yesterday. I'm sure it's fresh."

Coletta sniffed. "When I was living up here, I knew this man who used to go fishing up in Gloucester. He brought me fresh fish every time he went out. Will, what was his name?"

"Solomon something," William Shields said evenly as he ate the fish.

"Maybe I can get you his number," Coletta said, eyeing the fish on her plate and then Melinda. "Fresh fish tastes so much better than the kind they sell in the store. They don't tell you how long it's been lying around."

Melinda tapped her feet on the floor impatiently. But before she could say what was on her mind, Coletta's attention had turned toward her granddaughter. "What are you using on Taylor's hair?" she asked. "It looks a bit dry."

"Mom. Her hair is not dry."

"My hair's not dry!" Taylor's five-year-old voice filled the room, surprising everyone and causing a ripple of laughter across the table.

Once Coletta got over the shock, she laughed, too. *She's not worth the anger,* Melinda thought, laughing and watching her mother happily feeding Taylor a spoonful of rice. *She probably doesn't even know she's doing it. Making me crazy.* This dinner was a ruse Tari had cooked up to get them out of her hair while she slipped out for a gig. Melinda could not believe she had allowed herself to get wrapped up in the scheme. But she had relented after Tari had begged and pleaded with her to not tell Coletta. She still didn't understand why, at thirty years old, her sister was still sneaking around her parents. And worse, how Tari, a week before starting chemotherapy, could stand in front of a room full of people and sing.

Michael escaped upstairs with the kids as soon as dinner was over. He was uncomfortable around Coletta, and he made any excuse to flee anytime they were in the same room. It made Melinda want to laugh. *At least,* she thought, *he's reading to Taylor before she goes to sleep.*

"How you holding up, Mom?" Coletta was washing dishes by hand in the sink. "You know, these should go in the dishwasher."

Coletta snorted. "I've been washing dishes this way my whole life, child. I never needed a dishwasher." William Shields, as if sensing a fight underway, retreated to the living room, away from the impending fray.

Melinda took a breath. *Whatever, lady.* "So, how you and Tari getting along so far?"

"Getting along?" Coletta was evading her.

"Yes, Mom. Are you okay with all of this? Aren't you scared?"

Coletta didn't turn around, but her hands stopped flitting about the sink. "I'm not scared. God's not gonna take my child from me."

Melinda didn't know what to say to that. She had faith, too, but she could admit that she was scared sometimes. Cancer could be so insidious, so unpredictable.

"What kind of question is that, anyway?" Coletta turned around.

"I just wanted to know how you were coping, Mom." Melinda almost took a step back when she saw the anger on her mother's face.

"I'm coping! I hope you'll get your attitude right, Melinda. You shouldn't walk around making Tari feel like something bad's going to happen to her."

"I am not!"

"Then why are you asking me stupid questions? Didn't you hear what I said earlier? Tari's going to be fine, so stop being so dramatic." Coletta dried her hands and hurried off to the bathroom, slamming the door behind her.

Melinda sighed. Coletta was more upset than she'd been letting on; it was so obvious. But of course she wouldn't let Melinda see her break down. It was part of the unspoken rivalry between them. Who could be the strongest, the best cook, best mother, best homemaker? Melinda often told herself that she'd stopped trying to measure herself by Coletta's standards, but deep down she knew that was a lie. She wanted the woman to recognize her, dammit, for the great person she'd become. And the fact that Coletta still couldn't shed a tear in her presence hurt her deeply. *She still doesn't trust me*, Melinda thought. *She still has to put on the superwoman act in front of me.* She knocked on the bathroom door gently. "Mom, are you all right?"

"I'm fine," Coletta said, her voice betraying the fact that she was crying.

"I'm here if you—"

Coletta blew her nose loudly. A few seconds later she opened the door, and Melinda was still standing there.

"What?" Coletta asked, doing her best to sound composed.

Melinda hugged her mother tightly. It felt awkward at first; Coletta did not hug her back, but Melinda held on. "I'm scared, Mom," she finally said. And with this admission Coletta felt able, felt it safe to respond.

"There's nothing to be afraid of, Melinda," she said. "Tari will be fine. I'm not going to let anything happen to her. To either of you. Okay?"

"Okay." Melinda sobbed into her mother's shoulder, almost believing that Coletta had the power to save her very life. She thought she heard her mother crying over her own sobs, but she wasn't sure. Even if Coletta had let her guard down, Melinda would not watch. *Let her win; let her be the strongest*, Melinda thought. *I'm so tired of playing this game.*

CHAPTER
32

City lights glowered imperiously at the dark sky as Boston came alive on yet another Saturday evening. It was prime hunting season, and herds of single men and women prowled the bars, nightclubs, and restaurants looking for prey or positioning themselves to be preyed on.

Tari was nervous as she felt the excitement of the crowd. She couldn't help but worry about how her breasts looked, never mind how they felt. The swelling had come down and the bandage was off, but it didn't feel right, didn't look right. She'd tried on seven different outfits and settled on an ensemble that did not dip too low on her chest.

She could not pass up this gig once Manny had told her about it. The Jazz Hour in Faneuil Hall was slick and hip, and the clientele was a cosmopolitan, downtown crowd, certainly better dressed and more image-conscious than the geeks and bohemians she had grown used to across the river in Cambridge. This crowd was strictly State Street Bank, John Hancock, Fidelity, and Mass. General types; no academia lifers or lab rats that she could spot from the stage.

She felt them judging every inch of her as she took the stage. It gave her some satisfaction that they were at least

looking at her, and she was glad she had not worn something too revealing. She felt naked enough.

Shawn had been friendly but cool toward her, and she
wondered if she had done something wrong. Was it those
phone calls she hadn't returned? Nah. He couldn't be that
sensitive, she thought. She had been trying to play it cool
and had barely spoken to him during the short rehearsal.
But she wanted him to flirt, show some interest, at least
smile at her in that way again before they got onstage,
where it would be all business. But no cigar.

A few whistles from the audience as she hit the high
notes of "My Funny Valentine" built up her confidence,
and soon she began to lose herself in the music. She forgot
about the itchy scar on her breast, the audience of doctors,
bankers, and executives, and began to sing out the pain that
she was feeling.

All was not well, though it looked that way from the chocolate off-the-shoulder blouse and pants that fit her every
curve nicely and the way her hennaed hair curled around
her face. With her eyes closed, she saw the wig that sat on a
mannequin head in her bedroom. She remembered the
oncologist describing the medicines to her: Adriamycin,
Cytoxan, and Taxol. Yes, the doctor said, her hair would fall
out. Quickly. And all of it. Eyebrows, probably, nose, and
even down there. *Well, at least I won't have to shave,* she'd
laughed. The doctor had looked at her, expressionless, as if
she had heard that one many, many, times before. In less
than a week, she would have her first treatment. The doctor
had given her a stack of papers with a list of side effects:
early-onset menopause, nausea, fatigue, joint and muscle
pain, sore throat, mouth sores. The way Tari saw it, she
would be sick for four months straight.

After the first set, she sat backstage with Manny and the
rest of the guys talking about the lineup for the second set.
She was trying to treat Shawn just like any other member of

her quartet. Like Al, her drunk drummer, Mike, her weird sax player, and Manny. She hadn't returned his calls because she just couldn't see herself getting into that right now. She had erased each message breathlessly, regretfully. The sound of his voice could still do magical things to her that didn't help her insomnia one bit, but it wasn't fair to drag him into her life. Not now. So she tried to be the professional, joking with the guys but keeping her distance from him. Playing it cool. Still, hoping that he'd at least say something to her.

Soon, Manny and the guys answered the call of free drinks at the bar, and she and Shawn were the only ones left. The room was not big, and it was crowded with broken bar stools, a few tables and chairs, and other discarded restaurant furnishings. Tari sat on a creaky bar stool sipping lime juice with honey while Shawn stood inches from her, rubbing his fingertips.

"So, how have you been?" he asked as she tried to busy herself with a sheet of music.

"I've been okay. Busy, you know. Work and stuff."

"I know, I've been reading your stories."

Tari looked up, pleased. "You have?"

"Well, who isn't? A lot of people are taking their money out of that bank."

She nodded and tried to downplay her satisfaction.

"But you must be working pretty hard," he said, observing her intently. "You've even lost weight. Don't tell me you're dieting."

Tari pondered this for a moment and decided to go with it.

"Well, yeah. Summer's coming and I just want to look good. You know how that goes."

He shook his head. "You looked perfect the way you were."

Their eyes met and something unspoken was said. But she decided to change the subject to something innocuous.

"You're sounding really good out there, Shawn." She willed her eyes to stay on the sheet in front of her.

"What are you doing tonight after this?" he asked.

She looked up from her music. "I'm actually so zonked I think I'll head home and go straight to bed."

She saw the disappointment in his eyes, but his lips smiled. "I'm pretty tired, too. I may do the same thing."

The guys entered the room loudly with beers in their hands. The spell was broken.

"Shawn, you want a Heineken?" Al handed Shawn a green bottle.

"Nah, man. I don't touch the stuff," Shawn said.

"More for me," Al slurred. Tari glared at him. *Just don't screw up my second set*, she thought.

The performance went well, everyone said. She even did an encore, a first in many, many years. The owner of the place was beaming as she walked off the stage. "Oh, you have to come back. You just have to!" he said.

"Hey, I'm really sorry that I didn't return your calls," she said as Shawn packed his bass into its case.

He shrugged. "You said you were busy. Right?"

"Um . . . right," she said uncomfortably. He said good night curtly, as if she were his boss or a stranger.

She considered the Shawn problem as she drove home. It wasn't that he made her dream dreams she hadn't dreamt since the good times with Roger. It wasn't that she never pictured herself, 5'2", walking down the aisle with him, 6'4". Already. It wasn't that she didn't wonder how he felt about kids and if he would be okay with not having any and whether he liked West Indian food or whether he cooked and would welcome a woman into his life whose culinary skills were a bit lacking. She had to put things in perspective. She wasn't the woman who first saw him months ago in church praying, loud, strong, and unashamed. Back then she'd been among the eligible, hot, smart, and single. Now she was damaged goods. She had a dent in an imperfect right breast. In a month she would have no hair. God knew what else chemotherapy would take from her.

She didn't want to see the pity in his eyes when she told him that she had the big C. Nor did she want to shame him into admitting that her illness made her somehow less attractive to him. That the one breast, misshapen and grotesque, would be difficult to admire, lust after, to caress, kiss.

She sighed. At least she'd had a good performance. The Shawn problem would go away because she would not encourage it, cultivate it, or feed it. She would treat him as she did the other guys in the band. Sooner or later he would get the message.

CHAPTER
33

Sleep was eluding her again. She sought refuge in a chat room that she found herself visiting, sometimes four or five times a day, even while at work. She had never posted anything, but she gobbled up all the words that the other women brave enough to post would leave. It was there that she learned that too much soy was not the best thing for her type of cancer, and that while her hair would definitely fall out during chemotherapy, her nails would grow probably twice as long as their normal length, and that she should probably get all trips to the dentist out of the way now. She had learned so much from these faceless women with names like kathismom, marytexas, and nevagivup.

But tonight she felt burdened. She felt restless, and the urge to hear Shawn's voice was almost unbearable. She had to focus on the present, the reality, cancer and what it was doing to her mind. She had to post a message. It was something she had asked her doctor about, but the woman was never able to quell her fears enough for her to take that step. She wanted an opinion from someone who had been there.

The response was quick. Within five minutes Marla29 replied. Hon, you've got to do what's best for you. I've been on antidepressants since I was diagnosed four months ago. I am not ashamed. And frankly, if it weren't for my happy pills, I probably would not be sleeping a wink either. You have to make the choice, sleep or fear. And at this point, your body can't afford to lose any sleep.

Tari sighed as she reread the message. She could just hear Melinda's reaction. Although her sister was a psychotherapist, she did not advocate psychotropic drugs. And Tari herself had always thought people who took mind medicines were weak or somehow flawed in character. She believed that such drugs were just a few short steps down from heroin or cocaine or any other illegal mood enhancer that could be purchased just a block or two away on Norfolk Street or Blue Hill Avenue.

But she hadn't had a good night's sleep in ages. Her doctor had given her a prescription, but she had refused to fill it. Her insomnia, while physically taxing, made her feel virtuous, as if she had a special power to resist the lure of the evil pharmaceutical industry. But she was failing fast. And it wasn't just the bags under her eyes. She could barely make it through yoga class. At work she found herself nodding off at her desk.

She wrote back to Marla29. I just always imagine people who take those pills as bored suburban housewives or depressed young girls looking for a legal high.

Well, I'm 29 and I have cancer and I'm depressed. So if anybody needs a high, that would be me. But I'll take a good night's sleep instead.☺ Marla29 wrote back.

Tari laughed out loud. Twenty-nine. *Younger than me*, she thought. She typed up another message to Marla.

The two of them conversed back and forth as the minutes went by. Tari found out that Marla was an associate at a New York City law firm. They both were exercise junkies. Marla had even run the Boston Marathon and the New York

City Marathon. She, too, was a shell-shocked Stage II cancer patient.

You know what the hardest thing about this is? Marla wrote. I'm not even married yet. I don't even have a boyfriend. And I'm afraid I never will. I mean, who wants to be with someone who has had a near-terminal disease? I was dating this guy and things were going so well. But he turned out to be such a jerk. When I told him that I had breast cancer, he was so good about it. At first he was so comforting, always there. He even came with me to some of my doctor's appointments. But slowly he stopped calling. Then he said it was too much for him to deal with. He said that he was afraid that I'd never be able to have kids. Can you believe that?

Tari wrote back: Marla, that guy was a jerk. But he wasn't the one for you. And I don't agree with you that no one would want to be with us just because we've had this disease. I'm still hopeful. I just want to get through this treatment and then get on with my life the way I did before.

The words were meant strictly for Marla's benefit, because Tari herself did not believe them. She felt the same way as Marla did. She would be a liability to any man; who wanted someone who had this disease hanging over her head, who might not be able to have kids, who had to worry about recurrence, metastases, surgical scars? She sure wouldn't. But she didn't want to make her new friend feel worse.

That's great that you can be so optimistic. And I have to admit, sometimes I am, too. But today is just not one of those days. I had a really rough day at work. People are really nice. Really great. Too nice, as a matter of fact. I hate the pity I see in their eyes. You know? Poor Marla, alone in the big city with cancer. One lady actually told me that I should go home to my parents in Georgia. I'm like, heck no! I'm staying here. This is my life and I'm doing fine on my own. I have some good friends who take me to my appointments and who help me out with stuff I need. But I feel that it would be easier on other people if I had a husband or boyfriend. That way they wouldn't have to feel so sorry for me.

Tari wrote back: Yeah. I know what you mean. It's like you don't feel as sorry for yourself as other people feel sorry for you.

Tari continued this cyber conversation, laughing out loud sometimes as she shared her fears and frustrations with Marla. When she finally turned off the computer she felt cleansed, as if she'd just had a monster session with a shrink. She realized that Melinda was right about having support from other women who'd been there and who could share her experience. It wasn't enough to talk to someone sympathetic but who had no idea what she was going through. No, she wasn't the type to sit around in a circle and sing "Kumbaya" with a bunch of other women. But this on-line support thing, she could hang with it.

CHAPTER
34

On Tuesday, May 23, one day after the attorney general recused himself from the investigation, Donald Meehan, CEO of MetroBank, caved into the pressure and resigned. While the self-important swindler announced to the press that he was quitting his position to spend more time with his family, Tari was sitting in Room 32H at Harvard Pilgrim Medical Center. Her parents, Melinda, and Rebecca sat on plastic chairs around her, crowding the tiny room, one of many in the chemo center.

The nurse was a chatty, cheerful woman who was doing her best to lift the family's solemn mood. But no one wanted to talk. Not about the splendid weather, not about the sorry Red Sox. So she gave up, quietly pumping two large syringes full of a red liquid into Tari's vein. "Does it burn?" she asked for the fourth time. Tari shook her head. "Okay. Just sit tight. This other drug will take about an hour." The nurse winked as she left the room.

"That was the Adriamycin," Melinda said authoritatively. "That's the really powerful stuff. How you feeling, Tari?"

Tari shrugged, ignoring Melinda, as her family peered at

her. Every few seconds she inventoried her physical well-being, hoping to feel pain, an itch, anything would tell her that toxic drugs were coursing through her bloodstream. Deep breaths. Shallow breaths. Listening for a rise or fall in heartbeat. But the steady drip, drip, and the gradual deflation of the IV bag hanging over the leather recliner were the only indications that the drugs were traveling through her.

The television was tuned to the local news station, and the room was still as Donald Meehan made his announcement. Melinda looked at her as if daring her to rip the IV out of her arm and run off to cover the story. Tari glared at her sister defiantly. *What makes her think she knows what I'm thinking?*

When Donald Meehan finished his lame speech about taking time off to spend with his young second wife and toddlers, Tari looked through the faces as a camera scanned the reporter pool. It flashed on John Weston for a second as he fired off the first question at Meehan. She clenched her fist.

"Tari, come on," Melinda said. "That should be the last thing on your mind."

She rolled her eyes at her sister. "You don't know what's on my mind, Melinda."

Rebecca put her hand on Tari's arm. "You'll get your story back when you go back to work."

"I don't know why you don't just take some time off," Coletta said, wringing her hands and looking worriedly at the IV bag as if it could explode at any moment. "This is serious. Serious. I don't understand your attitude."

"If she wants to work, let her work, Coletta," William Shields said patiently. "What's the point of staying in the house feeling sorry for herself?" He made a sound of exasperation that Tari knew well, because she often made the same sound.

Tari found herself smiling at the sudden burst of conversation in the room. But they were wrong. If anyone would understand what she was feeling, it would be her father. He was the one who had taught her to give everything—work, school—her very best effort and to not give up no matter what. "Thanks, Dad," Tari said.

She felt only a sliver of regret as she beheld the scene on the television screen. Weston's face only reminded her that she hated competing with people like him who, no matter how hard she worked, would always be the star. Sure, she might get some recognition for breaking this story. But there would be others, bigger ones that would belong to him. And there had been so many other stories that had his name all over them. What bothered her most was that he would not keep his hands off her one little victory. She was angry that she was not there to ask the first question at the press conference. She was angry because *he* was always there. He or someone else who looked like him and had had a clear, long head start in life, plus the glittery future that was the birthright to people like him. Bad things never happened to people like John Weston, Tari thought. Then she sighed. *I need to stop feeling sorry for myself.*

"I think it's finished, Tari," Melinda said, looking at the almost-empty IV bag. Tari looked at her watch as Melinda went off in search of the nurse. The two hours had flown by; this hadn't been too bad at all.

"Oh, yuck!" she said, screwing up her face. "My mouth tastes like I just chewed on a soup can."

Coletta stood quickly. "Nurse!"

"Mrs. Shields, that's normal. I read that in my research," Rebecca said, laughing.

"Yes, it's normal, Mom," Tari said. "But it tastes like hell!"

The nurse popped her head in the room. "Are we all done here?"

Tari closed her eyes as the nurse pulled the needle from the vein in her left hand. When she stood, her head felt full and her bladder was overflowing. She noticed the slightly drunken sensation when she took her first steps. But the face staring back at her in the bathroom mirror looked the same as the one she'd always known. *I'm going to be fine*, she thought. *One chemo down; seven more to go.*

But on the drive home, she was still waiting to feel sick. "I don't feel anything yet," was her answer every few minutes when Coletta asked, concern in her wide eyes. *Aaargh!* Tari bristled after the fifth time. She even began to silently pray that she at least would retch or something. Just to give the woman some satisfaction and shut her up already.

They just wouldn't leave her alone. Even when they had dropped off Rebecca and had gotten her home, they hovered over her, looking curiously into her face.

"Tari, I'll stay here as long as you want me to," Melinda said, fluffing up the pillows on Tari's bed.

"Actually, I just want to rest. Alone."

"But what if you start to feel sick?" Coletta asked, standing on the opposite side of the bed. Tari looked at her mother and sister, both standing tall and erect like sentries on either side of her bed.

"Y'all need to stop," she said, shaking her head. "Just stop standing over me like this. Please."

Coletta sighed. "I'm going to get dinner started for your father."

Melinda sat on the bed as Coletta walked out of the room.

"You sure you want her over here, breathing down your neck?"

Tari restrained herself from screaming, *You're breathing down my neck, too!*

"I feel okay, Mel. You can go home."

Melinda looked at her and put a hand on her leg. "Don't be like that."

"Like what?"

"Like all independent and strong. You're probably gonna start crying the minute I walk out of this room."

"No, I'm not," Tari said. "Stop trying to make me cry, though. I'll hit you if you keep it up."

"At least you haven't lost your violent streak," Melinda said.

Tari leaned back into the pillows. "Please, go home. Go home and take care of your family. I'm fine."

"Are you sure?"

"I'm a hundred percent sure."

"I'll call you when I get home."

"Don't call me when you get home, Melinda. I'm gonna be fine. Mom's right downstairs."

Melinda stood up reluctantly. "Don't wait for things to get bad before you ask for help."

Tari groaned. "Thank you, Melinda. Now, please leave. I'll call if I need you."

Melinda leaned over and kissed her on the forehead. The gesture touched Tari so deeply she had to bite her lips to hold back the tears.

"Go away," she said.

"Fine," Melinda said. "I love you, too, weirdo."

"I'm telling Mom you called me a weird ho."

"Not funny," Melinda said as she closed the door gently behind her.

Tari closed her eyes and took a deep breath. What a day. All the attention had been too much. There were times when she was a young girl that all she dreamed about was leaving her family, getting as far away from them as possible. They never let her be her own person; she was always the baby. Today had been a prime example. But what if they weren't here? What if Coletta weren't here to fuss over her? What if Melinda didn't care enough to cancel her appointments and be there for her? They were a pain in the butt. But she was so glad they were there now. She couldn't imagine facing this all by herself.

CHAPTER

35

The nausea was sudden and violent, waking her from slumber at 3:12 A.M. She barely made it to the bathroom.

Coletta must have heard the retching and was at Tari's side within seconds. "Did you take the antinausea medicine?"

Tari could only move her head sideways from where she knelt, bent over the toilet bowl. Her entire body heaved up and down, and she felt as if she would give up all of her internal organs to the American Standard in front of her.

It was an hour before she was able to get off her knees, wash her face, brush her teeth, and limp back to bed, weak and shaking.

"Why didn't you take the nausea pills?" Coletta stood over Tari's bed, her hands knitted together.

Tari closed her eyes. She did not have the heart to say that she did not feel sick, so she did not take them. The doctor had admonished her, "Take them even though you don't feel sick. It's easier to prevent nausea before it starts than to stop it." As those thoughts went through her head, she felt another wave of nausea. She bolted for the bathroom and spent another hour kneeling on the bathroom rug. That would be the remainder of the night. Her stomach had emptied but the retching continued, punctuated with her prayers: *Make it stop, please. Make it stop. I'll do anything you want me to do, God. Just make it stop.* Long after her father had gone to bed, Coletta sat with her as she lay waiting for either the pills to work or the nausea to hit again. The sun came up, and they were still wide awake.

"Mom, I'm so glad you're here," Tari croaked.

"Mmmm-mmmm," Coletta said, thinking, *I told you so.*

Later, Tari clutched her hollow belly as she swallowed spoonfuls of noodle soup, thin but tasty, thanks to Coletta's expert seasoning.

"Tari." Coletta looked squarely at her daughter.

Tari looked up but kept on eating her soup.

"I'm sorry if I was . . . you know, hard on you when you were small." Coletta joined her fingers together and studied them. "You were just so . . . willful. I know you got that from me, but it's not always a good thing. I just see you now . . ."

Tari stopped eating.

"You're still too stubborn. Still always trying to get your own way against everything and everybody else, and maybe it's my fault." She sighed. "I should have shown you how to be soft, how to let other people help you and not feel bad about it."

"Mom . . ."

"I wasn't a good example," Coletta said. "But I had it hard, Tari. Really hard. You know my mother died of that same thing, and then I had to help raise all my sisters and brothers. Before your father came along . . . I had to be strong, Tari. I didn't have anybody, so I didn't have a choice. But you don't have to carry all this weight on your shoulders, by yourself."

Tari sighed. "Mom, what weight? I'm letting you help me, aren't I?"

"Yes, but you don't like it. If you had your own way, I wouldn't even have known you were sick."

Tari thought for a minute about how right her mother was. How all she could think about was being normal again so she wouldn't need all these people—her parents, her sister, Rebecca—fussing over her, making her like an invalid.

"Mom, it's not about being strong. I just know that I can take care of myself, that's all." Defiance was turning into fury. She didn't really want to talk about this now. Not when her throat felt like a gravel path and her every breath made a painful echo in her sternum.

"And I know that, too, Tari. You don't have to prove it to me. You don't have to prove that to anybody, not your job, not your friends. Everybody already knows you're smart, you're strong, and you can make it on your own. So, why don't you just take the help you're getting now and concentrate on getting yourself better?"

Angry tears thrust their way into her eyes. "I just hate feeling so weak, so sick!" The rage in her voice surprised even her. "This is so unfair, Mom. I didn't do anything to deserve this!"

Coletta tried to hold back her own tears. She moved from her chair and leaned over her daughter, taking her in her arms.

"I know. But we'll get through it together. You'll get better and then you'll be even stronger. You just have to be patient. And let somebody help you."

Coletta held her daughter and thought back to her own youth. At Tari's age she'd already raised her youngest sister and brother and was raising her own two daughters and a young son. Her mother's death was the long, slow, and painful kind that could have turned her heart inward, away from the rest of the world. But she never, ever thought of it now if she could help it. She was not the type to dredge up painful old memories just for the sake of "dealing with it." She had moved on with her life as best she could. Thank God, Will had been there with her so she wasn't alone. And she'd never leave her little girl to go through this all by herself. She would be here no matter what. Coletta held Tari tightly to her as they both cried. *This family's been through rough times before*, Coletta thought. *We'll get through this one, too.*

CHAPTER

36

Melinda laced up her sneakers quickly. Tari was waiting in the driveway.

"Your sister's here," Michael called out again from downstairs.

She ran down the stairs. "Be back in a couple of hours," she said.

"A couple of hours?"

"We're gonna do a long, long walk today. Maybe six miles, if she's up to it."

Michael's eyes turned back toward the TV, Bulls vs. Hawks in Chicago.

"Michael, please. I've been home with the kids all day. You can watch them for two hours, can't you?"

"I didn't say anything, did I?" he grumbled. "Don't start with me."

"Start what?" She put her hands on her hips.

He didn't answer and she waited. She watched him ignore her for a long time, then she grabbed her keys and made her exit. "Lazy bastard," she said under her breath.

"Girl, you need to thank your lucky stars you're not married," Melinda said as she jumped into the passenger seat of Tari's 4Runner.

"Uh-oh," Tari said. "Trouble in paradise?"

"He's trying to pull an attitude 'cause I said I'm gonna be gone for two hours. Two hours!" Melinda shook her head in exasperation. "He can't watch the kids for two hours without complaining. I'm the one out there working all week and dropping off and picking up the kids. You'd think when the weekend comes he would give me a break."

Tari had been hearing tirades like this for years. At first her advice to her sister had been "leave him." She liked Michael, but she thought he was a boy wrapped up in a man's body trying to hide from his responsibilities. But over the years she had seen the dynamics of the marriage change. She was no expert, but she could see that Michael saw his role as provider and head of household being usurped by his more ambitious wife. And his way of reacting to this was to become even more boylike, shirking his goals, his duties as a father and a husband, and pursuing his childish desire for daily golf and nightly ESPN. She'd vowed long ago to try to remain as neutral as possible.

"Well, I've said it before, but I'll say it again. You've got a situation on your hands. You gotta just keep praying that God will give you the strength to endure." Tari didn't like her answer. But it was what the church preached, what the Word said. And who was she to go up against that? All their lives it had been the same thing. There were solutions that looked clear-cut and easy. Worldly solutions, their father called them. And Tari had tried those solutions when she left home. But now she was back and she knew better. Leaving Michael would not solve a thing for her sister. What would happen to the kids? To the love that Melinda held for Michael despite his flaws? She had to stay and solve the problem or at least find a way to live with it. *And if she leaves him, I certainly wouldn't want her crying on my shoulder every night.* Melinda was right on one thing, though. Tari would rather stay single the rest of her life than be in an un-fulfilling marriage.

"Sometimes I just want to just go, just get in my car and go and keep on going." Melinda sighed.

Tari laughed. "I know. I know. Move to New York or London or Paris and become a carefree single gal, right?"

"Don't laugh at me, okay?" Melinda pouted. "You don't have my life. You don't know what it's like to have two kids and a lazy husband."

Tari laughed again. "Yeah. And my life is a bed of roses."

Melinda stopped. "Tari, shoot. I'm sorry. With your atti-tude . . . I forget sometimes . . . and then I feel so guilty."

"Guilty? Are you nuts? I forget, too, sometimes. But I can't be anything but carefree, Melinda. If I focused on this thing 24/7, I'd probably be dead by now. I have to keep on living like I'm not sick."

She parked at Ponkapoag Pond, one of the majestic won-ders of the 5,800 acre Blue Hills Reservation. There was a four-mile trail, overshadowed by a bounty of trees and shrubs, and several types of wildlife ruled the vicinity. The early-summer sun shone high and bright in the sky, which was untidy with scattered clouds, hanging suspended from the calm blue like torn bedsheets.

"What a gorgeous day," Melinda said, stretching her long arms wide open. She was wearing brand-new sneakers and an Adidas track suit that had been sitting in her closet for at least two years. She wore a Boston College baseball hat over her chin-length hair. *If nothing else,* Melinda thought, *at least I get to wear these workout clothes.*

The lot was full with cars belonging to picnickers, walk-ers, and joggers, whom Tari eyed enviously. They walked along the trail, inhaling infant leaves and new, dewy grass. A jogger ran past, leaving salty sweat in Tari's nostrils and a jealous fury that forced her to quicken her steps.

"I should be in kickboxing today."

"Tari, please. You're on chemotherapy. There's no way you should go anywhere near a gym."

But the doctor said. . . . It was no use, Tari knew. She doubted she possessed the energy to walk the six miles she had boldly set as her goal. Six miles of walking. Hmmph. Six months ago that wouldn't have been a goal; it would have been a joke. But her body was protesting; it would do no more than keep her alive and functioning, would take no more of those high kicks, and refused to even jog for more than five minutes. She'd tried to ignore its warnings but it would rebel, leaving her breathless, light-headed, and faint, needing to sit down. Another jogger ran by.

"You'll get out there again." Melinda touched her shoulder. "Before you know it you'll be in kickboxing, you'll be jogging, you'll be skating. You'll be doing everything."

"I just wish I didn't get these looks from these runners. As if they're so superior. So fit. I have cancer, for goodness' sake. If I didn't, I'd leave them all in my dust!"

"But, Tari, you're not even a runner," Melinda said, laughing. "Why are you getting all worked up over this?"

"I just hate them all!" Tari said.

"You're crazy, you know?" Melinda said. "You think those runners even noticed you? You're out of your mind. What you need to do is concentrate on getting yourself well instead of worrying about running or kickboxing."

"Don't tell me what I need to concentrate on, okay? I know what's important to me."

Tari walked even faster, forcing Melinda to up her pace. Maybe this had all been a mistake. What made her think she could tolerate Melinda for an entire morning anyway?

They walked in silence, Tari hoping that she could at least break a sweat and Melinda struggling to keep up.

"Tari, slow down," she finally said.

Tari turned to look at Melinda's face. She was crying.

"Mel, what's wrong?"

Melinda shook her head. "I'm just tired. It's not just you. It's everything. Work, Michael's crap, the kids, the house, Mom. Everything is just making me crazy. I'm so freaking exhausted." She wiped her eyes with her hands. "What if it had been me, Tari? What if I'm next? Who's gonna take care of my kids if I get sick?"

Tari looked down at the pebbles on the trail. "Melinda, you're not going to get sick. Just because I have it doesn't mean you'll get it."

"But the likelihood—"

"Forget the likelihood, okay?" Tari said. "I'm thirty, healthy, and I don't smoke, so there's no likelihood or un-likelihood. Just . . . Just don't think about it."

Melinda nodded and they walked slowly.

"Mel, we have so much to be thankful for," Tari said. "Michael's who he is, but look at your life. That's what Pastor Terry told me when I spoke to him that Sunday, to look at my life. You have the career you always wanted, two beautiful kids, a nice house, cars, not to mention your crazy extended family, your health, your sanity. . . . Just concentrate on enjoying your life, girl. Forget about what could happen."

Melinda took Tari's hand and squeezed it. "I know. I just worry sometimes. And Michael's so irresponsible." She sniffed.

Tari shook her head. "Let God do His thing with Michael, 'cause there's nothing you can do to change him yourself. If you want to hop over to London for a weekend, we'll go together. We'll let Mom watch Taylor and Jared so Michael won't bawl you out."

Melinda laughed, still sniffing. "You're right. It's not that simple, but maybe . . ." She sighed. "I should know this stuff. It's just so hard to apply it to my own life, you know?"

Tari nodded. "I know. I know."

"So what are we doing next?" Tari asked after they'd finished their walk. She felt that she had another couple of miles in her but didn't want to push it.

Melinda shrugged. "Are you sure you don't want to go home to bed?"

"I feel fine; sun's out, it's a gorgeous day." Tari inhaled the clean air deeply. She really wanted to stay outside all day long if she could.

Melinda shook her head in wonder. "Guess we could get something to eat."

"Not hungry much these days. Let's just go to Starbucks. I could use a soy chai latte."

"Yum," Melinda said, hopping in the passenger side of Tari's truck. "How's the nondairy, vegetarian thing going?"

"It's not that hard anymore. I just hate having to pay so much for groceries now. Man, it's expensive to eat healthy. No wonder poor people are the first ones to die."

"Don't forget to treat yourself once in a while, though," Melinda said. "A little ice cream now and then ain't gonna kill ya."

"Yeah," Tari said dreamily. "Kahlua crunch from Kimball Farms on a huge waffle cone."

Melinda turned to her, a mischievous glint in her eye. "Wanna go?"

Tari laughed. "Nah. My taste buds are too screwed up. It wouldn't taste the same."

They drove to the Starbucks in Canton, gazing at the cute houses on Main Street. "Didn't you want to buy here?" Tari asked Melinda.

"Yeah, once upon a time. But I'm glad we decided to stay in the city. In the community."

"Even though it's costing you an arm and a leg to send the kids to private school?"

"We've been through this before. I love my house, Tari. And I like the neighborhood."

"Sure you do."

"I do. More people like us need to stay in the community."

"Hmmph," Tari said. "If I made your kind of money, I'd be in some tony suburb somewhere."

"No, you wouldn't. You know you like living in da hood."

"Whatever."

Tari pulled into the Starbucks parking lot and watched an older couple shuffling into the coffee shop.

"They remind me of Mom and Dad," she said. "I can't believe they're getting old." She'd been shocked to see that both her father and mother walked much slower these days. Like old people. She'd never really thought of them that way, but if they were someone else's folks she'd sure think they were old.

"Yeah, what did you think? They're still thirty-five and we're still in our teens?" Melinda asked.

"It's just weird to see them so slow."

"I think the chemo's making you sentimental."

"Ha. Not really. Maybe more observant."

"So, you wanna head to Neiman's for Last Call after this?" Melinda asked as they got in line at the Starbucks.

"Woo hoo!" Tari said.

"You sure you up for this?" Melinda glanced at her.

"I'm always up for a sale, Miss Big Spender."

"Who said I was treating?"

"Well, I don't have any money, and my credit cards . . . Well, you know."

"Cheap bastard."

"It was your idea, not mine."

Forty minutes later they'd made it downtown and were giggling like little girls as they made a beeline for Neiman

Marcus in Copley Square. "Oooh, I even love the way it smells in here," Tari said as they entered the store. She'd forgotten about chemotherapy; she'd even forgotten that she'd had cancer.

"I think I need to stop at the Mario Badescu counter. My skin is a mess," Tari said. "But after we do clothes."

"I'm long overdue for a spree anyway," Melinda said as they prowled the sportswear section.

"Michael's got your funds on lockdown?" Tari joked.

"Please. He knows better. Nah, the women's conference is coming up, so I need to get a couple of outfits. I have to lead a panel and I'm on the dinner committee."

Tari rolled her eyes. "I thought you were going to quit. How do you stand being around those women? They're like black wannabe Stepford wives."

Melinda sighed. She had guiltily reconsidered after her little outburst with Stephanie and was now back on the hook for the women's conference. "Not all of them are like that, Tari. Lucy's not like that."

"Yeah, Lucy's cool. But that's 'cause she's a badass lawyer and she doesn't care what anyone says about her. But that Stephanie Strong, Michelle, Hilary, and the rest of that gang . . . They're all crazy."

"They do a lot of work for the church. And in the community."

"Doesn't mean they're not crazy."

Melinda paused and inspected a pair of pants. "Well, if they're crazy, doesn't that mean I'm crazy, too?"

"No comment."

Melinda poked Tari in the back with a hanger. "When you get married, you'll see what it's like. You're probably gonna be worse than any of them. You'll probably be the mom all the teachers hate because you're always hanging around the school telling them how to do their jobs."

"Ha!" Tari said, holding up a Catherine Malandrino dress

against her body. *Too long, darn!* "I don't think that kind of life is for me."

"Yeah, right."

"Seriously, Melinda. Especially now, with all this stuff. I think I just want to get well, then travel the world and sing for the rest of my life."

Melinda stared at her for a few seconds. "Yup. That chemo's definitely doing a number on you."

Tari shrugged. She was being serious, so why was Melinda making a joke out of it? She didn't want to be anybody's wife or anybody's mother. What if she did get married and had kids and then had a recurrence? Who would take care of her kids? Or even worse, what if she died and left her kids without a mother? Her ebullient mood began to spiral down.

Melinda held out a skirt to her. "That looks like you."

Tari shrugged. "I'm getting kinda tired."

"You okay?"

"I guess. Just tired."

"You wanna go back home to bed?"

Tari looked around at all the clothes, the mannequins, the beautiful store. *I need to suck it up*, she thought. *Live in the moment.*

"Nah. Let's hang out for a while."

"You sure?" Melinda asked, looking genuinely worried.

"I'm sure." She grabbed the skirt from Melinda. "I'll go try it on."

A couple of minutes later she came out of the dressing room wearing the skirt and a top she'd grabbed on her way into the fitting room.

"Looks nice," Melinda said, her arm full of dresses.

Tari raised her eyebrows. "You gonna buy all these?"

Melinda nodded. "I hate trying stuff on in those little rooms. Those mirrors give me a false sense of slimness. If I looked like you . . ."

"If you worked out as hard as I did, you'd probably look a lot better than I do."

Melinda shrugged. "True. I can't imagine spending all that time in a gym."

Tari let it slide. "Okay, Ms. Moneybags," she said as she returned to the fitting room to change into her clothes.

"You can go ahead and get something else," Melinda called out.

Wow, Tari thought as she changed into her own clothes. *She must be feeling really bad for me.* Not that Melinda wasn't generous. She just wasn't always *this* generous. *I should take advantage of her emotional behind and let her buy me this whole store,* she thought, laughing to herself.

When she walked out of the fitting room Melinda was already at the register, paying for her truckload of dresses and suits. Tari added her one Vivienne Tam skirt to the pile. The sales girl looked at them and smiled. "Sisters?" she asked.

"Yes," they said in unison.

"She's the rich one." Tari pointed to Melinda.

"Yeah, and she's the silly one." Melinda rolled her eyes.

"Thanks, babe," Tari said, putting on her sunglasses as they pulled out into traffic minutes later. "That was a good idea. Especially since I didn't have to spend my own money."

Melinda looked at Tari, smiling. "I knew that would cheer you up. You're such a clothes whore."

"You know it, babe."

"What do you think they're doing?" Melinda asked.

"Mom and Dad?"

'Yeah.'

"Dad's probably trying to read or watch the news, and Mom's probably talking his head off."

They laughed. "At least you won't have to worry about having to listen to old Charley Pride records when you get home."

"Oh, my God," Tari said, and they laughed long and loud as they remembered their parents' favorite country music artist.

"I still can't believe I know all these songs by heart. They just won't leave my brain," Melinda moaned. "Remember that one?

"You've got to / kiss an angel good morning / and let her know you think about her when you're gone / kiss an angel good morning / and love her like the devil when you get back home." They sang together, then burst into laughter.

"Can you believe she let us sing those lyrics but she wouldn't let us watch BET?" Melinda said, wiping her eyes.

"Man, we had some weird times," Tari said.

"Tell me about it," Melinda said.

"I don't know any other black kids who knew as much country music as we did. But it was fun. Sometimes," Tari said.

Melinda looked at her. "I'm having fun now."

"Me, too," Tari said.

"Know which one I really miss?" Melinda asked.

"Which one?"

"Hank Williams."

"Nooooo!" Tari groaned.

"Come on, Tari! 'I'm So Lonesome I Could Cry' is probably one of the best American songs ever written."

"You mean the most depressing American song ever written."

"I wish I had that record sometimes," Melinda said wistfully.

They sang and giggled all the way home, both forgetting the fear and sadness that sat way at the bottom of their hearts.

CHAPTER
37

The phone rang, and before she even had a chance to turn over in bed to grab it, Coletta had already answered it. Tari rolled her eyes. *Why in the world does she feel the need to answer my phone?* Seconds later, Coletta knocked on her door.

"You have a phone call," she said. "Some man named Shawn." There was a question in her voice and her eyes. Tari decided to ignore it.

"Mom, you really don't need to answer the phone."

"I thought you were sleeping."

"Well, just let it go to voice mail."

Coletta affected the most injured look she could muster. "Fine, then. I won't answer your phone. I don't know what kind of man calls a young lady so late anyway," she mumbled as she walked away.

"It's not late!" Tari yelled after her.

She sighed and picked up the phone.

"Was I interrupting something?" Shawn asked.

"No, it's just my mom being a pain."

"Is she visiting from the islands, or did she move in with you permanently?"

"Ha!" Tari said. "They're visiting, but they're leaving

pretty soon." She truly meant the last statement. It was time to cry uncle. She'd shown them that she could be broken and helpless. They had seen her vomiting, ravaged by diarrhea, with thinning hair, chills, hot flashes, a blue tongue, and blue fingernails. And she let them baby her through it all.

But that didn't mean she couldn't have her home to herself. Couldn't not have Coletta Shields doing her laundry, folding her underwear, ironing her clothes, reminding her to take the daily injections that built up her white blood cells, making her bathroom smell like spring-fresh Lysol. It was too much. She wanted normal. She wanted to go out to lunch with someone who wanted to talk about the world, about child slavery in the Sudan, or about music, like what was the deal with Cassandra Wilson's latest CD anyway. No cloying parents who watched religious channels and the news nonstop, who had their friends walking through her house, talking about old days, old people, dead people. No more comforting, stomach-padding home-cooked meals. No more warm, childlike feelings induced by too much parental love. She wanted her cool, independent, rushed lifestyle back.

"How have you been?" she asked. She was dead tired. It had been another chemo week and she was on her worst day, Day Three after treatment. It had taken all of the willpower in the world to call in sick to work that day, but she hadn't had a choice. It took so much energy to even walk from her bedroom to the bathroom.

"I'm fine. And you? Are you getting over your cold?"

Cold? What cold? She realized that she must have been telling him white lies again. She cleared her throat. "For the most part."

"Well, when you're completely over it, we should probably do something? Maybe get some dinner or something else."

She sighed and rubbed her itchy scalp and ignored the feel of thinning hair. The thought of food made her want to vomit. "Okay. I can't promise anything. . . . You know, work and all."

"Wow," Shawn said. "For a while there I thought I was making progress."

"No. You are!" Tari blurted out a little bit too eagerly for her tastes. "I mean, I really want to go out, I'm just not feeling too up to it."

He laughed. "Good. I'll see you at rehearsal in a few days?"

She said yes, but the way she felt at that moment, she didn't even know if she'd survive through the night. She hung up the phone and pulled the covers over her head. *Why is it that when I finally meet a nice guy, I'm too sick to even enjoy it?*

First things first, though, she thought.

Two days later, she had finally come up with a plan to get rid of her parents. The last straw was when she crawled home from work and found some old lady cooking in her kitchen. She'd run to the living room, where her parents sat watching television.

"Mom, who's that in my kitchen?"

"Oh, that's Sister Walsh. She wanted to come over and have dinner and a prayer meeting when you got home from work."

Huh? What? "Mom! I'm tired. And the last thing I want to do now is eat, never mind have a prayer meeting with some strange lady."

"Tari, keep your voice down!" Coletta hissed. "Sister Walsh is an ordained minister. She just wants to pray for you."

Is she out of her mind? Tari wondered. "Mom, I'm going upstairs to my room, and I don't want to be bothered!"

Coletta looked at her daughter in shock. "But you can't do that! You'll hurt her feelings."

"What about my feelings? I'm sick as a dog, Mom. Why didn't you call me, and ask me about this?"

Coletta shook her head, flabbergasted. "I didn't think you'd mind. And you told me to stop calling you at work."

Tari clenched her fists. Why even bother arguing this further? "I'm going upstairs. Give Sister Walsh my apologies."

As she walked up the staircase she could hear her father saying, "I told you not to do that."

That day she'd decided they had to go, and tomorrow was the day she would tell them. *Once they're gone I'll start to feel like my old self again*, she thought.

The three sat at Tari's dining table, eating a Sunday dinner that Coletta had cooked. A belly-deep desire drove Tari wild as she sat, mouth watering, eating pita bread and hummus while her parents devoured fried chicken and baked macaroni and cheese.

"Mom, you guys should probably think about going home soon." She couldn't help it. The teasing aroma of the food she would not allow past her lips made her say it.

Coletta stopped, midbite. "I think it will be better if we stay till the end of the chemo."

"Mom, that's not necessary. I'm already halfway through and the doctor said as long as I'm consistent with the shots and the antinausea pills I won't have any problems."

Coletta sighed. Even she understood that she'd outstayed her welcome. "But what if something happens to you and you're here all by yourself?"

"Mom, Melinda's ten minutes away. And Rebecca can be here in less than twenty. I'll be fine. Besides, don't you guys have stuff to do back there?"

They were silent, polite perhaps, but Tari knew her parents. They wanted to go home, too, though they would be reluctant to admit it. They probably missed their church, their friends, their house. She felt guilty for getting sick and taking their retirement away from them. It wasn't only that she wanted them out of her hair. She didn't want to cheat them out of their normal lives, too. At least that's what she told herself. Deep down, she knew she wanted the hovering to stop. She wanted Coletta to stop answering her phone. And she wanted their friends to stop dropping by with food and prayers.

"Well, if you're sure . . ." her father said.

Coletta glared at her husband. "William, you can go home. I'll stay with her!"

Tari was horrified at the thought. Her father served as buffer between the two of them. With her and Coletta alone in the house, who knew how long she would last before committing herself to a mental institution?

"No, Mom. Please. If I need you, I'll send you a plane ticket, okay?"

Coletta sighed but did not make any promises either way.

As the night died down insomnia showed up, dependable as the mail, and Tari reached for the surety of her laptop. That flat silver little box opened up a world where someone else was always awake and there was always something worth talking about. And Marla29 was there again. Tari noticed that she seemed to be in good spirits, despite her recent weeklong hospitalization for a high fever and mysterious viral infection.

I'm so glad to be home from that stinky hospital, Tari. I swear. The people on the oncology floor are either these elderly, sickly people or these little kids with leukemia and other types of scary cancers. It's so depressing. I felt so guilty. I just wanted to be away from them. I had to keep reminding myself that I'm a cancer patient, too. I'm not better or different from them.

Tari typed quickly, echoing Marla's feelings and telling her about her own experiences in the "chemo room."

I feel so selfish for not feeling some type of kinship with them, Tari typed. We all have the same killer disease. But just being around them makes me feel worse off. Even with all this going on, I can't believe I still manage to be a shallow snob.

Blech! You're too hard on yourself, Marla wrote back.

Tari wasn't so sure. Instead she turned the topic back toward Marla and how she was feeling.

I just want to be among the land of the living again, Marla wrote. I so want to be over this infection so I can go back to work. I don't care how funny they look at me. Some of the girls there are actually saying that they're jealous because I've lost so much weight. Can you believe that? I'd rather be fifty pounds overweight than to have this freaking disease, Tari. I'm so tired of cancer. So tired of all these stupid pills, blood tests, nasty chemo, doctor's appointments; I'm just sick of all of it. I want my life back.

Tari wiped her eyes. Marla, don't get mad at me for saying this. But maybe you should go home for a bit. My folks are here for a few weeks and it's the best thing that's happened so far. Yes, they drive me crazy sometimes. But it's so nice having them to spoil me and take care of me. I felt less scared and less alone. Since I got this thing, my house has just seemed so big and empty. I don't know what I would have done without them here. Just take a few weeks off from work. Let your docs give you a bunch of meds and just go home to your folks.

Marla's response came minutes later. Tari, I took a while to answer because I just can't stop crying. I just don't know what to do. A part of me is scared to go home. I'm so afraid that if I go back to Georgia, I'll never ever come back to New York. When I think of back home, all I think about is my warm room with my Barbies stacked up in a corner, my dad taking me fishing, and my mom and me baking pies on Saturday afternoons. Yes, I know it sounds corny. I want to go so bad sometimes it hurts. But I'm just so afraid that I'll get so comfortable there that I'll never come back. That I'll never want to stand in front of another mean old judge again; never want to go on another date with another shallow, critical Manhattan guy; never get another credit card bill from Bergdorf's. You know? All the stuff that I thought I wanted so much when I was in college and law school. The big-city life. Now that I'm sick, I'm scared that I don't want it anymore. And going home will be kinda like I'm surrendering. You know? 'Cause I really don't think I'll come back if I ever leave New York.

Tari typed furiously. And what would be wrong with that, Marla? If being home is what makes you truly happy, that's where you should be. The dreams we had when we were in college, well, after a while real life shows us that they were just that. Dreams. We change. Things change. I know I'm definitely tired of competing for and chasing after stories that just fizzle out and die after a couple of weeks. And once I get better, I'm not doing that again, even if it means I get stuck writing obituaries for the rest of my life. I don't think it would be surrender if you went back home. It would be your way of being true to who you really are. Who said you couldn't practice law in Savannah anyway?

I'm thinking about it, Tari. I'm really going to consider it and give it some thought.

Tari wiped her eyes as she logged off the computer. Had she really typed those things? The more she thought about it, the lighter her chest felt. Yes, she'd said it and meant every word. She was darned tired of all that running, trying to have the perfect career, the perfect body, the perfect everything. Nobody would give her a medal for getting through another chemo treatment. And that was a zillion times harder than getting on page one every day or making it through kickboxing class or fitting into those size four pants.

It wasn't anything Rebecca or Melinda wouldn't have

told her, but seeing it in the mirror of Marla's life made it clearer because Marla *knew*.

Over several late nights of mutual sleeplessness they had formed a bond that made them forget that they even couldn't point each other out in a crowd.

Chapter

38

William Shields had managed to keep his wife so busy with packing and making all the travel arrangements that she seemed to forget she was leaving her sick daughter to fend for herself. Therefore Coletta appeared a bit dazed as she stood in the airport terminal, her large frame slumped under her worries. Tari tried to be reassuring and put on the brave face she usually reserved for work these days. She wanted that woman on that next plane out of the country.

"Tari, if anything, anything, happens, call me first, okay?" Coletta said, holding her daughter's hands in hers as they stood near the security check point. "Don't wait so long like you did the last time."

Tari nodded. "I will, Mom. I mean it." She looked her mother squarely in the eye. She would try, she thought. To stop resisting, to be more accepting, softer. To let Coletta help her.

"Your hair is really long," Coletta said, smoothing her hand down Tari's hair. "It seems to be hanging on."

Tari smiled. It was thinning, though, she wanted to say.

Melinda stepped in and hugged Coletta. "Thanks, Mom," she said, "for coming."

Coletta looked at her oldest tenderly. "See, I behaved

myself this time." Melinda restrained herself from crying as she hugged her mother good-bye. "Me, too, Mom."

A momentary panic struck Tari as she watched her parents disappear beyond the security gate. What had she just done? She'd be going home to an empty house with just her breath, her footsteps, her puttering to fill its vast spaces. She fought an irrational urge to call them back, to say, *I made a mistake. Stay.*

"Let's go," Melinda said.

They were silent as they pulled out of the airport and into a tepid, gray afternoon. Tari pushed work out of her mind as the *Statesman*'s building loomed on the downtown skyline. Joe had been understanding when she'd asked for yet another day off because of her "virus." She just couldn't stand to be there, not when her body was erupting like a volcano, unpredictably and violently, every hour or so. The hot flashes would leave her physically spent, with sweat pouring down the sides of her face, her chest shiny, her blouse sticking to her back. Mariska had noticed and looked away, embarrassed. Tari didn't know what to do.

"I'm not going to miss her." Melinda interrupted Tari's thoughts.

"Are you ever going to make your peace with her?" Tari asked as they were swallowed by the brand-new tunnel heading toward I-93 south. "I thought you guys were starting to get along. Or was that just for me?"

Melinda sniffed. "I've made peace with the fact that she'll never approve of the choices I've made."

"Choices or choice?"

Melinda shifted in the passenger seat. "She's just so self-righteous. The way she looks at Michael . . . He's my husband, her son-in-law, for goodness' sake. She's just so condescending to him."

"Maybe she's taking her cues from you?" Tari ventured, chafing at the bottleneck of vehicles on the roadway and surprised that rush hour seemed to start way before three in the afternoon these days. Who were these people, and how in heck did they get out of the office so early?

"And what does that mean?"

"Well, Mel, you're always mad at Michael, and it's not that hard to pick up on that. If you're not satisfied with your own husband, how do you expect her to be?"

Melinda was quiet as she mulled this over. "I just hate that she was right."

"Right about what?"

"Right that I shouldn't have married Michael. If I'd married John Sykes or Thomas Stilton—"

"Oh, please, girl!" Tari said laughing. "If you had married any of those guys, you'd really have something to hate her for then. You know you love Michael. You guys just need to tell each other what it is you want from each other. That's all. Just talk to the man. Tell him it's time he gets a job and stop playing around all day. Just be up front with him instead of trying to shame him into acting right. You've been trying to do that for years, and it ain't working."

Melinda sighed. "Tari, I've tried. He doesn't listen to me."

"Hey." Tari held up one hand. "I don't know the answer. I'm no relationship expert; that's your area. But maybe you could at least try a *different* approach from what you've been doing."

Melinda shook her head and looked out into a sea of cars. What did Tari know? The girl was right; her last relationship had been no stellar success.

"And give Mom a break. She's doing the best she can," Tari added.

Melinda turned to her. "You guys must have really gotten deep over the last few weeks."

"We did," Tari said. "It's the same story about how she raised Auntie and Uncle and all of them after Granny died, but this time I really listened when she told it. She had some rough times, girl. And I think I'm starting to see her in a totally different way now. I think she just wants us to see how easy we have it, you know?"

"I know that," Melinda said. "But her attitude still bugs the heck out of me sometimes. Such a martyr."

"What!" Tari snorted.

Melinda cast an innocent glance her sister's way.

"Melinda, you're the biggest martyr in the world!" Melinda protested.

"Okay. Truth?" It was a game they always played when they had to be brutally honest with each other.

"Truth," Melinda replied uneasily.

"I think you were just itching for a big fight with Mom because you're too afraid to deal with what's really bugging you. Michael. But it's not her fault, you know. It's not about her being right or wrong. And you have to take some of the blame. Things wouldn't have gotten this far with Michael if you hadn't let them."

Melinda didn't answer, but she knew Tari was right. She hadn't gotten what she'd wanted. She didn't get to take out all of her frustrations on her mother; those feelings were still building up inside of her. Instead she turned to the window again as Tari took Exit 18 off the expressway.

"What about that guy?" she asked, wanting to change the subject. "Shawn?"

Tari shrugged. "He's okay. Playing the bass, looking good. What else do you want to know?"

"I thought you said there might be something there," Melinda said.

"No. I said he was cute."

Silence, then, "A boyfriend might be a nice distraction."

"I can't get into that right now, Mel. I need to have things nice and simple right now."

"You think he couldn't deal with it?"

"I don't think I can deal with him dealing with it."

"Know what Mom said about him?" Melinda said.

"She talked to you about Shawn?" Tari was incredulous. "She doesn't even know him except for one conversation on the phone!"

Melinda giggled. "Her exact words were: 'I don't know what kind of man calls a woman after nine o'clock at night. American men are so ill-mannered.'"

"'Did you tell her he was born in Barbados?"

"I did." Melinda laughed. "That shut her up real quick."

They laughed. "Know what it is?" Tari said. "It doesn't matter if you or I find the most perfect man in the world, he still wouldn't be good enough."

"Yeah." Melinda giggled. "He would have to be Jesus himself for her to approve."

"Even then," Tari said, "she'd probably say he needs a haircut." They laughed, stalled in the rush-hour traffic.

CHAPTER
39

Rebecca threw ice cubes, strawberries, cantaloupe chunks, blueberries, and vanilla yogurt into the blender on Tari's kitchen counter. She salivated over the swirling concoction. No guilt in a healthy smoothie, she thought, especially right before yoga class.

Tari heard the blender's roar over the drizzling sounds of the shower, and she tried to work her stomach into some enthusiasm for sustenance. *Maybe after yoga,* she thought, closing her eyes to the lull of the warm water. It was the only activity worth looking forward to since chemotherapy had decimated her energy, throwing her beloved cardio out of the equation. Yoga made her feel just a few shades away from her old strong self, even for just that one hour. And sometimes she was able to forget that the effort would require ten hours of sleep for her body to recover, but it was well worth it.

Rebecca herself had found that she, too, was beginning to undergo a physical transformation. It wasn't consciously planned. But she did think twice before using a stick of butter in her famous pineapple upside-down cake or ginger cookies. She would shut her eyes and sterilize her taste buds with pep talks as Ravi devoured cheese puffs, deep-fried pakoras, and blankets of potato-stuffed nan. The pay-off was that she didn't feel wiped out after her yoga class anymore, her walks to and from work took less time, and she slept more soundly. Ravi, to her disappointment, did not notice the new tightness in her body, only the new lightness in her cooking.

Tari hummed in the shower. She had sung the night before, and she replayed the one-set performance in her head. And the wink from Shawn that had made her blush. That had been fun. And he had looked good, too good to allow herself to be alone with him. She'd watched him closely. He closed his eyes when he played sometimes. And he bit his lip, too. What had he been thinking about? Manny liked him a lot. Said he was talented. Tari had agreed, offhandedly, and tried to appear casual in his presence. She worried that the other guys would notice that she couldn't even look him in the eye for more than a few seconds without having to turn away. . . .

She was massaging her scalp when she felt it. The water. It was creeping up to her ankles rapidly. She pushed her face under the spurting water to rinse the shampoo off her eyes. She looked down, and pieces, chunks, of her beautiful hair lay at her feet, swimming like dark fish in her bathtub.

She opened her mouth to scream, and water from the shower went down her throat, making her cough violently. She touched her head, really touching it this time. There were spots, here and there, bald spots. And if she tugged just a little bit, more of her hair dropped into her hands in soggy pieces.

She bent down and freed the drain, gathering the clumps of hair. Water poured over her back and down the sides of her face, mixing with tears, as she picked up hair that had been on her head.

All the books she'd read said that most women lost their hair within two weeks of treatment. But it had been over a month, and she'd begun to get comfortable with its thin-ness. Maybe, just maybe, despite what the doctor said, she was in the 1 or 2 percent who could get out of this looking like a perfect ten. She had not minded too much when her oily skin became dry and yellow; makeup and moisturizer took care of that. The sore throats were constant but only mildly annoying. And the fatigue, well, she just slept more. But the hair had been her last hope. The one thing she felt that she might have held on to. And it wasn't that she wasn't trying now, all of it now in her hands.

Rebecca knocked on the bathroom door. "Tari, you okay in there?"

When Tari came out of the shower and looked at herself in the mirror, she gasped. It had to be somebody else with that crazy, lopsided haircut, long on the left, chopped short on the right, a few spots where she could see her brown scalp peeking through.

Rebecca knocked again.

"I'll be out in a few minutes. Use the downstairs bath-room if you need to." The calm in her voice surprised her.

"No, I was just worried about you. You've been in there awhile."

"I'm fine."

Tari took out a pair of scissors from a cabinet under the sink and began to make big slashes, starting from as close to the scalp as possible. She looked intently into the mirror while she did this, concentrating, wanting to do it right. She felt pieces of hair brush against her skin as they fell softly to the towel she had placed on the floor. It took less than five minutes before it was all gone.

Her arm was tired, and there wasn't much left, nothing the scissors could grab on to. Her head looked big and round, like a honeydew melon, but with a man's three-day stubble in some spots and smooth as a baby's butt in others. She ran her hand over it, and it felt rough and uneven.

"Oh, my God!" Rebecca's hand flew to her mouth as Tari entered the living room where she sat watching Saturday-morning cartoons.

"Don't cry," Tari said sternly.

Rebecca nodded, her eyes full and bright.

"I guess I'll start wearing that stupid wig today." Tari sighed. She turned around and walked up the stairs to her bedroom. As she got dressed, she evaluated. She felt betrayal, mostly. It was as if her hair had failed her—it just couldn't stay the course, it just wimped out on her. After all these years. Weak, trifling hair! She was so disappointed. She picked up the bag into which she had chucked the wet, dead strands and she tossed it in the wastebasket. Stupid hair!

"To hell with it," she said, reaching for the six-hundred-dollar wig she'd bought good-naturedly enough, hoping that she would never have need of its royal fakeness. Her insurance company called it a hair prosthesis. To the health care industrial complex, losing your hair must be equivalent to losing a limb, she thought grimly. Who decided that there would be no deductible? "It looks exactly like your hair," the woman in the shop had said when the thing had finally come in from wherever in the world they made such things. But Tari was not fooled as she looked in the mirror. The color was off. Her color was chestnut with a few randomly placed gold highlights. There was nothing random about that thing on her head. It was some kind of dark brown with deliberate highlights of the most unnatural dark gold, and it felt thick, heavy, like the wool hat she wore in the dead of winter. "To hell with it."

She pulled on her yoga pants and tank top quickly, grabbing a Gap baseball cap. "You ready?" she asked Rebecca, who had turned off the television and was sitting straight up on the couch, red eyed and sad faced.

Tari turned up the radio in the car, Dan Schorr on NPR,

to fill the air with something other than Rebecca's silence. With one hand on the steering wheel, she smoothed the wig, again and again, and after a few minutes she began to get used to its texture. She sighed. She would never be one of those women who walked around bald, proud, and happy. Call her vain, but she had to have hair. Even if it meant wearing this fake thing.

"So, what did I look like with my bald head?" Tari asked as they made their way through the deep Saturday-morning traffic at Codman Square.

"Tari, I . . . I was so shocked. What happened?"

"It just started coming off in the shower, so I cut it down all the way."

Rebecca looked ahead. "If you shaved it off, you know, like Meshell Ndegeocello, it would probably look good."

"No way," Tari said. "My face is too big for that look."

Rebecca didn't know what to say, what to do, to make Tari or herself feel better. "It's not that bad. It wasn't that bad. I . . . You should have warned me."

"I can't believe I'm having this conversation," Tari said, waiting for red to turn green at Melville Avenue.

Rebecca took a breath. "Tari, you're beautiful, and strong, and courageous. And I'm so mad this is happening to you. This is just so crazy. It's just crazy."

"I'm just pissed. Do you know how much I hate short hair? Do you know how happy I was when Halle Berry finally started to wear that weave?"

Rebecca looked at her. "Halle Berry? Either you're taking this really well or you've lost your mind."

Tari sighed. "Girl, I'm so tired of this freaking cancer and all the drama that comes with it. All these treatments, doctors, nurses, hair issues, skin issues. I'm ready to kill somebody right now. That is, if it doesn't kill me first."

Rebecca sighed. "I don't know what to say, because if I were in your shoes, I'd probably be feeling the same. But look at it this way: you're almost done with chemo, and you're still working, still basically healthy. You just have a little bit left to go and you'll have your life—and your hair—back."

Tari rolled her eyes. "You don't know how long it took to grow that hair."

"Get a weave, then."

"Rebecca, do I look like the weave type?"

Rebecca shrugged. "What's the weave type?"

Tari shook her head. "Never mind. I like the real thing."

"I see," Rebecca said, looking at Tari's wig. "Whatever."

They looked at each other and laughed. "Do you think Shawn will notice it?" Tari asked.

"He won't. Men are totally clueless about that kind of stuff."

"I hope so," Tari said, smoothing the wig again.

"So, you haven't told him what you're going through?"

"Nah. Not yet."

"Waiting for?"

"I'm waiting to get better."

Rebecca didn't answer.

"You know, I think I could really like this guy. But his timing is so off. I mean, these days I just don't want to be around a man. I'm all self-conscious, and on top of that I feel crappy. It's like my body's become my worst enemy." Tari smoothed the wig again. "Sometimes I wish I could just get another one. You know? Just call up God and say, can you send me another body? Or just trade this one in and get a new one with a perfect right boob and a sane mind."

"My right boob is not perfect either, Tari," Rebecca said. "I can show it to you."

"No, thanks," Tari said, laughing.

She was sad for her hair. Missed it terribly every time the foreign thing on her head brushed against her cheek or grazed her shoulder. But grateful that it was Rebecca who was there with her for this moment. Grateful that Coletta would not have to see her hairless and alien looking, magnifying the tragedy with her emotional outbursts. Grateful, too, that she did not have to appear weak in front of her father again and have him look at her, half worried, half bewildered. Grateful that it was just her hair she had lost. Tari smoothed her hand over the wig again. "Yeah. And my real hair. A new body with my real hair."

CHAPTER
40

The jar of superchunky peanut butter was half full, and Tari feared that she might polish off the rest of it. But it was the perfect antidote for a day that had left her exhausted and depressed. The taste, the smell of it soothed her insides, and the effect was a bubble bath for the mind. She needed that after a day in which John Weston took the lead on MetroBank again. She'd been too tired to even argue with Joe and even a little relieved when he told her to go home early.

She watched TV idly, Diane Sawyer interviewing a young, blond pop star. The girl was so . . . so young, so fembotlike with those tight abs and those teeth. And there she was, crying, because she was hundreds of millions of dollars rich and her heart had been broken and oh, the pain of it all. At first Tari couldn't turn away from this one-car wreck, wouldn't switch to something else.

"I'm not perfect," the girl was saying.

Tari moved her hand to her right breast and pulled out the thing, the contraption that she used to get her tops to fit right, so that both sides would appear even. She felt the half breast with the four-inch-long scar on it. The doctor said that she could have it "done." She didn't consider herself the kind of person to have anything "done."

"I'm not that perfect," the blond pop princess recited again, as if it were a line she'd practiced many times before a mirror, making sure that her eyes and casual body language conveyed just the right amount of modesty while she said those words.

Those words, "I'm not perfect," coming out of that young, inexperienced, pampered mouth made Tari want to throw something at the television and see smoke come out of the place where the silly girl now preened and posed for all of her adoring viewers. What in the world was wrong with these people? Why would that question even arise anyway? The girl looked nothing near perfect to Tari, with her overbleached hair, starved-out, wasted body, and desolate eyes. Nor did she sound perfect, with her off-key singing voice and her eighth-grade vocabulary. Stupid. Stupid. Tari used to really like Diane Sawyer, but the woman was fawning over some little girl who actually believed that she needed to issue a disclaimer: I'm not perfect, lest anyone be confused.

Tari was disgusted. The whole interview reminded her of that kickboxing class days ago. She had gone the day after chemo, feeling good, but mostly in her head. In a moment of sheer stupidity she misread as gutsiness, she took her usual spot in the front row. The first fifteen minutes went by smoothly enough. Her body followed along with the thumping music, giving in to Donna's commands. But thirty minutes into the class, heaviness had begun to travel from her shoulders slowly down her body. Her legs felt like twice their usual weight when she lifted them to kick. Her neck grew rigid, and her head felt as if it were slowly filling with water. She slowed her movements a bit.

Donna noticed and must have been in a particularly nasty

mood. "Don't clog up my front row if you're tired," she barked into her strap-on microphone. "You're making folks in the back tired, too."

The words stung. Tari could feel the entire class's attention shift to her as she tried to get her fading breath under control and the sweat out of her eyes. She could not keep going. Her body was screaming at her to stop. Stop right now. And she did. But she should have known better. The room began to spin. She staggered over to a side wall and leaned on it, her eyes closed. Gasping. Everything was turning black.

Donna walked over and removed her mic. "Hon, you okay?" Tari nodded, unable to talk because breath was still being expelled from her body in violent rasps. She let Donna guide her to a sitting position while the rest of the class watched. "Just sit here for a minute and rest, okay?" Donna said and ran off to continue teaching the class.

Tari sat on the floor, her knees drawn up to her chest, head on her arms. *Oh, this is rich*, she thought amid her despair and the blackness that was taking over her brain. Tari from the front row, one of the strongest in the class. Sitting on the floor. Head in her hands. Weak.

It took more than a minute—a few, to be exact—but then her head began to feel lighter and the darkness began to lift. She opened her eyes and she wasn't seeing double anymore. She almost laughed when it dawned on her that the class hadn't stopped for her. The girls, even the ones in the back row—the heavier ones with the baggy sweatpants— were still kicking and punching. She noticed that some of them threw glances her way, probably to make sure she was still alive. But she thought she saw them laughing, and she wanted to disappear into the mirrored walls forever. She thought their looks of concern were pity or, worse, could have signaled some kind of schadenfreude. *Who's in the back row now?* She walked out of the class, her body soaking with sweat, tears poking the back of her eyes, and shame in every step she took. She would never go back, she swore to herself. Never.

What was perfect, anyway? She watched the sorry confab between the pop star and Sawyer come to a giggly end. Starving yourself or working out till you dropped so you could be a size six? A four? A zero? And then hair, makeup, nails, clothes, accessories, job, boyfriend, husband, kids, house, neighborhood, SAT scores, top-tier school, Fortune 500 company, vacations, retirement, and then a well-attended funeral in a respectable cemetery. Was that what perfect was?

She would settle for a whole right breast and half the energy she used to have, she thought, as she scraped another spoonful of peanut butter from the jar.

She switched off the television; why was she wasting her time? She looked at the laptop sitting on the coffee table. Nah. She could not, would not go on that site to talk about breast cancer tonight. What she wanted now was something that felt good. Dark chocolate with almonds. A Snickers bar. Then she thought of sex. Delicious and hot with someone who really knew her and really knew what he was doing. She thought of Roger Levine. He would know. And she almost called him, selfishly disregarding his fiancée, but then she realized that he probably *would* come over. Out of pity and nothing else.

Where were these thoughts coming from, anyway? she wondered, sinking deeper into the couch. Even during healthier days she had subjugated those desires just because it had seemed a futile exercise. But now that she wanted to hide her body from the rest of the world, she found herself wanting some.

She swallowed peanut butter and allowed her mind to

roam down Carnal Lane. *I have cancer, so aren't I allowed? Shouldn't it be okay with God if I sin just this one time?* Yeah. Just to feel big, strong, rough hands all over her and a deep voice saying something sweet. She dialed.

He answered groggily, and she almost hung up when she heard his voice struggling against sleep. But he seemed a bit more awake when she said hello in a high, uncertain voice that was part acting, part embarrassment.

She decided to forget every rule written for when it came to those things, number one being the wrong of calling a man in the middle of the night. A man you were not dating. A man who was attractive and no doubt had his fair share of desperate late-night calls from women like her, lonely and afraid but trying to sound casual and hide the shame in idle chatter. Giggling and being coy. Like a teenager with delusions of being perfect.

She heard him turn his body over in bed from the way his voice heaved and then settled and the rush of breath through the receiver.

That kind of desire was wrong, she knew. Carnal, lustful, and sinful. And she had long stopped being the kind of person who made excuses for herself like, "Well, I'm only human. The spirit is willing but the flesh is weak." It had taken time and perseverance, but she had put those feelings away. She could say proudly, "I don't masturbate anymore, like I gave up cheesecake. And how in the world did I do it? It was God"—that or the same determination that made her who she was. She would conquer it, she would tell herself after every episode, breathless and ashamed. It took only six months. She prayed it out, stopped watching certain things on TV, stopped reading certain kinds of books, and before you could say the word, she no longer struggled. But Shawn threatened all of that with his goodness, his tall, beautiful goodness, especially now, in her weakness and wanting. She could hear the wariness in his voice as he held back, as she led him, or tried to lead him, down the path of iniquity.

"Do you want to get some coffee? I just really need to talk to someone right now."

He sighed, and that made her want him even more. She imagined him shirtless in his bed, with those big arms of his that could encircle her three or four times and probably swallow up her cancer and smother it into nothingness. She thought of his eyes, warm and inviting, which would tell her, *you're beautiful to me, despite that scar on that part of you that makes you a woman, and I like women with short, short, barely there hair. No, take off the wig.*

"It's late, Tari. Are you sure?"

"Yes, please, Shawn."

She waited in the twenty-four-hour Dunkin' Donuts on Morrissey Boulevard. She was two sips into her hot chocolate when he arrived. Hoyas sweatshirt and jeans, sneakers. He rubbed his head and sat next to her. Bewildered.

"Are you okay?"

She felt silly now. This was wrong, what she had done. It was almost 1:30 in the morning. Why had she gotten this man out of his bed to tend to her stupid impulses?

"I was just feeling really . . . really down. I just needed—"

He put a big hand on her small one.

He understood, he was saying, and what was it that he could do to help?

But how could she put it into words? She dug deep and furiously for the right phrase. All the words she'd learned from reading, writing, and listening could not articulate in any language: make it all go away. *It* as in what? And how to make *it* go away? He was no magician. He was a man like she was a woman. And what special powers did his maleness give him to make her *it* go away?

So she didn't speak and he stared at her as she sipped her cocoa, nauseatingly sweet. But she didn't want to betray even that with her face.

"I just don't know if I can keep on singing. I mean, I think I need to take a break for a while," she heard herself saying. It was the best she could come up with. And it sounded genuine. It was a valid concern that he could identify with. Maybe.

He only nodded and then asked why.

The unspoken other question being, *why did you have to wake me out of bed to tell me this?*

"I'm just going through a rough time right now, Shawn. Everything around me just seems to be falling apart. My health, work, everything."

He looked at her deeply, wanting her to go on and reveal more. Tari bit her lip and blinked back the tears. She did not look up, but she felt Shawn move in the tiny chair. He leaned forward and tightened his grip on her hand.

"Why don't you tell me what's going on, Tari. Tell me why you wanted me to come here."

A tear had somehow escaped and she wanted her other hand, the one he was holding, to wipe it away. She sniffed.

"I just need some . . . some strength. I was just feeling so weak."

It sounded strange to her, and she imagined it would to him. But it was the truth and she had not practiced it, had not even anticipated opening up to him in that way.

"Look at me."

Her wet eyes obeyed. When he looked at her, he did not judge her or question.

"You have strength," he said. "Remember, God says that in our weakness he makes us strong? Tari, you have strength. You just have to tap into it." His voice was steady and lacking in the kind of emotion she wanted to hear from it. But he did not remove his hand from on top of hers.

She nodded. "Thanks, Shawn. I needed to hear that."

She wiped her eyes, using a napkin, and then looked up at him and smiled, composing herself. Common sense began to flood back, washing away the dross of desire. She sat up straight.

"I've just been having a rough time." She cleared her throat, trying to regain her aloofness. "I'm sorry I woke you up. But I thought . . . I don't know what I was thinking." She was trying to salvage her pride, but she had no idea where to even start. This whole fiasco was already a major disaster, she thought. She felt embarrassed and silly. Like one of those women who revealed all their deepest psychoses to a first date and then stayed up all night wishing those words away.

"It's okay, Tari," he said. "I'm glad you called me. I've been thinking about you a lot lately. I noticed you've been looking a bit tired." His eyes were still questioning. It was as if he didn't know, couldn't see through her ploy. Most men, Tari thought, would have taken full advantage of the situation. She'd made the first move. Wasn't it his natural role to take it from there? Say *let's go to my place?* But all she got was the inquiring eyes.

"It's just something I'm dealing with. I'll be fine," she said quickly. There was no way she would tell him that she had cancer. No way in hell.

"Well, anytime you want to talk. Call me. I'm more than happy to listen. Preferably before midnight." He smiled.

She felt his eyes still on her as she climbed into her truck, her jeans, now a bit too big, creeping down her hips.

What a big mistake, she thought as she drove out of the coffee shop's parking lot. *Impulsive. Impulsive.* She had just embarrassed herself again in front him. And he had been too nice to take advantage of her.

"I'm not perfect," she said out loud as she drove up Gallivan Boulevard. Two-fifteen in the morning, going home empty-handed from a would-be booty call that she had initiated. *Aaack!* She burst out laughing.

CHAPTER
41

"You called him and asked him to meet you at two o'clock in the morning?" Rebecca's incredulous voice came through the phone. "Oh, Tari. Oh, Tari."

"Don't sound so . . . so dismayed, Becks. I know I screwed up. Okay?"

Rebecca sighed. "Well, how did it end?"

"He sent me home. But he was really nice about it." Tari laughed again, keeping her voice low so that Mariska's eavesdropping ears would not pick up a signal.

"Tar, I'm sorry. Oh, man. How awful. You should have called me instead!" Rebecca shook her head and flipped through the messages that were on her desk.

"It's no big thing," Tari said in a half whisper. "You know what the worst part was, though? He quoted a scripture to me. Here I am, trying to get this man to comfort me with his big, fine self and he's quoting the Bible to me. Talk about embarrassing. I felt like the woman at the well."

"The woman at the who?" Rebecca asked, turning her eyes to a pink message slip that was beginning to absorb most of her attention.

"Oh, it's, a prostitute in the New Testament," Tari said,

then sensed her friend's inattentiveness. "What's up with you?"

Rebecca was silent a moment, then, "Tari, you will not believe this!"

"What?"

"That woman, the recruiter from *Gourmet Today* magazine, she wants me to call her."

"Oh, my goodness, Becks! Call her. Call her now!"

Rebecca turned over the pink message slip in her hand. "I can't. What do I say?" Rebecca began to doubt herself, dreading that she would say the wrong thing, worrying that this possibly was not even what she hoped it would be.

"Girl, you hang up and call the woman right now. Do you hear me?" Tari ordered.

"Okay. Okay," Rebecca said meekly, hanging up the phone. She took a few deep breaths before she picked it up again.

Shoot, Tari thought. Rebecca was finally getting hers. And she deserved it, too. There was no doubt in her mind that Rebecca would get whatever job it was that she wanted at that fancy food rag. *But where does that leave me?* It was a selfish thought, and she quickly tried to put it out of her mind. She couldn't ignore the fact that she had alienated every single girlfriend she'd had in her adult life. Rebecca was the only one who could stand her upswings, downswings, and jagged sideways moods. Friends like that did not come along every day. She felt abandoned already. She dialed Melinda's number.

"Wow," Melinda said. "Good for Rebecca."

"Well, it's not like she's gotten the job yet," Tari said.

"I'm sure she will. She's a good writer."

"So, you wanna hear what your crazy sister did last night?" Tari said, realizing that Melinda was the last person in the world she should be telling this story.

"Oh, Lord. What did you do?" Melinda asked.

Tari told her about the late-night encounter with Shawn.

Melinda listened, not interrupting and not saying anything. When Tari was finished, she waited for the lecture.

"Are you there, Melinda?"

Melinda breathed out through her mouth. "I am here, Ms. Tari."

"Well?"

"I'm not gonna say anything. You know what you did was shady. But you're a grown woman."

Huh? What? "Melinda, are you feeling okay today?" Tari asked, laughing.

Melinda rolled her eyes. "What? You expected me to go off on you because you acted all desperate—"

"See! Acted desperate! I knew it!" Tari said triumphantly.

"Slow your roll, okay?" Melinda protested. "I'm not gonna judge you. I probably would have done the same thing."

"No, you wouldn't have," Tari said.

"True. But that's because I'm not as brave as you."

"Nice save."

"I mean it. If the guy likes you, he's not thinking about this the way you are. Let it go. So what? You felt bad; he made you feel better. That's what men are here for."

"Really?"

"I think so," Melinda said. "I hope so."

"You're a pathetic excuse for a married woman," Tari said.

"Don't I know it." Melinda laughed.

They chatted for a few minutes, and Tari gained a new perspective on the night before. It hadn't been an entirely bad thing. She had reached out, swallowed her pride and reached out, and for her that was something to laugh about.

Later, she checked e-mail blindly for the third time in five minutes. Pathetic. She could see John Weston across the room. He was on the phone, speaking into the receiver, an intense look on his face. She could recognize it. That look meant that he would be on A1 tomorrow and not her. Someone was talking to him. She felt resigned. *Let him have it.* She was tired and didn't have the energy to care anymore.

Since Bill Boggs had been subpoenaed by the attorney general's office and was prohibited from speaking to the media, she had nothing to go with except run-of-the-mill quotes from bit players in the scandal who couldn't tell her anything that would break any new ground.

The story just isn't hot news anymore, she told herself. *No one's going to care about what Weston's got.* It would be months before the state finished its investigation of the bank. She had done her job, and justice was being done. She had nothing left to give to this story, so let Weston do all the digging. She checked e-mail again, in vain.

"So, what's new with MetroBank these days?" Mariska, in one of her sudden bursts of friendliness, swiveled her chair in Tari's direction. She peered deep into Tari's drawn face, her fashionable granny glasses sliding down her nose.

"Nothing much." Tari sighed. "Just waiting for the investigation to be over." *Now please go back to your Internet shopping,* she wanted to say.

"Hmm," Mariska said primly. "Are you okay? I don't mean to pry, but you look pretty exhausted."

Tari bristled. "Just a bug I've been fighting."

Mariska turned fully around. "My husband's sister, who's a doctor over at Mass. General, well, she had this unexplained virus for what seemed like forever, and then before you know it she was hospitalized for three weeks. You should be careful, Tari. Don't work yourself too hard."

Tari nodded politely. "Thanks, Mariska. I'll try to take it easy."

Mariska then launched into a full-blown account of her husband's sister's mysterious illness, and Tari tuned her out as she felt the dreaded warmth start to spread all over her body. Sweat began to spill out of her pores.

"So, later this week?" Mariska's large brown eyes were boring into Tari's inattentive face.

"Huh?"

Mariska repeated the question. Did Tari want to have dinner or lunch sometime?

"Um . . . I don't know. We'll see. My appetite's—"

Mariska's countenance grew defensive. "I was just asking. No big deal." She turned back to her PC, then must have thought better of it. "Are you sweating? Are you okay?" She looked at Tari incredulously, as if she'd never seen sweat before.

"Uh . . . It's really warm in here." Tari began to fan herself.

"Really? I don't feel that warm. Are you sure you're okay?" Mariska looked doubtful.

"I'm fine." Tari desperately tried to change the subject. "Yes, let's do dinner sometime. It should be fun."

Mariska's face softened. "It's on me. I know you've had a rough time lately." She paused. "With the virus and all."

Tari smiled but silently wondered what Mariska knew as they both returned to pretend work.

She was doing her best to fake it, but the chemo drugs were draining her, allowing her only enough energy to put in a lackluster performance at work every day and then go home straight to bed. She could hear the whispers in the office about her haggard appearance and her frequent sick days. She deflected their misguided compliments—"My God, you're so skinny"—with offhand jokes. But questions were being asked behind her back about her physical and mental health. And Mariska sat right next to her. Maybe she'd overheard some of the hushed conversations with Rebecca, Melinda, the doctor. . . . She lifted her eyes from the news wires as she heard the quick, heavy footsteps of Joe Martone.

"Tari, do something with your face, okay? You need to do TV today." He stood in front of her, trying to hide his dismay at seeing the mask that had taken the place of Tari's face.

"Are you kidding?" she asked wearily. Another MetroBank executive, the chief financial officer, had resigned. *Shoot. Why isn't John Weston doing the TV spot?* She was in no mood to answer that anchor's questions.

"Don't give me a hard time, okay? You have ten minutes." He lowered his voice and narrowed his eyes. "Go put some makeup on or something."

But five minutes later, Tari was kneeling over the toilet in the ladies room, retching. This time she could not blame herself for not taking the pills. She wracked her brain for an explanation, and then it hit her. The tuna sandwich. It must have been the mayonnaise. She could barely lift her head to look at her watch, but she knew that the time was flying by and that she would miss her slot on the news roundup.

A few minutes later someone knocked on the door of the stall. "Are you okay in there?"

She didn't recognize the voice, probably one of the college students who worked in the newsroom. "I'm fine," she croaked, waiting for the next round of dry heaving.

Another fifteen minutes of violent retching went by before she walked out of the ladies room. Her throat was sore and her body felt as if it had been dropped from an airplane. She looked down the length of the newsroom through red, irritated eyes and saw Joe Martone talking with Steve Bluesteed. John Weston was sitting in the TV booth, doing the spot that she'd been asked to do. Her chest began to pound. She wasn't sure whether she should hurry over and explain herself or run off and hide.

Instead she walked slowly to her desk. She felt eyes on her from other desks as she moved down the hallway, her head still swimming. She had barely sat down when Roger Levine came rushing over.

"Tari!"

She looked up at him.

"You were throwing up in the bathroom?"

She didn't answer. But she realized that her suspicions must have been true. The students could spread gossip faster than a supermarket tabloid in a beauty salon.

Before she could explain herself, Joe hurried over and Roger bolted, sensing a showdown was about to occur.

"So what was that about?" Joe demanded.

"I had some bad tuna at lunch and I got sick. I'm sorry," Tari said flatly.

Joe looked at her long and hard. "I don't like this new attitude, Tari. I'm not liking it one bit. And I'm not the only one who's noticing."

"What attitude, Joe? I told you, I'm sick."

"Whatever you want to call it, I don't like the constant calling in sick, leaving early, and the way you walk around here looking like a zombie. If you need help, you should come out and ask before it's forced on you."

Tari sighed as Joe walked away, refusing to look her in the eye.

She'd been thinking about telling, coming out of her cancer closet. But pride kept her mouth shut. She saw the way they looked at her now, the questions they asked silently as she walked by. "What's wrong with her?" And she could only see it getting worse if she ever came clean. They would pity her, see her as less competent, see it as justice for that one time five years or two years ago when she said something that hurt their feelings or put them down. They'd probably say it was probably good for her stuck-up little butt. No, she couldn't tell them. Besides, this would be over soon enough. No one had to know.

CHAPTER
42

Melinda's breakthrough came in the most unusual way. It was the day of Tari's last chemo treatment, a Friday that she decided she would just spend with her little sister and forsake all of her other obligations. The house was quieter than usual because Jared was off at Bible camp and Taylor really had no one to torment for those three weeks, so she was off playing quietly in her room.

Melinda's goal, once the summer began, had been to schedule more time just for herself, and today would be her "me" day. But it was hard. There were things that needed to be done. Stephanie had been breathing down her neck about the two panels she was supposed to lead at the women's conference. And she needed to find a new ballet school for Taylor; her old teacher had moved to Philadelphia and there was something just plain weird about the new instructor.

All these things tugged at her mind, telling her that she should just stay home and take care of business. But no. She had to ignore the guilt and at least attempt to reconcile it to the fact that it was almost impossible for Michael to tear himself away from the golf course when the temperature rose above seventy degrees. He didn't care about what needed to be done, so why should she? His three-times-a-week game had stretched to four and sometimes five, and their ensuing fights contributed a stoniness to the silence in the house.

And she'd asked him nicely. "Just one day, Michael. For me. And Tari. Just watch the baby for one day." His answer was, "Didn't you and Tari just go shopping the other day?" Melinda had gritted her teeth and held her ground.

But it was too bad that one day, today, was a perfect late-July day, not a cloud in the sky, no breeze to throw off his game, the temperature a balmy eighty-two. A day like that, well, they just didn't come any old day. It was a day to play golf. Fore!

And the fight was on.

"You know, my mother was right about you," she said, stomping off to the kitchen after he flat-out refused to cancel his game.

"What's that supposed to mean?"

"That you'll never grow up and take responsibility."

"Oh, just cause I want to play golf means I won't take responsibility?"

"You play golf almost every day, Michael. Every day! And I work every day!"

"We agreed—"

But she cut him off. "Don't give me that we agreed crap! You're a man, aren't you? You're supposed to be taking care of me. Of us. At least you should want to. How could you just want to live off me like that?"

"Live off you? I'm raising my kids—"

"Raising your kids? You mean babysitting your kids. When was the last time you took Jared out to play golf with you? You don't even make sure he does his homework. I have to make sure his work is done when I get home from working all day."

"Every time I try to help, you criticize. I never do anything the way you want me to."

"Oh, cry me a river, Michael! You're a pathetic loser. I made a huge mistake when I married you!"

She looked into his face, which was aghast, his mouth gaping, shame in his eyes, his shoulders slumped.

"You're setting a bad example for your son. You're not showing him how to be a man," she snarled. "You should be ashamed of yourself!"

She'd thought these things in her angriest moments but never imagined they would ever boil over to her surface and spill out of her mouth. But she wanted him to hurt. She wanted him to feel how she felt sometimes: abused, tired, and humiliated. And as she looked at his wounded face, she felt satisfied.

She ran up the stairs and grabbed her overnight bag. She slammed the door behind her, and she didn't tell him when she would be back.

"Girl, we gotta go somewhere," Melinda said breathlessly as Tari slowly climbed into the car.

Tari looked at her sister. "Where? I can't go anywhere in the state I'm in. I'm not going anywhere that's farther than fifteen minutes away from my doctor."

Melinda looked at her. "I thought we were gonna celebrate. It's your last chemo."

Tari shook her head. "Not today." She had cried when that final IV was taken out of her vein. Jubilation and relief did not contain enough meaning to define what was in her heart. She'd hugged the nurses and gamely recited the poem given to all chemo patients at the cancer center at the end of treatment. The thing had been so corny.

I leave this place today
Stronger than I came

Ready to live life
With a sharpened aim

The worst phase was over, the doctor had said. "Your hair should start coming back in a couple of weeks." The only treatment left was six weeks of radiation therapy. She had cleared the biggest hurdle. But Tari did not have the energy to jump for joy, and Melinda's mood was wearing on her. All she wanted was the comfort of her own bed and to be away from Melinda's marital drama.

"Well, I'm going somewhere," Melinda said resolutely. "I'll celebrate for you."

Tari had listened to every detail of Melinda's fight with Michael as she'd sat captive in the chemo room, grunting and nodding at all the right moments. But she'd been only half listening. She had been taking in the sights and surroundings, wondering how it was that she had managed to do this every two weeks for four months and not lose her mind. She so wanted to be out of there, away from the sickness, the needles, the drugs. She had no interest in her sister's prattling. Melinda would have to find a way to solve her marital problems on her own.

"I think you should," Tari said. "It's Friday. Drive down to New York for the weekend. It'll give you time to think." Tari didn't care whether or not she was making sense, but at least she was saying what Melinda wanted to hear.

"Really?" Melinda's uncertainty began to fade as she began to picture the escape. "Do you think so? He can watch the baby for the weekend. Right? And Jared's with his friends at camp in Carver; he doesn't need me."

Tari sighed. "Melinda, stop trying to rationalize it, okay? Just go. You need to go off on your own for a couple of days. I'm scared of what you'll do to that man if you go back to that house anyway."

Melinda laughed. "Girl, I almost hit him over the head

with a pan this morning. Made me so mad. Telling me he can't watch his own daughter and to take her with me. Like I can take my daughter to see her aunt getting chemotherapy.

"You know what I'll do?" Melinda said as they approached Tari's house. "I'm doing this in style. I'm gonna go jump on the US Air shuttle, stay at the Paramount, get room service, maybe go to a play, get a little shopping done. Oh, Tari," she said, her voice brimming with excitement, "I wish you could come with me!"

Tari smiled wanly. "Me, too. But the only place I'm wishing for right now is bed."

Melinda sighed. "I understand. But I'm so excited. I'm doing something fun. Something bad. We could be like Thelma and Louise." She put her hand in front of her mouth and giggled like a little girl who had just spilled her fruit punch on white carpet.

Tari's sparse eyebrows furrowed. Thelma and Louise? "I don't think you're doing something bad. But if that's what makes you happy, then go ahead and think that. And I'm not the one having man trouble, so I'm not getting involved in your mess." She looked at Melinda and shook her head. The girl was all slaphappy and giddy, as if she had just discovered the word *freedom*. If that's what it was like to be married, Tari thought, then she really wasn't missing anything.

Melinda sat in the terminal at Logan Airport waiting for the boarding call for the three o'clock flight to LaGuardia. Her heart was pounding. *It's only for a weekend,* she kept telling herself. She pictured Michael sitting dejectedly in front of the television set watching ESPN, his perfect golf day evaporating right before his eyes. And her little baby daughter missing her mommy.

On an impulse, she dialed home from her cell. Five rings and no answer. She dialed again. No answer. Where was he?

She called his cell phone. He answered after the sixth ring. He was outside. She could hear a breeze whistling through the receiver and male voices in the background.

"Michael, where are you?"

She could hear the hesitation in his voice. Then she heard a familiar voice in the background, one belonging to Sam Albrecht, his favorite golf partner. "Busted!" She could hear Sam laughing.

He was on the links. Her heart fell.

"Michael, where's my daughter?" she asked, panic in her voice. She feared the worst, her baby left all alone in the house.

He sighed, her tone telling him that he had been caught. "She's fine, okay? I paid the babysitter next door to watch her for a couple hours."

Melinda felt relief and then anger. She felt sheer disgust for her husband's childishness, his inability to deny his whims. That he could not even take one day. One afternoon.

She hung up without saying good-bye and walked to join the line for the first-class passengers on the flight heading to New York City.

Tari lit candles and placed them around the bathtub. She grabbed a three-week-old copy of the *New York Times Magazine* and placed it at the head of the tub.

Before she stepped in, she removed the hat she'd worn all day that had made her scalp itch and sweat in the summer heat. She thought she could see the scattered sprouts of stubble darkening her shiny scalp. But maybe it was just wishful thinking. It did not immediately bring tears to her eyes anymore to see the nearly bald head in the mirror. She had almost grown used to that alien-looking person looking back at her. She had made peace with that girl, the sick one who was now so tired physically and mentally that she had no energy to smile even though she actually looked funny. Ha-ha funny. Her body itself had lost most of its tightness and muscle tone and her skin was now slack; her gym-bunny body was now just average, her entire being frail and vulnerable. Five months had been all it took.

She wondered if she would ever be the same again as she stepped into the hot water. If she would ever feel normal, look normal. If the tingling in her lower legs would ever go away. She wondered what it would be like to not feel dread every two weeks before chemo treatments, to not have an army of prescription bottles standing sentinel on the kitchen counter, to not have to worry about white blood cell counts. What was normal, anyway? She could barely remember her life before this cancer coup d'état. Health. Hair. What would it be like to have those things again? Could she now throw away her thermometer and stop fearing an infection like the one that might or might not have done in Marla29?

She paged through the thin, glossy magazine. She remembered Sundays BC, before cancer, reading the *Times*'s Books, Fashion & Style, and then the *Globe;* she'd save the *Times* magazine for last—always with a chocolate chip cookie and Irish cream coffee. But cookies still tasted like backyard mud cakes. And she saw the devil in every tempting cup of coffee, strongly suspecting that her years-long addiction had somehow brought all of this on.

But she felt grateful and tried to tell herself that she should be proud. She'd made it through the toughest part without getting herself too sick, not even once. She'd stuck to the schedule and finished on time. No one at work knew. And that was worth celebrating, she thought. Once she had the energy to do so. The phone rang, and her heart rapped at her chest wall when she answered.

It was Shawn.

He wanted to know what she was doing.

"Uh . . . I'm in the tub."

He paused. "Do you . . . Are you heading out some-where?"

"Uh . . . no."

"Did you want to get dinner or something later?"

She looked at the wooden clock on her beige bathroom wall. It was six-ten. She had no appetite. But she wanted to see him. But then seeing him could rouse all kinds of emotions.

"Are you there? Tari?"

"Yes, I'm here."

If she saw him, she might just open her mouth and tell him everything. She couldn't see herself sitting across from him and not telling him, forcing him to take on her burden. "I'm sorry, Shawn. I'm not up to going out tonight. Maybe another time."

"OK. Another time. But this rejection thing . . . It's not a lot of fun," he said. "It's really bad for my ego. Just so you know."

She laughed weakly. "I'm not rejecting you, Shawn. I really am just exhausted. You don't know how much I'd love to go out tonight."

"Right, your three-month-old cold."

She ignored the sarcasm in his voice. "Once I get better, I'll cook dinner for you. How's that?"

"Can I have that in writing?"

"You have my word, Shawn," she said.

He sounded disappointed as he said good-bye. She picked up her magazine but her eyes didn't work; they wouldn't cooperate with her brain to join the words together so they'd make sense. She threw the magazine on the floor and closed her eyes. *Another time*, she thought.

Later, as she piled the covers on top of her, she wondered

if she'd made the right decision. Maybe she should have dragged herself out of the tub and gone out with him. *Then I wouldn't be here all by myself. Why didn't I go to New York with Melinda? I just need to sleep*, she thought. *Tomorrow, everything will be clearer and better. And I'll be less tired. Darn! Why didn't I go out with him?*

CHAPTER
43

Rebecca sat straight up, belted into her aisle seat on the US Air flight back to Boston. She was only pretending to read the article titled, "Edam vs. Gouda: Even You Can Tell the Difference." The slight variations between Dutch cheeses was the furthest thing from her mind.

Once again she'd landed herself in serious trouble. She had acted before thinking. The interview that she'd spent days prepping for, grilling herself on her knowledge of obscure marinades for game meat and which wines went best with whatever was on the table, had turned out instead to be a big party. The editorial assistant who'd picked her up from LaGuardia had been friendly to the point of sisterly. On the way into Manhattan, they'd stopped at Starbucks so the woman could pick up her customary midmorning lemon bar and mocha something-or-other. The editor who'd interviewed her was a young-looking and even younger-acting fortysomething, single, urbane type who just "loooooved" everything about Rebecca, most importantly the pieces that she had written for the *Globe, Boston Magazine,* and the *Improper Bostonian.* The other staffers were friendly, all members of the food snob sorority, and Rebecca immediately felt as if she had come home after a long sojourn in the foreign, hostile land of career purgatory. There were fancy kitchen gadgets and utensils speckled through the messy, homelike office and two small kitchens, equipped with the most high-tech ovens, small appliances, and refrigerators that Rebecca had ever seen. She was in foodie heaven, and she did not want to leave.

The following day, the editor picked her up from her hotel room near Times Square in a Town Car and whirled her off to one of the city's fashionable bistros, where Rebecca had the most sinful omelette she'd ever tasted. Lunch was the same; a good table at La Boite en Bois on Sixty-Eighth. She had the seafood in puff pastry, the editor had the saucisson en brioche.

They offered her the job on the spot, and she accepted it without thinking. And how could she have not? she asked herself. In two days she'd glimpsed the life that she always knew she was meant to live. Not the one her parents had mapped out for her in a stuffy, cutthroat law office. Not the compromise she had created, begging to get her work published as she wasted away in a thankless, brain-numbing job. This was it, the big time, what she was meant to do. But she feared that tying up the loose ends would not be easy.

The plane landed and she walked toward the airport exit, her apprehension growing with each step. She had no idea what she would tell Ravi. What she had done was wrong on so many levels. That she had not checked with him first before making a decision that would affect them so profoundly was at the top of that list. The long subway ride into Boston, Blue Line to Orange Line to Red Line, offered her no more clarity than she'd had when she first walked out of the sleek offices of *Gourmet Today*.

An hour and a half later, her shoulders drooped and her head felt heavy as she took timorous steps up the staircase that led to their apartment. Ravi had cooked pasta, and she could smell the tomato sauce as she walked into the apartment. It looked small and dreary compared to the plush hotel room she'd slept in the previous two nights. She wondered why they had never even discussed getting some real furniture instead of the old orange couch that looked like a giant, wet tabby cat and the blue leather armchair, which had a huge slash the entire length of its armrest. It occurred to her that her valiant effort to make this place a home had not amounted to much.

"Babe, how did it go?" Ravi called out from the kitchenette.

She dropped her garment bag on the orange couch and followed the aroma to where he stood over a pot of burbling red sauce.

"It was incredible." She hugged him from behind.

He turned around to kiss her.

"So, I'm guessing they offered you a job," he said lightly, stirring the sauce with a wooden spoon they'd picked up at a yard sale on Brattle Street. It had a green plastic handle shaped like a shamrock leaf. It was ugly, she decided. "They did."

"And?"

"I want to take it."

She was looking at him but he was not looking at her. The sauce had his full attention.

"I thought about it, Rav. You have only one year left in business school. And then you'll come meet me there. We'll get a place in Brooklyn. Brooklyn Heights."

He laughed. "A year? You say that as if it's a couple of weeks. And what about staying here and waiting for the *Globe* to come through?"

"Ravi, I'll be up here every weekend. The *Globe*. They may never call."

"Did you already accept the job, Rebecca? Because you're sounding as if this is a done deal."

CHAPTER

44

The house was quiet when Melinda walked in. She had taken the first flight back, desperate to see her baby and to a smaller degree Michael. But they were not home. She walked through the neat living room; the kitchen was clean, no dishes in the sink. She walked up the stairs and picked up one of Taylor's dolls. The bedroom was tidy, bed made. She went back downstairs and made tea.

The one and a half days away had not changed a whole lot for her. Tari had been wrong. Actually, she had been wrong. This hadn't been the great escape she'd hoped it would be. She hadn't left the hotel once. The anticipation and excitement evaporated once she landed in LaGuardia. As the cab crawled into Manhattan, she saw the big, bad city and at once she missed her cozy house, her precocious little girl, and the presence of her husband. She was too ashamed to admit it, but she felt nervous about hitting the town on her own. Fear crept into her mind. What if she were attacked, robbed or worse? She tried to remember the last time she'd ever done anything like that, and she could not recall a single episode in her life when Michael was not at her side. She had taken his presence for granted, and in that brief moment when he was no longer there, she felt alone and scared.

She thought of Tari that night as she lay in that unfamiliar, too-firm king-sized hotel bed. *This is the kind of thing that Tari excells at; not me.* She cried when she thought of what her little sister had gone through. On her own. Melinda knew that her own strength stretched far but had its limits, because no matter how bad things got with Michael, she knew she would never, could never leave. She had never been alone, not in that sense anyway, and she didn't want to be. She needed her family; without them she didn't even feel that she could exist.

A key turned in the lock.

"Melinda?" Michael's voice boomed from the foyer.

She walked out of the kitchen, cup in hand. He was all dressed up, and he had dressed the baby well, too.

"You guys went to church without me?" she asked, holding her arms open for Taylor. She felt victorious at the relief in his eyes. *At least he missed me.* She had fought herself all weekend, resisting the urge to call him just to hear his voice.

He shrugged. "I wasn't sure when you'd be back. You didn't say in your message." He was humble, apologetic, his eyes down. She had expected him to be angry, to accuse her of abandoning her family on a whim. But he just stood there, his eyes traveling back and forth from her face to the floor. Was that fear she read in his body language?

Melinda buried her face in her daughter's unruly hair. "I missed you so much, honey bunny." She had missed Michael, desperately. But she would not fling herself into his arms. He would not get off that easy. Michael stood awkwardly, watching his wife bond with her daughter.

He had played golf while Melinda was gone. But he was terrified when he came home to the empty house and that message from her: "I'm not coming home tonight and probably won't be back until Monday. And don't you dare leave my daughter at the neighbor's house all weekend."

He'd sulked around the house at first, but before he knew it Taylor absorbed most of the gloom he felt about Melinda's wrath. He played with his daughter, read her stories, tried to style her hair and failed, made her breakfast, and was startled that this five-year-old little girl made such great company.

"I did some thinking while you were gone," he said.

"Yeah?" Melinda asked, still playing with Taylor.

He folded his arms and cleared his throat. "Some of the things you said really, really hurt. I didn't know you felt that way."

She looked at him. She knew she'd been cruel, but she had been right. He wouldn't guilt her into taking it back.

"I like being with my daughter, Melinda. A lot of guys don't get to spend time with their kids the way I do, and I know I'm lucky. I may not be the best father in the world, but I'm here for them. That's why I think you're wrong . . . about that and a lot of other things. Just because I don't do things the way you want them done doesn't mean I don't do them right. You're not the final say on what's right or wrong."

"I didn't say I was."

"Let me finish," he said, holding up his hand. "And don't ever call me names again, especially in front of my daughter. I know you were angry, but don't ever think that you have the right to insult me because you earn more than I do. I'm your husband and I deserve respect."

"I'm sorry," Melinda said softly. "Taylor go upstairs," she said, putting the baby down. Shame made her want to hide her face from him. *But I was right*, a tiny voice still insisted in her head, *he doesn't pull his weight around here.* She gritted her teeth and tried to force out an apology. "I shouldn't have said those things in front of Taylor. But this is not what we agreed to, Michael." She watched Taylor scurry up the stairs. "Everything's just too much for me now."

He cut in. "I know you're going through a lot with Tari being sick, and I understand that. It makes me scared, too. But we have to keep this marriage together, Melinda. I know what your mother thinks about me, and I don't care about that. But you can't all of a sudden go to her side because things aren't going your way. When we got together we decided it was till death do us part, and this running-away stunt you pulled this weekend. . . . Don't let it happen again."

"I . . . didn't run away."

"Right. You were trying to teach me a lesson," he said.

"Michael, I just wanted you to know how I feel sometimes. I'm so tired all the time, with the kids, work, and everything else."

"But, Melinda, you put a lot of that stuff on yourself. Nobody's forcing you to be in all those church groups. Tari's not forcing you to worry about her. Hell, you probably worry about her more than she worries about herself. Why can't you just chill? Handle the things you can handle and let everything else go?"

"But that's what you don't get, Michael. I can't just chill. Know why? Because you're chilling all the time. Somebody has to worry, somebody has to pay the bills, somebody has to stress about making sure the kids get picked up, that our family is represented well in church. If we're both chilling, none of that stuff is ever gonna get done!"

"Why do we have to be the best at everything, then?" he asked angrily. "Why are you always putting all this pressure on us? To impress your friends?"

"No, Michael. I want to be the best I can be." She pointed to her chest and she felt that her voice was about to explode.

"The best mother, best wife, best therapist, best sister, best daughter. That's how my parents raised me, and there's nothing wrong with that. I know I can't ever be perfect, but that doesn't mean I shouldn't try to always give everything my best." She paused as she remembered their dreams, the plans they'd made, years ago when this fight, this wedge, didn't even seem possible. "I thought you were the same way, too, when we married. I thought you wanted to build something with me, Michael. I thought our family, our marriage, our lives would be a powerhouse because the two of us would be giving our best. But I'm the only one trying, and now you're telling me to chill?"

He sighed. "I talked to Pastor John today about substitute teaching at the Adventist school. . . . Math. Fifth grade."

Melinda took a deep breath and nodded. He was avoiding what she said and throwing her a crumb. It was a start, but he would have to do more than just make promises. This would not placate her. "It sounds like a good opportunity."

"But you're going to have to give some things up so we can spend more time together as a family," he said. "If we're both going to be working, things have to change in this house."

"I want things to change, Michael." *Fine,* she thought. *Let him assert the one shred of authority he thinks he wields around here.*

"I'll give up the women's group," she added quickly. And she couldn't wait to call Stephanie Strong to tell her that she quit. For good this time. "But you're going to have to cut down on golf and your gym time."

"Fine. All right," Michael said. She could see something in his eyes that was still defiant, and it bothered her.

"So, are we gonna be okay?" Michael asked. "I'm tired of this arguing."

"I don't know."

"You don't know?"

"Michael, we've lost a lot of ground in the last few years. I have a lot of anger. It's going to take some time before I can honestly say we're okay."

"What do I need to do, then?"

"Help me. Take some of this load off my shoulders."

"I'm trying. I'm going to try my best."

"Okay," she whispered, looking at an ever-widening gap between them, hoping that this time he really meant it but not getting her hopes too high. *We have to be okay*, she thought, *for my kids, my life, for the vows we made to each other.*

"I'll do my best," Michael said again. "I'll change."

"I believe you," she said, only half believing herself.

Chapter

45

It was time to take the short afro out for its first public airing. The wig, the heat, it was just too much. Forget it, Tari told the mirror, and cast its royal fakeness aside. Two diamond studs in her earlobes made the look reminiscent of a circa-'80s Whitney Houston, in her *Seventeen* modeling days. *This could work,* she thought, checking the mirror for the millionth time. *This'd better work.*

And, to her surprise, no one gave her a second glance. Some of the girls in yoga class even said they liked the haircut. It was cute. Super cute.

She could feel her scalp through the purple yoga mat, its grooved plastic on her cool skin. The room was quiet, like an empty schoolyard on a Sunday afternoon or a mall on Christmas Day. Her hand often went to her head, flat, nappy, and real where long, silky, and fake had been.

"Just let your mind float free for a few minutes," Dee said in her soft breathy voice. "Just let go." Tari did.

On the other side of Tari, Rebecca was trying. But inside her head it was loud and jumbled like pieces of a puzzle, maddening because some pieces were missing. When she and Ravi finally reached détente, everything had come gushing out like a geyser. How inadequate she'd been feeling, how she dreaded telling her parents that she had been lying to them all along about her nonexistent job at a nonexistent law firm, how she wanted a better life, a nicer apartment, maybe a car, a child, some security, that she didn't want to be one of those women who didn't contribute to the relationship, who relied on their man for everything, including validation as a human being. . . .

He'd nodded and said he understood. But he never looked at her the same anymore. No matter how much she promised that this year of long distance would work, that she would do everything in her power to make it work. She was not getting through to him.

This yoga class with Tari only distracted her more. Of all people, she expected her to understand. But these days she could never tell with Tari. "What's done is done," Tari had said. "You just have to convince him now that everything's going to be okay." Then, "Frankly, Becks, I'm surprised and a little disappointed in you for doing something so impulsive. Never mind not telling Ravi first. You didn't even try to bargain with them for more money?"

Rebecca had fought the urge to yell, "Who are you to lecture me? You're the queen of impulsive behavior!" But she'd held her tongue, ignoring this new anti-impulsive-behavior Tari. She didn't want to deal with this new imbalance between them. She, Rebecca, had always brought the common sense, the restraint, the strength, the composure to the friendship. She expected, depended on, Tari to be immature, petulant, and pouty when things didn't go her way, berating waitresses, fussing over high-heeled shoes, tight skirts, and the state of her abs. Rebecca did not know what she would do if Tari no longer cared for those things. If she became more like her.

After the class, they sipped Bai Hao oolong at the Tealuxe on Newbury and watched people who did not appear to be thinking about anything but the fine sunny summer day. Tari was philosophizing about the weather again and how it was a metaphor for her own life. She wore a silly smile on her face, but Rebecca let her finish her thought before telling her to stop being so Pollyannaish.

"They're free, you know," Tari said of the sun, sky, air. "For everybody, black, white, sick, healthy. And it would be selfish of me to not count that as a blessing, you know, Becks?"

Rebecca nodded, waiting to find out where Tari was going with this newfound bright-eyed optimism.

"I just . . . I'm just realizing now how much of that I let pass me by for so long. I just need to slow down, you know? Take note of all the beauty that's around me."

"Hmmm," was all Rebecca could say, and she strongly resisted the urge to ask, *Who are you and what have you done with Tari?*

"So, where are you mentally with the Ravi thing?"

Rebecca shrugged and sipped the hot tea carefully. "I don't think he's convinced that this is going to work. He thinks I'm walking out on him or something."

Tari slowly leaned back in her chair and touched her barely there hair again. "Becks, don't stay here just because Ravi's scared he's gonna lose you. This is the man you're going to marry no matter what. I still think you went about this the wrong way, but you had to take this job—for your own sanity. I don't know how you lasted this long with those loony tunes in your office anyway."

Rebecca laughed. "They are not loony tunes!"

"I'll miss you, girl," Tari said pensively.

"Don't say that. I could still change my mind."

"You'd better not. Ravi'll come around. He has to. Besides, New York is only a four-hour drive away. Three and a quarter if you drive like me." Tari snickered. "That's not really long distance."

Rebecca shrugged again. "It is if you're used to waking up next to somebody every morning."

Tari rolled her eyes. "Well, I don't know much about that. . . . So what about the wedding, is that officially postponed?"

"Not really. We still have to go home so he can meet my parents."

"Well, at least now that you have a job you're proud of, it'll be easier for you to face them."

Rebecca nodded. "Yup, but I still have to convince him. So what about Mr. Bass?"

Tari sighed. "Don't even go there. I'm trying to just get over it."

"Why? You're getting better every day. So now's the perfect time to start a relationship."

Tari shrugged. "I don't know. I don't know if I can tell him I have . . . had cancer."

"You don't have to tell him right away."

"I have to. It's a part of me, Becks. I can't just not talk about it."

Rebecca nodded. "I understand. So, tell him. What makes you think he won't be understanding? You're the one who said he's a nice guy and that he's got depth."

"I said those things?" Tari smiled.

"Maybe it was your alter ego," Rebecca joked.

Tari shrugged and looked off into the distance. "It's not that I don't think he'd understand. Of course he would. But I just don't want him to see me that way."

"What way?"

"Sick. Damaged."

"You're not sick and you're not damaged, Tari! Geez, what is wrong with you? Just a minute ago you were Ms. Sunny Outlook, now you're Girl Interrupted again?"

"I know . . . My boob's got a dent in it, Becks. What do you think he's gonna think about that?"

"He might not even notice. Listen, if this guy really likes you, it's not going to matter. If I had your body, I wouldn't care about a little dent in my boob."

"I just hate being defective."

"Oh, give me a break! Stop it already. You're such a narcissist. What's next? Move to a leper colony because you found a stretch mark? Lighten up."

"That's easy for you to say, Becks. You've never—"

"Been perfect?"

"That's not what I was going to say."

"But it was probably some variation of that. I've never cared about my body as much as you care about yours, Tari. And Ravi still loves my big butt and sagging thighs. I just don't understand what you're worried about. Maybe the real problem is you don't like yourself enough the way you are, so you don't think this guy can like you."

"Thanks, Oprah." Tari rolled her eyes.

"Hey, make fun if you want. You can be all alone with your so-called defects, or you can stop being so prideful and give the guy a chance."

Tari looked at Rebecca. Could she be right? "I'm not prideful."

"Of course you're not. And I don't eat curry, either."

Tari ran her hand over her afro. It had taken some courage to go out in public with this short, stubby hairdo. She didn't think she could do it. But there she was. And it wasn't defective. People thought it was a fashion statement. Maybe, just maybe Rebecca was right. Maybe she didn't have to have perfect parts to be perfect. Maybe she didn't even have to be perfect at all.

CHAPTER
46

Steven Bluesteed, editor in chief of the *Boston Statesman*, had a round head, big brown eyes with long, thick baby eyelashes, and pink lips, a look best suited for a Gerber baby food jar. He was telling Tari, who was sitting cross-legged before him and worrying about whether her skirt was too short, that he didn't do this sort of thing often, but that he had been so pleased with her work the last few months that he felt that it was his responsibility to call this meeting with her—not only as her editor but as a concerned friend. *In other words,* Tari thought, *what's eating you, kid?*

His speech was so long, so meandering, that she had plenty of time to formulate a response. As the wheels turned in her head, she noticed that his eyes nervously jumped from her face to the large portrait of Truman on his wall. *What is this?* she wondered. *Am I being fired?* She felt like a cornered rat. But she steeled herself. *Stay calm, or at least appear that way.* The more he talked about how important it was to ask for help when faced with a "serious" issue, the more she realized she had to come clean. Bluesteed was too shrewd to accept the old "I've been under a lot of stress" line.

Here goes, she thought, as she unleashed her unrehearsed and unplanned response.

"Actually, Steven"—she cleared her throat importantly—"I've been trying to avoid this for months, but I guess I have no choice but to be honest with you. I've been diagnosed with breast cancer." She didn't pause when his eyebrows shot skyward and sympathy clouded his doggy eyes. "Anyway, I've had surgery and I've just finished chemotherapy. But I still have two months of radiation therapy left." She uncrossed her legs and bound her knees together. "I was hoping that I'd be able to continue my normal work schedule during treatment, and in all honesty I have, though I've been sick a few days here and there and exhausted, for the most part. But I've done my fair share of work. I didn't want to tell anyone because I didn't want . . . I didn't feel that it was appropriate . . . I didn't want anyone to feel sorry for me . . . or to think that I couldn't do my job." She looked at him defiantly. She would not break down in tears. She swallowed. She did not need or want his sympathy.

"Tari, I don't know what to say. I am so, so, shocked. So sorry," Bluesteed stuttered, but it was Tari who felt sorry for him. She could see that his plans to give her a good talking-to had gone awry and that he was at a genuine loss for words.

"Well, thanks, but I'm doing fine, Steven."

His cheeks looked as if someone had dabbed tomato sauce on them with a blush brush.

Can I go now? she wanted to ask, but he launched into another monologue after nervously offering her as much time off as necessary and inviting her to come to him if she needed anything. She thought she saw shame in his eyes. And whether he meant it or not when he said he admired her strength and courage, she would deposit that statement in her memory bank forever.

Well, it's only a matter of time before everyone else knows, she thought as she walked out of Bluesteed's office with hundreds of curious yet furtive eyes trailing her.

She stood over Joe Martone's desk, interrupting his lunch.

"What now?" he asked, narrowing his eyes.

"Joe, I have . . . had cancer."

She had expected a loud, dramatic reaction, but she did not get it. He put down his rye bread sandwich and looked at her thoughtfully.

"I knew it was something like that," he said. "Jeez, kid. Why didn't you tell me sooner?"

" 'Cause I was scared," Tari said and felt tears pricking at the back of her eyes. Joe looked around and saw that his colleagues were only pretending to mind their own business.

"Let's go for a walk," he said.

They stood outside in the warm day, talking for a half hour.

"Why didn't you come to me, Tari?"

Tari had never thought she would do it, but she cried. She cried in front of a tough, veteran newspaperman who had tears in his eyes, too.

"I didn't want people to feel sorry for me. I didn't want to lose the MetroBank story." She blew her nose.

Joe snorted. "Come on, kiddo. This is a newsroom, people here are not sentimental. You know that. No one's gonna feel sorry for you for longer than a minute. You could have at least told me. I would have had your back."

"Sorry, Joe. I guess I wasn't thinking straight."

He looked at her. "What's next for you, kiddo?"

She shrugged. "Next big story?"

He shook his head. "If that's what you want, I know that's what you'll get. I wish you'd just give yourself some time, though. You've been through hell and back."

"It wasn't that bad," she said, smiling.

He laughed. "You can stop trying to show me how tough you are now, okay?

"Come here," he said and she let him wrap his big, hairy arms around her.

"Joe, you know how this would look if someone saw us now," she said in his shoulder.

"Yup," he said. "I'll probably have divorce papers waiting for me when I get home."

They laughed and looked at each other. "I'm glad you're okay, kiddo. But don't pull that again. You need to take care of yourself first. There are always gonna be big stories out there; there's only one of you."

Joe's right, she thought as she walked back into the building. This whole secret had been silly on so many levels. Rebecca was right, too; she was always making things harder than they had to be.

Her next target was Roger, and it wasn't hard to find him. He sat in the cafeteria reading the *Times* and eating French fries one by one, no ketchup. She sat in the empty chair at his table.

"What's up?" he asked.

"I have to tell you something big."

He put down a fry.

Tari sighed. "I have—I had cancer. Breast cancer."

"What!"

She shushed him as other people looked their way.

His eyes immediately traveled down to her bust line, and she rolled her eyes. "I still have them, Roger. Okay? They're still there."

His face reddened. "Well, do you have to have chemo?"

"I'm done with chemo already." Tari smiled, proud to be able to say those words.

"But how? How long have you known?" Roger was confused.

"A long time. Months."

"You've been keeping this to yourself all this time?" Realization spread across his face. "And everyone thought the MetroBank story was driving you off the wall . . ."

Tari nodded. "I found out right about when MetroBank broke."

He looked right into her, and she thought she saw a look of admiration mixed with worry. "Why didn't you tell me? I would have liked to have been there for you."

She shrugged. "I wasn't thinking straight. I just wanted to pretend that I was fine. And I thought that if people didn't know, then it was easier for me to believe that I was okay."

Roger nodded. "Well, are you okay?"

She shook her head. "Not really. I'm exhausted, I still have this weird tingling in my fingers that won't go away, and this wig is really itchy."

Roger's eyes opened wide. "It's a wig?"

Tari smiled. "Thanks, Roger."

"Are you going to take some time off now? Do you need me to do anything?"

"Like what?" She laughed. "I'm going to think about taking time off, though. Nothing too interesting going on here anyway."

Roger nodded.

"Oh, Tari, I just heard, I'm so sorry."

Tari looked up into Mariska's sympathetic eyes.

"Why didn't you tell me?"

"Uh . . . I . . . Mariska, I'll talk to you—"

Before she could say anything else, another then another, came up to her. The news was spreading, and the pity party had officially begun.

CHAPTER

47

The increased frequency of compliments was beginning to wear on Tari's nerves, but she couldn't lie—it touched her deeply. "You look great," colleagues said in the hallways at work, on the stairwell, in the parking lot, in the cafeteria. At first it was amusing. *Okay,* she thought, *maybe they're saying those things because they think that breast cancer took away all of my confidence. Sweet. Or maybe I'm supposed to be insecure about my femininity because I'm missing a huge chunk of boob.*

"Mom, I feel like everyone's talking about me!" she wailed to Coletta on the phone. "It's sweet, but it's strange at the same time! It's like they all like me now. I'm not used to that!"

"Oh, get over yourself," Coletta scolded. "I don't know why you're so proud. You didn't get that from me."

"Ha!" Tari replied.

But a tiny part of her regretted "coming out" for various reasons. Even John Weston had misplaced his ever-present smarmy, condescending manner. Now he treated her gently and was even uncomfortably friendly. She flinched at the smiles in the hallway from people she barely knew. People said strange things like, "If you need me to come over and clean up or cook or run errands, just let me know." It made her want to scream. *If I couldn't do my own errands, would I be in this office every day?* But she tried to take it all with a sense of humor. *Maybe I should have someone come over and do my laundry,* she thought, glancing at Mariska. *Yeah, I could have her clean my whole house!*

Let somebody help you, she heard Coletta's voice say in the recesses of her mind. *Well, the house is a filthy mess, and Mariska does want to help me. . . .*

"Tari, I just know you're going to be fine," Mariska had said to her earlier, smiling. "You're just so strong. I can't believe you went through all of this and kept on as if nothing was wrong. You're just so courageous."

She tried to put away doubts about Mariska's sincerity. *She's just trying to be nice, relax!* But still . . . She couldn't understand what Mariska wanted from her. To see weakness, some sweetness emerge from all that anger, maybe a bit of fear? She sniffed as she wrote a news brief, a pointless thing that would run deep inside the paper. *I'm still the same,* she thought. *A little dented, but I'm still the same. I've never been a victim. Never will be.* "Courageous" was what Mariska said. And she searched for layers of meaning in the word. Did Mariska really consider her some kind of heroine, or was she secretly wondering, *What is she trying to prove? That's it! She's cleaning my house this weekend,* Tari thought deviously.

"So are we going to have dinner soon?" Mariska asked as Tari turned off her PC for the day. Tari looked at Mariska; there was no mistaking. The woman was genuine and sincere, almost pleading. *I can't play games with her,* Tari thought.

"Yeah, sure. Maybe some night next week."

Later that night she looked at the clock—ten minutes till ten—and felt alone. *I can call him and make a fool of myself again, or I can not call him and save my dignity.* But the phone rang, jolting her out of her internal argument. *Wow! Is that him? Do we have some weird mental connection that he knows when I'm thinking about him?* She cleared her throat and picked up the handset.

"Tari, I hope I didn't wake you." It was Melinda.

"No, what's up?" She couldn't disguise her disappointment.

"Well, sor-ry, missy. Expecting someone else to call?"

"What's on your mind, Melinda? Shouldn't you be in bed?"

"Actually, I'm packing. I'm taking the rest of the week off; we're going down to Newport."

"Oh, how romantic," Tari said. She'd heard all about Michael and Melinda's makeup and was glad for her own sake that the drama was over and done. But she couldn't deny that she felt a little envious. Now that Melinda was all happy and in love, where did that leave her?

"I know," Melinda said giddily. "It was Michael's idea. What are you doing with yourself these days?"

"Nothing." She wondered that, too, sometimes. Now that the radiation treatments were almost finished, she was in emotional limbo. What would she do with herself?

"Summer's over, Tari, and you haven't been to the beach once."

Tari sighed. "Don't remind me of all the things I could be doing, Melinda. I'm not in the mood for the beach."

"Okay, fine. I'm just going to make one suggestion, then I'll leave you alone."

"Fine, suggest away."

"Now that you've told your coworkers what's going on, why don't you take a couple of months off? It would give you some time to decompress from all the stress you've been under and you'd get to escape their pity, which we all know is your paranoia in disguise."

Tari sighed. "I don't know . . . What would I do with myself for two months?"

"Go on vacation somewhere exotic, sing, write bad songs. . . ."

"I don't write bad songs."

"Whatever. Just do something nice for yourself. For me? For Mom?"

"I'll think about it," Tari yawned.

She noticed that by eleven-thirty she was already nodding off halfway through the news. *Am I getting my sleep back?* she wondered as she snuggled under the covers. When the alarm went off at seven-thirty the next day, she hit the snooze button. She tried to rouse herself out of bed, but she couldn't. The office. Ugh. Deadline. Double ugh!

She tossed and turned and looked at the clock. *So tired.* She yawned, not opening her eyes. The alarm went off again nine minutes later. She hit the off button and sleepily called Joe's voice mail. "Joe, it's me. I think I'm going to take some time off. Maybe a month. Or two."

CHAPTER
48

Ravi had cooked dinner again. Rebecca was touched, especially by the veggie meatballs, because Ravi loved meat, all kinds of it. They were not as perfect a match as they appeared. Ravi had grown up on the Pennsylvania Main Line, as American as any Abercrombie & Fitch model. When they met at NYU he had found Rebecca exotic, with her heavy Caribbean accent and her modest fashion sense. He knew Indian girls, more Indian than she, from proud families in Mumbai and New Delhi who had come here and assimilated all the way. Those girls he loved, too. But Rebecca, boy, she was something. She didn't speak often, but when she did it was always to say something you'd never forget. He had resisted her at first. He was too young, too unsettled for a girl like that. But she wouldn't wait until he finished business school, got a job at a respectable firm, and had the means to buy her a house in whatever suburb it was that she chose. He had to make haste now, while she was still there with that faraway look on her face, wearing her long skirts and unflattering shoes, her hair all over that pretty, pretty face.

"I really wish we could have gone to Trinidad, despite

everything else," he complained as they ate at the tiny, creaky dining-room table with the mismatched chairs.

"We'll go," Rebecca said.

"When?" he insisted. "You're just starting a new job."

"Well, I was thinking . . . I don't start there for another month. So why don't we go in a couple of weeks?"

"But I thought you wanted to go with Tari to her radiation treatments."

"She's got her sister. Besides, Tari's a big girl. And she hates it when I fuss over her."

Ravi tilted his head to the side. "So, okay. We're going to meet your folks in a couple of weeks, and then you're moving two hundred miles away."

"But we'll see each other every weekend."

"What if there's a blizzard?"

"Especially if there's a blizzard." Rebecca laughed.

She was being impulsive again. She had not thought this Trinidad trip through, but the idea of it seemed to already warm things between them. *Oh,* she thought, *I'm getting more and more like Tari every day.*

It would be better this way, she thought as they ate dinner, occasionally holding hands between bites. They would surprise her parents. It would work, she suddenly realized, because she would be in full control.

She pictured her wedding now—the way she wanted it: an old church, one with a steeple, and herself in a white wedding dress, a big, fussy one. And a small reception in a hotel ballroom. She wanted plain vanilla. No gold bracelets jangling on her arms. No elaborate days-long feast.

"What are you thinking?" he asked as they cleaned up after dinner.

"About how great our life is going to be," she said. "I can barely wait."

CHAPTER
49

Rico was captivated. This was a sad song that he hadn't heard before, and he worried that it would dampen the mood of his customers. He quickly scanned the room, and all eyes were on Tari. Couples held hands or leaned into each other as the sound of her voice drenched the room.

> *When all I have is gone,*
> *Can I turn to you?*
> *When I can no longer depend on me*
> *Can I count on you to be you?*

When she finished, she bowed her head and the crowd rose, applauding and whistling. She noticed Rico standing by the bar; their eyes met and he clapped and winked at her before he disappeared into his back office. Her throat still ached, and she popped into her mouth a mint that she had grabbed from a table near the bar.

She felt Shawn's eyes following her to the dressing room, but she did not look back.

She sat on the creaky chair and looked into the cracked mirror. There was no way she would make it through the next set. Her head felt heavy, and she was so tired she could almost feel the blood straining to travel through her veins and to her organs. The can of Ensure she kept in her bag was warm, but she cracked the top anyway. Her eyes closed as her taste buds anticipated the chalky taste that would probably give her just enough energy to make it through the next half hour. She swallowed it without tasting.

Her pragmatic, practical side asked, *Would you seriously date a man who had prostate or lung or liver cancer, survivor or not?* Her answer was always yes. But that was the new her who saw things a bit differently. And that same Tari was no fool. She knew what men were like. Sure, they could pretend otherwise, but they all wanted the perfect little package. And though she had never been that perfect package, at least before this thing she could have put on the act. Be sweet and acquiescing, get her nails done, wear painful, sexy shoes and flattering outfits, fake nice meals in the kitchen, laugh out loud at his jokes, especially when all his friends were watching and listening. But now those tricks wouldn't mean much. When would she tell him? On the first date? "Well, my favorite color is pink, which is really kinda funny because you know that's the color they use in all those breast cancer awareness ad campaigns, which, incidentally, I have had." Then what would he say?

The semidark room made her image in the mirror appear all of her thirty years. *No one will ever mistake me for a college student again,* Tari lamented. Whoever said radiation therapy was a breeze was a bald-faced liar. The daily zaps to her breast left her almost as drained as the chemo. The skin on her breast was leathery and sensitive, as if she'd lain out in the sun for five days straight. She could see the dark circles under her eyes and the lines at the corners. Her scalp itched from the hairs that were sprouting from her follicles daily.

Only two more weeks of radiation therapy, she told herself, and this chapter of her life would be closed, and hopefully there would be no sequel. But the future held its own problems. Everyone thought she was fine now, and she'd been unprepared for that. Even Coletta's phone calls dwindled from daily to triweekly. Melinda was busy with her own life, seeing patients, being the perfect wife and mother, and all the other things in between. Rebecca was busy planning her vacation with Ravi and finding a place to live in New York. She felt out of everybody's loop and completely alone in her own tiny circle. It was if her army had deserted her in the middle of the battle. *I'm still fighting this thing,* she thought. *I still need pep talks, company, encouragement, help. Somebody!* She had not seen the inside of the *Statesman*'s office in weeks, and she did not miss it. But she missed the sympathy and attention she'd gotten from her coworkers. Even Mariska.

She took another sip of the protein drink. *This feeling has to end,* she thought. *This feeling that I'll always be terrified of cancer.* She imagined her life taking a different turn. Maybe she could turn her back on all frivolous things like dating, shopping, and even her career and become a full-time activist. A living martyr for the cure. She could run support group meetings out of her house. Organize charity runs and walks. Be a spokeswoman, a champion for other "survivors." She'd be one of those women who gave interviews to TV reporters every October during breast cancer month, reminding women to do their breast self-exams monthly. Or was it weekly? She didn't know, because she checked her breast daily for lumps. Maybe she would say things like, "Breast cancer was the best thing that ever happened to me because it made me find out who I really am." But she knew that wasn't who she was. There had to be a comfortable middle, where she could just live her life and not be consumed by cancer. *Okay. Forget normal. Forget going back to the way things were before the diagnosis,* she thought. *But there's got to be a better way than having this always hanging over my head.*

There was a knock on the door, and it was only then that Tari realized her head was in her hands.

Shawn, always self-assured, looked embarrassed to be standing there.

"I hope I'm not disturbing you."

She shook her head, glad to see him but worried he might notice how tired she looked.

"You really killed that song," he said. "In a good way." He laughed.

"Thanks." Her voice was lukewarm.

"Tari, are you all right? I wanted to talk about . . . I mean, I just feel that there's something here, you know?" He pointed his index finger from his heart to hers three or four times.

"I don't know what you mean," she said, sitting up fully in the chair.

He sighed. "Okay. You haven't returned any of my calls. Is this how you want things to go? You want me to leave you alone or beg?"

"Shawn. I'm sorry, but things have been . . . kinda busy. I'm really not up to doing a lot of socializing these days."

He narrowed his eyes and looked at her intently. "That's not really true, is it? The busy part. It's more than that, but you don't have to tell me if you don't want to."

Tari sighed. *Why is he trying to back me into a corner?*

"You can't tell me that I'm wrong. I know there's something between us, Tari."

She couldn't tell him everything. But she had to tell him something. "Shawn, I'm dealing with some things right now. And my feelings, whatever they are, have to take a back seat to the facts. I'm just not at a point in my life where I can pursue something like that."

He nodded. "Can't you at least try to talk to me about it? I can help. Or listen."

She looked at him; he wasn't acting. This guy was just too nice! Too damned nice. "Shawn, I appreciate it. But it's just not a good time. I have to get my head straight."

He nodded and closed the door quietly.

Whatever, she thought. *Too perfect for me; he needs a nice, sweet girl. Better for someone like Melinda. Or even Rebecca.* She picked up her scarf and threw it against the mirror. *Whatever!*

At the end of the night, she chatted with Manny and the guys.

"Everyone, we're playing for Jimmy Gurstein next week. Mars guy," Manny reminded them. "This could be our big break, so make sure y'all show up for rehearsal."

"Yeah, right," Al the drummer mumbled.

She avoided looking at Shawn, although she could feel his eyes on her. *What is he staring at?* She gathered up her things and rushed out of the bar.

She sat at a red light, looking at her rearview mirror. The streets were brightly lit but were desolate. The city seemed like an abandoned movie set. *Ugh. Why did I blow him off? Why couldn't I take Rebecca's advice and at least go out with him tonight?* She didn't look forward to going home to just her thoughts. *How many times is he going to keep asking?* she wondered. *What if tonight was the last time?* She ran her hand through the wig and quickly pulled it away. *I've made a huge mistake.*

Chapter

50

Tari knocked on Rebecca's door at 7:45 A.M.

"Oh, my goodness, you're all dressed up." Tari laughed, looking at her friend.

"Well, you're the one who said people in your church really dress up," Rebecca said, looking embarrassed. "Besides, I want to practice walking in heels. I think I'm expected to wear them on my wedding day."

Tari was amused to see Rebecca nattily outfitted in a tan suit with ivory satin blouse, pearls, and tan leather pumps.

It had taken some convincing, but she'd finally decided to let Rebecca accompany her to church. She did not know what made her agree to something she'd always been so against, though she suspected it might have had to do with her sadness about Rebecca leaving for New York.

"You promise you'll behave yourself?" Tari teased as she drove toward Boston.

"You mean I can't raise my hands and ask questions during the sermon?" Rebecca shot back.

"Sure you can. As long as you don't sit next to me."

"You okay?" Tari asked minutes later as they walked into the already full sanctuary.

Rebecca tried not to stare in awe as the congregation

erupted in emotion at the hymn that was being sung; she felt self-conscious as the congregants joined in, singing with the choir, Tari, too. She hadn't heard Tari sing in a while— she never did get out to see her that much anymore—and she was surprised to hear her friend's soprano voice spiraling high above the other voices around them.

She decided then that Tari had been right all along. She had no place here in this church full of people who knew all the words to the songs, who knew when to say *amen* and *God is a good God* all the time. It made her feel like a stranger at a family dinner table where everyone was joking and reminiscing about old times. She had nothing to add. She smiled politely and tried not to stare at the worshipers. She sat awkwardly, unfamiliar with the cues that regular churchgoers did not need. In a gesture of what might have been guilt, she dropped a $50 bill in the offering bucket.

Then the pastor took the pulpit, and she couldn't tear her attention away from him despite her resolve to remain an objective observer. All she really wanted to do was to watch but stay removed from this church thing that Tari was so committed to, but now she was taken in by the man on the pulpit and his obvious intellect and rock-solid faith.

He paced the pulpit like a professor. He didn't preach; he taught. "How do you live your life, the best life you can?" It was nothing she hadn't heard before: treat others well and, of course, yourself. But he didn't just say that. And later when she tried to remember exactly what it was he had said that made a seemingly pedestrian message seem like something far more profound, she couldn't put a finger on it. But she would never forget the experience. Oh, she had to have a wedding. In a church. This solidified it for her.

On the way home, Tari was triumphant. "See, I told you. Don't you feel like your eyes have been opened?"

Rebecca didn't answer. It wasn't that simple. It wasn't as if she'd suddenly stepped into some divine light. But a door that had been shut had certainly opened a crack. "Hmm. I'd like to come back again," she said.

Tari laughed. "Maybe you could bring Ravi."

Later, as they waited for a table at Baker's Best restaurant amid a thick, hungry crowd in Newton, Tari said it. "You're changing, Becks."

"Me? How?"

"I don't know. You're just so much more . . . assertive? Is that it?"

Rebecca shrugged. "Ravi says it's impulsive."

"One man's impulsive is another woman's assertive," Tari said. "I kinda like it. Except when it's directed at me."

"Well, if you behave yourself, you won't have to worry," Rebecca joked.

"Okay, Miss Thing"—Tari held up her hands in mock surrender—"maybe you should take your assertive butt to New York in a hurry, then."

"You know you're going to miss me. No one else will put up with you the way I do."

Tari felt a pang of sadness. "What am I gonna do without you, Becks?"

"It will be like before I moved to Boston. We'll spend all day Sunday on the phone."

"I don't want you to go. I think Ravi's right." Tari mocked a pout.

"Nice try. Oh, I forgot to ask you . . . or tell you . . . you're going to be my maid of honor, so start working on your social graces."

"Becks! Really?" Tari was both startled and ecstatic. "I haven't been in a wedding party since Melinda got married! Do I get to go to Trinidad?"

"Probably not. It'll probably be in a church somewhere in Boston or New York."

"You're no fun. You should have it in Trinidad. That way your folks will be happy and I'll get to lie on the beach."

Rebecca shrugged. "Sorry, but the new assertive me doesn't want that."

Tari laughed. "Babe, I'm gonna miss you so much. We had some good times here."

"We'll still have plenty of good times, Tari. It's just beginning. Our kids will be kissing cousins."

"Yeah, right! You think I'll let my kids play with your boho, vegan, lacrosse-playing kids?"

"Blah blah blah." Rebecca rolled her eyes. "Our table's finally ready."

The hostess led them to a tiny table in the corner of the restaurant, and Tari started to protest, but Rebecca stopped her.

"This is a great table," Rebecca told the smiling waitress.

Tari sat down. "You know what I'll really miss, Becks?"

Rebecca glanced up from her menu.

"The way you let me know when I'm out of line without even telling me."

Rebecca smiled knowingly and her eyes went back to the menu. But Tari knew they were both thinking the same thing: *I could never find another girlfriend like you.*

CHAPTER
51

The Mars Recording rep was in the audience again. He'd called Manny asking when and where he could get another look at Loose Change. And though she had spent the whole week preparing for this night, Tari knew she was not at her best. Her voice just could not reach as wide or as far as she willed it. She stuck to less challenging, well-known songs that would win the audience over just because the melodies were familiar.

She grabbed the mike stand as dizziness faded in, then out. Her fatigue surprised her. For weeks she had been doing nothing but sleeping late every day, going to yoga, and reading bad novels. It seemed that her energy tapped out just when she allowed her body to rest. Why now? Why didn't she run out of gas during chemo, during MetroBank? She felt betrayed again, this time by her body. She'd hoped that by now she would have her strength back. *When is this going to be over?* she wondered as Manny threw her a dirty look.

"What's wrong?" he mouthed as she missed a note.

She shrugged and turned her attention back to the audience.

Shawn noticed it. He heard the weakness in her voice

and saw her try to clear her throat on the fly for the tenth time.

During the second set she swayed involuntarily. Then she stopped dead in the middle of the song. Manny quickly stepped in with his piano, picking up where she left off with a solo.

As the song ended, she walked off the stage, head down, breathing through her mouth. The audience murmured in protest. Shawn was there first, catching her before she collapsed at the door of the dressing room. She was nearly unconscious. He picked her up and carried her to a chair. Amid all the running and the calling of the ambulance, Tari managed to open her eyes and say a few words. "Don't take me to the hospital, I'm fine. I'm just tired."

But it was too late. Before too long she was lying in a bed at Cambridge City Hospital, a few blocks away. Liquids were being pumped into her body. A serious case of dehydration was what the doctor said.

"Don't call anyone," she begged Shawn when he asked if she wanted to call her family.

It was ironic, she thought as she lay in the hospital bed, that she had gone through four months of poison being pumped into her body without an incident, but she had to collapse onstage. From dehydration, of all things.

"Tari, what can I do?" Shawn asked, sitting beside her bed. She shook her head. She wanted to talk to the doctor, but she couldn't with him standing there. "Nothing. You don't have to stay."

"That's not what I mean."

She knew what he meant. And she wanted him to stay. But she wasn't sure . . .

He was asking her again. "What can I do to make you tell me what's going on with you?"

She resisted. "Now is not the right time. I can't talk about this right now. It's not that simple."

"Why not?" he insisted.

Silence. *Not the right time,* she thought.

"Okay," he said. "I know you're sick. My sister died from leukemia when she was sixteen, so I know that yellowness in your skin is from chemo drugs. And everybody could tell from the way you've been acting that you have some kind of serious disease. Everybody knows, Tari. Everybody. I just wish you'd told me instead of making it come to this. I don't want to embarrass you, but I'm tired of playing this game."

She clenched her stomach muscles. He knew she was sick?

"Have it your way, then." He shrugged when she didn't say a word. "I'm going to leave. If you want to stay here by yourself, that's all on you."

"Shawn, I'm sorry," she said, not wanting him to go but not really wanting to stop him.

"For what?" He stood up.

"I was just so . . . I don't know. Yes, I had breast cancer, but that's not why I passed out. I'm just tired. I didn't tell you because I didn't want you to feel that . . . that you just had to stay, else I'd feel worse about . . . my situation."

"That's the kind of person you think I am? You don't really know me, do you? You've never even given us a chance to get to know each other."

"I'm sorry. I'm really bad at this sort of thing."

"At relationships or at letting people get too close to you?"

"Both."

"You could at least try to learn. You know? Just let go a little bit. You have nothing to lose. And I'm not going to hurt you. Matter of fact, I feel like I'm the one at risk here. You make a brother feel as if he only gets one chance with you. And if he screws up, you're outta there."

Tari grimaced. "I'm not that bad."

"Do you still want me to leave?"

She shook her head and patted the bed. He sat next to her. "You've been confusing the hell out of me since I met you," he said.

She tried to smile. "How?"

"Sometimes I thought you were really into me, other times I thought you wanted to kill me or something. I hope that's because you were sick and that's not the way you are all the time."

"I'm not that way all the time." *At least not anymore*, she thought, crossing her fingers. "And I was always really into you," she said. "From day one."

I'll behave, she told herself. *This is a good guy.*

"So when do I get to kiss you?" he asked, smiling.

"Not now," she said, horrified. "I . . . My breath . . ."

He laughed. "Okay. I'll wait. I've had a lot of practice waiting for you."

"I can take a hug," she said.

He smiled and leaned over and took her in his arms.

Oooooohhh, Tari thought, closing her eyes, as she lost herself in Shawn's embrace. *Oooooooh! This feels just the way I thought it would.*

CHAPTER
52

"I can't believe it's almost winter again," Melinda said as she and Tari stopped by the small pond in Franklin Park to snap pictures of the wildly colored leaves that formed a canopy over the water, adding gold, red, and orange flecks to the water. "The leaves are already falling off the trees."

Tari sighed. "What a crazy year."

"Yeah, but you made it through. Didn't I tell you you'd beat this?" Melinda put her digital camera back in its case and they continued their Sunday-afternoon walk. "So did you hear from that Mars Recording rep again?"

Tari nodded. The night that she'd fainted, the representative from the Mars Recording label had left his card with Manny. When she spoke with him, he sounded excited. He asked for a demo CD, which she still hadn't gotten around to recording.

"I don't know. I'm still not sure if that's what I really want."

She touched her short, curly hair, which she had spent all morning coloring. Chestnut; the gold highlights would come later. She was still asking herself exactly where it was she was going. She felt like she had just been through hell, and she wanted her life back, albeit a scaled-down, slow-motion version. Work loomed; her three months of leave were almost up, and she wasn't sure that she wanted to go back to the same thing. She remembered the tip Mariska had passed on to her at lunch the week before. The jazz critic was retiring, so his job would be open. Maybe it was a sign, she'd thought. Maybe.

"I don't know if I'm up to recording a CD and all of that. Besides, I think I wanna give choir a try."

Melinda was snapping pictures of yet another oak with golden leaves and quickly put the camera down. Her eyebrows shot up.

"I kinda promised God one day while I was puking my guts out that if he got me through this I'd start singing in the choir."

Melinda narrowed her eyes. "You made a deal with God? That's so . . . you."

Tari shrugged. "So, where's Michael today?" She wasn't in the mood for a lecture on the wisdom or lack thereof of making deals with the Almighty.

"He took the kids to the aquarium," Melinda said, a carefree grin on her face. "You know, Tari. I'll never stop telling you that if you hadn't gotten sick, I'd probably be divorced by now."

Tari snorted. "Please. That doesn't even make sense."

"Girl, you don't know how close I was. But—"

"But you love that man," Tari finished for her.

They walked in silence for a few hundred yards.

"And Shawn?" Melinda asked slyly.

Tari blushed. "Gosh, you are nosy!"

"Come on, now, you know all the gory details of my marriage, you need to share your stuff. Now spill it."

Tari sighed dramatically. "Fine. We're dating. Involved."

"Yeah?" Melinda stopped. "And?"

"And it's fun. He's fun. We make beautiful music together." Tari laughed.

"Oh, boy. Do I want to hear this?"

"It's not what you think. We're still waiting—or trying to." Tari giggled and Melinda shot her a look. "Sorry, Mel. But we have this chemistry . . . It's like I wanna get naked every time I see him."

"Please stop now. I don't want to aid and abet your little fornicating behind." Melinda laughed.

"But we're not . . . We haven't quite gone there. Yet," Tari said.

"Hmmm. So you've discussed the future?" Melinda asked.

"Sort of. It's still kinda soon, but we're getting there."

"I see," Melinda said. "So little Tari went and got herself a man," she added as if thinking out loud.

"I guess she did." Tari smiled happily.

"I'm sure Mom would like him," Melinda said. "He's from the islands, educated, gainfully employed."

"Yup, he sure fits her criteria," Tari said, laughing. "Except for the late-night phone calls."

"It's so funny that you would be the one to end up with the guy she'd approve of," Melinda said.

" 'Cause I was always the rebel?"

"Um . . . yes," Melinda said.

"Hey, don't write me off so soon. It's not like we're married yet or anything. I might end up with a gangsta rapper next year."

"Yeah, right. I could definitely see that," Melinda snorted. "It's just a matter of time, though," she said, "before you break down and walk down the aisle. I can't wait till you start having kids so my kids will have some cousins."

Was it only a matter of time? Tari wondered. Did Melinda even know what she was talking about? *Well, she does tend to be right most of the time*, Tari thought. *Scarily so.*

A tinge of regret crept through Tari's body as she read the 8,000-word story that started on the front page of the Sunday paper and continued into a four-page spread with photos, graphics, and bold headlines. "Malfeasance at MetroBank," by John Weston, *Statesman* Staff Writer.

It was good. No. It was excellent, award-winning reporting and writing. Weston had put all of the tiny, scattered pieces together in the MetroBank saga, and the article was flawlessly researched and executed. Could she have done as good a job? she wondered. There was no question in her mind that she could have. But she knew that what it took to get such a huge project completed would have taken much more out of her than she had to give. And it didn't bother her too much that Weston had finished off her big story. After all, it was she who had created that first spark.

She chuckled at the picture of Donald Meehan, the bank's former CEO, being led away in handcuffs by two law enforcement toughs as his wife peered out from the window of their expansive home in Prides Crossing.

Tari couldn't put down the paper. Weston had gone through every line of every annual and quarterly statement of the bank over twenty years to ferret out every single penny that was stolen, misspent, and covered up by Donald Meehan and his band of thieving executives. Weston was a jerk, but he was good at what he did, she had to admit.

"Weston did a really, really good job with this," she said, turning to Shawn, who was reading the sports section next to her on her couch.

"Oh, yeah? I never thought I'd ever hear you say something positive about that guy." Shawn chuckled. "Maybe you should congratulate him when you go back to work tomorrow."

She playfully elbowed the man who had become the center of her world, not taking her eyes off the article, in total awe of the little story she'd started that had become the biggest story of the year. "Maybe I will."

Later in the bathroom, she put on her makeup carefully

as she prepared for their dinner outing. Her skin had changed forever; it was lighter, smoother, thinner. But her face had filled out some. Her upper arms and shoulders were beginning to get some definition again from her trepid foray back into kickboxing. She looked at her right breast. The scar was still there, but the indentation didn't seem so bad now. She touched the scar, moved her fingers over it, searching, and prayed that the evil thing would never come back. She looked in the mirror. *Thank you, God.*

She could hardly wait for tomorrow.